M000197926

SEALS
in
Paradise

GRIZZLY
BITTERROOT
RANCH

Riante
Romance

HOT SEAL, SWEET & SPICY

SEALS IN PARADISE / GRIZZLY BITTERROOT RANCH

CYNTHIA D'ALBA

For the staff at West Shores Senior Living in Hot Springs, Arkansas.
Thank you for all you do for my mom.

Hot SEAL, Sweet & Spicy

By Cynthia D'Alba

Copyright © 2021 Cynthia D'Alba and Riante, Inc.

Print ISBN: 978-1-946899-30-9

Digital ISBN: 978-1-946899-29-3

Cover Artist: Elle James

Editor: Delilah Devlin

Photographer: Tom Tyson

Model: Shane Rice

The thrum and vibrations from the cargo plane had almost lulled Navy SEAL Eli Miller to sleep. Or maybe it was the fourteen days of getting a maximum of two hours of sleep each night. Either way, he was drifting off when someone tapped the toe of his shoe.

"Wolf. You asleep?"

Eli, aka Wolf, opened his eyes and watched Romeo team leader Ted Brown, aka Bear, drop onto the seat beside him. "Nope. Just resting my eyes," he said, his tone dry.

Bear handed him a beer. They popped open the cans and took long swallows.

"You sure about your decision, Wolf?" Bear asked. "The Lieutenant can swear you in for another hitch right here, right now."

Eli chuckled. "Bear, you are without a doubt the best team leader I've had the pleasure to serve under. Romeo team is the strongest SEAL team of the bunch because of you. However, I've been at this, man, for twelve years—seventeen, if you count the years in the Navy before I joined the SEALs, and I've loved every minute. But you know when the time comes to move on, and my time is now."

"You'll be hard to replace," his team leader said with a frown.

Eli chuckled. "I've heard through the grapevine that command has lined up Nomad to take my place until you find my replacement."

Nomad, aka Sawyer Becket, was a SEAL floater who moved from team to team as help was needed. Rumor had it that every team asked him to stay, but floating was his choice. Eli had heard the man could shoot the wings off a butterfly from hundreds of yards away.

"True," Bear said and took a long gulp of beer. "However, he won't be you."

Eli laughed. "You mean, he won't have a house with a big yard for all the parties?"

"Yeah, and I'd be willing to wager he won't know the first thing about bacon-wrapped-cheese-mashed-potato-stuffed-meatloaf."

Eli snorted. "Are you going to miss my SEAL expertise or my cooking more?"

Mars, aka Jack Marsten, dropped onto the bench on the other side of Eli. "Both, but man, I'm going to really miss those cookouts. I will not miss the extra miles I have to run to use up the calories."

"What about staying in the area and opening up a SEAL-focused bar and diner?" Brian Anderson, aka Heartbreaker, said as he joined the group.

"Interesting, but there's already McP's, Danny's, and the Little Club. Can't see taking on that competition. Besides, I'm headed home to the ranch. Now that my brother Zane is married and my parents are spending winters in Florida, I feel like I'm needed there." He shrugged. "It won't be the same as living on the coast, running in the wet sand—"

"Doing HALOs," Mars added.

"And holding your breath underwater as the minutes tick slowly by," Heartbreaker said.

"And don't forget getting your ass chewed by command when you fuck up," Bear said. "Never mind. That's just me."

The guys laughed.

Eli studied his SEAL team. Bear, Mars, Heartbreaker, Joker, Zig, Gator, and Cash. Zane was his biological brother, but these guys were the brothers of the heart. He trusted them with his life, and they trusted him. He doubted he'd ever have a group of men around him again like these guys. Strong. Trustworthy. Honest. And he knew, if he called anytime to come anywhere and meet him, every one of them would make that happened.

He hadn't been around Zane for more than a few days at a time in years. Zane had left for college in Chicago when Eli had still been in high school, and he hadn't come back from Chicago until a little over a year ago. Zane had committed to staying in Gardiner, Montana and running the family horse ranch.

Last winter, his parents took off for Florida for five months, leaving Zane in charge. His mother was so thrilled with the Florida weather and all the new friends they made, they'd bought a place in Titusville at a gated community named The Great Outdoors, and were planning to establish residency there, meaning they'd be gone at least six months from the Grizzly Bitterroot Ranch. That also meant Zane had a lot on his plate, including having a new wife. In fact, seeing his brother and his parents at Zane's wedding almost a year ago was the last time Eli had been with family...or at least his biological family. The men sitting around had been family for so long, he worried he'd be lost without them.

"So, you're gonna cowboy up?" Joker asked. "Yee haw and all that shit?"

Eli laughed with the rest of the Romeo team. "I don't know about the yee haw, but that's the plan."

"Can you even still ride a horse?" Zig asked, his face furrowed with concern. Ever since Zig had married the widow of a fallen SEAL hero and taken on the role as stepdad to her son, his father gene had taken over.

"Yes, Dad. I can still ride," Eli answered with a grin. "But thanks for being worried about me."

Zig snorted. "Hell, Son. Not worried about you, but if you fall off and break somethin', it'll be inconvenient for the rest of us havin' to come check on you way up there in Montana."

The team laughed as Mars slapped Zig on the back. "Spoken like a true dad."

"Listen up, men," the commanding officer shouted over the roar of the plane.

The men straightened on the bench and turned their attention to the Lieutenant addressing them.

"Good work over there, men. Not only did you find Adeel Saade, you brought him in alive and with his laptop. The brass is extremely pleased with your hard work and wanted me to pass that along to you, and you know me...if the brass is happy, I'm happy. I know the hours were long and the work was stressful. You've definitely earned some time off, so the team is approved for ten days leave, starting tomorrow."

Loud cheers and whistles filled the belly of the cargo plane as the guys high-fived each other.

Their commanding officer waited until the celebration died down to add, "Go only far enough away that you can be back on base within twelve hours should the team be needed. But you have my word, you'll only be called back if all hell breaks loose."

The team chuckled and clinked cans of beer.

"Okay, we'll be landing shortly," the Lieutenant said. "One more item of business. I'm going home to be with my family. I do not want to have to bail any of you out of jail, so bear in mind that you *do not* want to pull me away from my wife. Got it?"

"Yes, sir," came the replies.

"Miller," their commanding officer said. "A minute of your time."

"Yes, sir." Eli pushed up from his seat and the two men stepped away from the team into an empty area.

"You sure you want to leave us, Miller? You're a hell of a SEAL. An integral part of this team."

"Yes, sir. It's time."

"You have some leave accrued. I checked before we boarded. Go ahead and go to personnel for termination. They'll walk you through all the various offices you have to visit to officially leave us. You're shy twenty, right? You could still earn that retirement. Transfer off teams if you feel you can't keep up and the Navy can find other ways to use your skills."

Eli wanted to laugh. He knew the Lieutenant was busting his balls with the "can't keep up" dig, hoping to push buttons to make Eli want to reenlist. He fought back a grin as he replied, "Thank you. It's a kind offer. I do have three more years, but Air Force Reserves will let me complete my commitment in Montana."

"Chair Force. Cushy, Miller."

This time Eli chuckled, knowing what the other branches of the military thought of the Air Force.

"Thank you for your leadership," Eli said. "I'll get with personnel today."

"Damn. I hate to lose a good SEAL. Best of luck."

"Thank you."

Eli rejoined his team.

"A little subtle pressure to stay?" Joker asked.

"Nothing subtle about it," Eli said as he pulled out another beer from the cooler.

It was close to seven in the evening by the time Eli reach McP's to join his team for his official going away party. He parked his truck loaded with items he wanted to keep in the back lot and walked around to the entrance. He paused on the sidewalk and studied the building. The American and Irish flags on either side of the McP's sign whipped in the breeze. The green evening lights were on even though the sun had yet to set. The flowers in the window boxes nodded toward him, bent by the wind.

He'd lived at McP's for what seemed like forever. There probably wasn't anything on the menu he hadn't ordered at one time or another. He'd learned to cook the ones he enjoyed, although, in his opinion, his version of shepherd's pie beat theirs hands down. Over the last couple of years, he'd also dabbled in making his own microbrews. The ones he'd produced had been good, but not great. Maybe he would perfect his craft once he was home in Montana.

His team waited inside for him, and yet, he stood frozen in place. He didn't want a party. Didn't want to say goodbye to the men he'd been closer to than his own biological brother. For a minute, he contemplated turning around, getting in his truck, and leaving.

He had a couple of weeks of vacation coming, and he could have hung around Coronado with the team, but that felt like putting off the inevitable. Good-byes sucked whether he left today, tomorrow or next month. The next phase of his life was waiting, and he decided he might as well get to it.

"You better not be thinking of walking out on your own party," his team leader said from behind him.

Eli whipped around. "Bear, I didn't hear you walk up."

Bear threw an arm around Eli's shoulders and forced him to walk toward the door. "You're the guest of honor. You have to go in."

Eli chuckled. "I guess so."

For the next couple of hours, beers were poured and stories told, some more risqué than others. Eli laughed and drank, but inside his soul, he'd already begun the hard task of breaking his emotional ties with the team. He'd always be there for them, just as they would for him, but he was ready to move on.

After a couple of hours, Eli stood and lifted his glass. "To the best damn SEAL team."

The men clicked bottles and drank.

"And I'm gone," Eli said, setting his empty mug on the table. "Don't do anything I wouldn't do."

"Well, hell, Wolf," Heartbreaker said. "That leaves the door wide open."

After a final round of back-slapping hugs, Eli walked out, followed closely by Zig.

"Man, you've had a lot to drink. Maybe you should sleep it off before getting on the road."

Eli loved Zig's dad gene. "I'll be fine." He leaned in close. "Don't tell the guys, but Ray the bartender has been serving me near-beer all night. So other than a full bladder, I'm good to go."

Zig slapped his back. "Take care, man. Stay in touch."

"Will do."

He climbed into his truck, ready to put some miles behind him. As he left the parking lot, he couldn't help but reflect. Damn, he would miss Romeo Team. The guys on the team had changed over the past couple of years, but they'd always had his back, and always would, he assumed, just as he would die for any of them. But their last few missions had been rough. Losing a Romeo team member and good friend during a mission had hit him harder than he'd expected. He'd spent the last year waiting for his bullet, but it never came. A couple of months ago, he'd decided the time had come for him to go home, and he'd put in his papers to the joy of his parents. His brother's reaction had been a little harder to read.

All the bright lights of Las Vegas welcomed Eli as he neared the gambling capital of the west. A hot, dry arid breeze blasted his face when he climbed from the driver's seat of his truck for gas. He stretched his lower back as fuel filled the truck's tank. He was in excellent condition, but after being in the same position for the past five-and-a-half hours, the muscles in his back had tightened.

After filling his truck, he went inside the truck stop to use the men's room and grab coffee. Instead of caffeine to wake him up, he decided to pull his truck between a couple of idling eighteen-wheelers and sleep. Lord knew he'd slept in worse places than the front seat of his truck. There was no reason to push himself until he dropped or had an accident.

He chuckled at the accident thought. Daddy Zig was living in his head.

Home would be there whether he got there in one day or three, or even two weeks from now, when his family actually expected him. He hadn't told them he was leaving early. When the team had been called out for this last mission, he'd had no idea how long they'd be gone. Completing the mission early had given him the opportunity to get a jump on his new life.

After four hours of sleep, he woke feeling like a new man. Coffee for the caffeine jolt, along with some sausage biscuits and a cinnamon roll from the store inside the truck stop, and he was ready to face the long drive to Grizzly Bitterroot Ranch.

After twelve more hours on the road, he was over halfway to the family ranch between Gardiner and Emigrant, Montana. The remaining portion of the drive would be on tight, two-lane, state highways, not to mention the fact he'd be travelling through Yellowstone National Park. At this time of the year, the drive from the West Entrance to the North Entrance could take anywhere from two to eight hours, depending on the traffic. Given it was the middle of July, his money was on eight hours. His timing for hitting Yellowstone could have been better.

It was early evening when he stopped for gas outside of West Yellowstone. The temperature wasn't as high as he'd faced in Last Vegas, but the humidity was distinctly higher.

As the gas flowed into the tank, he leaned against the truck's bed and studied the area around him. The town of West Yellowstone had changed in the years he'd been gone. It'd grown and added more tourist stops. People walked on the sidewalks and in and out of stores. Business appeared to be going well for the town.

With West Yellowstone full and busy with visitors, he knew the Yellowstone National Park tourism would be heavy. He worried about the wildlife in Yellowstone. Some tourists were idiots when it came to getting too close to the bears, buffalo, and elk.

On the other hand, the wildlife did like to take the path of least resistance, which meant walking on the paved roads, and blocking traffic for hours. For tonight, he hoped all the wildlife stayed in their glens and valleys and left the roads to the cars. It sure would make his trip easier and faster. Given that it was early evening, and figuring he would be facing a slow drive through the park, he found a café that was producing delicious aromas and parked. A maddening drive would be so much more pleasurable on a full stomach.

He lucked into a small table in the corner and let his mind drift to his brother and the family ranch. Zane had married a little under a year ago to a doctor from Texas. He'd bought out a couple of smaller farms and enlarged their ranch holdings. Their horse breeding and boarding businesses were growing in leaps and bounds.

The cabins Eli and Zane had planned to use as lodging for a dude ranch were staying booked as vacation rentals, which was excellent, but required some hands-on housekeeping from Russ's wife Lori with each flip. With his parents in Florida every winter, Zane was facing a lot of work with just his wife, Wendy, and their fulltime ranch hand, Russ and Russ's wife.

Plus, Wendy had bought into a small medical practice, so she was pulling double duty. And if that wasn't enough, Zane had broken the news that Wendy was pregnant with their first child, and his brother was insane with happiness.

To Eli, it felt like it was past time for him to pick up his share of the load.

Would he like being a cowboy again after being away for so many years? Would he miss the adrenaline rush of jumping from an airplane? Would he miss the ocean? The missions? His California friends? He had so many questions and so few answers. Only time would tell.

After dinner, he grabbed a Coke to go for caffeine and a couple of candy bars for sugar and got back on the road. At the rate he was going, he could be home around midnight and wake up in his own bed tomorrow. The idea spurred him to drive on.

When he reached the west entrance to Yellowstone National Park, he was glad he'd killed some time. Now early evening, there appeared to be more cars leaving than entering. July at Yellowstone was a traffic nightmare. Crazy to think he had to drive through this park to reach home, but straight through from the West entrance to the North entrance was the fastest route. At least at this hour, the traffic should be reasonable.

It was nearing ten-thirty when he rolled through the north exit of Yellowstone and into the city of Gardiner. Thirty minutes later, he turned off the highway and down the drive of Grizzly Bitterroot Ranch. A smile broke over his face, and a sense of peace filled his soul. He was home.

He parked his truck in the drive and slid out. His back cramped as he stretched his arms over his head and twisted from side to side. As he stretched, he studied the area. The lights were off at his parents' house. In the distance, he could see his brother and sister-in-law's new house. From where he stood, he couldn't see any lights there either. Cowboy Russ's house adjacent to the barn was dark. Ranch work started early, he remembered that, but he'd forgotten how early everyone turned out the lights.

When his parents built the newest, small feed storage barn, his mother had included a small apartment for her sister, if and when she came to visit, which wasn't often. The small, one-bedroom efficiency apartment was almost never occupied. His parents hadn't wanted to use it as a vacation rental because of its close proximity to the main house, so his coming home plan had included bunking there until he could get his house built, not that he had any idea of what he wanted to build or where. But there was no hurry.

Because their ranch was so far removed from the main road, the small barn apartment was rarely locked, and he doubted it'd be tonight. If it was, he knew where the key would be hidden. He'd surprise everyone at breakfast.

He stepped into the dark storage barn, stopping long enough to enjoy the aroma of hay, oats, horse liniment, and saddle leather. He smiled. Surprisingly, he had missed those scents.

The door that led into the hallway to the apartment was unlocked. He dropped his duffle bag in the laundry room and tried the apartment door. To his surprise, it was locked. He retrieved the key from the laundry room, unlocked the door and entered. Lights were on, which he found surprising, but maybe someone had left them on by accident. Or perhaps this was Zane's work. He had hinted to his brother that he could be home sooner than he'd planned. Inside the refrigerator was a six-pack of his favorite beer. Eli pulled one out, popped the top and took a long gulp. Bless his brother.

A woman's scream startled him and he dropped the beer onto the hardwood flooring. His head jerked toward the door of the bathroom and his mouth dropped open. Wrapped in an undersized towel, her left thigh exposed, and her hair wrapped in another towel stood the last woman who'd ripped out his heart and made him question love and marriage.

What the hell was Addison Treadway doing there?

CHAPTER 2

E ight Months Earlier – Zane's Texas Wedding
       It's not often that a Navy SEAL can be
caught flat-footed by a simple introduction. However,
Eli Miller's mother had succeeded in doing just that.

"Eli, over here. Come here." Betty Miller, his
mother, waved from across the room.

Eli lifted a hand in acknowledgment that he saw
her, then snagged the beer handed to him by the
bartender and made his way to where his mother stood
with a petite woman he did not know, but someone he'd
like to...very much.

His mother wrapped her arm through his and gave
him a bright smile. "Honey, do you know who this is?"

"Unless he lives in the Orlando area, he won't," the
woman said with a self-conscious laugh. "I'm Addison
Treadway." She extended her hand, but he had trouble
taking his gaze off her coral-tinged lips that had curved
into a smile when she laughed.

Taking her hand, he looked into a set of twinkling
jade-green eyes. He couldn't help but notice the

sparkles of gold mixed with the green of her eyes. With her three-inch heels, she was still a couple of inches shorter. When he squeezed her hand for the shake, he took care to be gentle. Her hand was slender, and she was as petite as he was muscular.

Wrapped in a multi-colored, one-shouldered, Hawaiian-inspired dress that hit just above her knees, she was a breathtaking beauty. Her wavy, long red hair was being tossed around in the ocean breeze, and she kept having to sweep strands off her face. Who was this incredible woman and why did he feel like he'd been waiting his entire life for this moment?

Eli smiled. "Eli Miller. How would I know you if I lived in Florida and, more importantly, should I move to the Orlando area immediately?"

She laughed, the sound wrapping around his heart and squeezing. "I have a morning show on WCDA, the local NBC network."

"She has the best show," his mother gushed. "It's funny, and informative, and well, something I just have to watch every day when we're down there."

"Thank you," Addison said. "I'm so glad you enjoy the show. I've had so much fun doing it for the last four years."

"Mom." Eli gestured with his beer bottle toward the door. "There's Zane and Wendy coming in the door. You probably want to go say hello."

"Oh, you're right," his mother replied. She looked at Addison. "It was so nice to meet you, Ms. Treadway."

"Addison," she said with a smile.

"Addison," Betty said. "I'm so excited to discover my soon-to-be-daughter-in-law has famous friends."

Addison rolled her eyes with a chuckle. "Not hardly, but thank you."

Betty Miller hurried off toward her son and bride-to-be.

"Can I get you a drink?" Eli asked, not ready to let this woman walk away.

"I'd like that."

They walked toward the bar, Eli's hand on the small of her back. The palm of his hand burned to slide up and down the flesh exposed by the deep, plunging vee of her dress. Reining in his strong emotional response to her was a struggle. This wasn't like him. He was Joe Cool, not some sleazy guy hitting on the most attractive woman in the room.

"What can I get you?" the bartender asked as they stopped at the open bar.

"Dry, dirty martini," Addison said.

"You got it. Another beer, sir?"

Eli nodded. "Sounds good."

Once they had drinks in hand, Eli gestured toward an empty table. "Want to sit for a minute? We've got a little time before the rehearsal."

"Great idea." She gestured toward the ground. "These shoes are beautiful, but not that comfortable." She sighed. "What we women do for beauty."

Eli's gaze searched until he found the perfect table for two, off to the side, and out of the patio's traffic pattern. He pointed with his beer bottle. "This work?"

"Perfect. You're the groom's brother, right?"

He nodded. "Right. Are you here as one of Wendy's friends or one of her bridesmaids?"

She lifted her foot and pointed to the sexy, high heels. "Bridesmaid. These are my shoes for the wedding reception. I've been wearing them all week trying to break them in and get used to them."

"Can I say how great they look on you, or would that be too much too soon?"

With a chuckle, she lifted her drink. "Thank you. A lady never turns down a compliment."

"I'm sure you've had many of those."

She shrugged. "Some more welcome than others." She looked at him with a smile, and his stomach flipped. "Yours being one of the welcomed ones."

"Glad to hear it." He lifted the bottle, returned her smile, and decided to jump into the deep end. "Are you here with a date or a husband?"

With a grin and arched brow, she said, "Neither one. No date, no boyfriend, no husband. You?"

"No husband either."

She snorted.

"Seriously, no fiancée, no wife, no date. I flew in for the wedding, and I have to fly right back out on Sunday, but there's no woman waiting at home."

"That's hard to believe, Eli."

"Maybe so, but true."

"What do you do? I'm sure Wendy must have told me, but I'm blanking."

"I'm part of the Naval Special Warfare Command."

She nodded. "Ah. A Navy SEAL."

"Good for you," he said with a grin. "Most people would have no idea what that meant."

"I worked at a small station in Norfolk for about six months. Impossible not to learn the lingo. Where are you based? California or Virginia?"

"Camp Pendleton, California."

"Oh, a surfer boy."

He chuckled. "I can surf, but that's not one of the talents I would list."

She started to say something when a microphone squealed.

"Can I have your attention, please?"

Eli looked in the direction of the voice. A man dressed in a purple shirt, pink jacket, and gray slacks stood with a handheld mic to his mouth.

"I know all of you are excited about tomorrow's ceremony and tonight's fabulous dinner," the rather flamboyant man said. "But first, we have to walk through the wedding. I need all the bridal party and parents up here now."

Addison leaned forward. "That's Mr. George. A tad fussy, but one of the best wedding planners in Texas."

He leaned closer. "Why are we down here in Port Aransas at Villa by the Sea instead of Dallas? Isn't that where she grew up?"

"Not really. She grew up outside of Dallas, but Dallas was where she had her medical practice. There was a major incident at her cousin's wedding when the groom announced he was in love with Wendy instead." Addison shook her head. "What a mess and embarrassment for Wendy and Mae." When he frowned, she added, "Mae is her cousin. She's here too and happily married now to someone else. Anyway, the Villa is kind of famous for being a great place to get married, and she wanted something small and intimate. She said that if she got married in Dallas, she'd have to invite way too many people. She wanted to elope, but Zane said no." She chuckled. "Said he was doing this once, and he was doing it right."

"Sounds like my brother," Eli agreed.

"We are missing a best man," Mr. George yelled in to the microphone.

Eli hopped to his feet. "Here." He looked down at Addison and winked. "Save me a seat at dinner."

The bridal party did a walk-through with Mr. George correcting, clapping, and smiling as each person conformed to his directions.

"At this point," Mr. George said, "you will be announced as husband and wife. You can kiss her and start down the aisle."

Zane nodded. "Got it. You got it, Wendy?"

Eli's future sister-in-law smiled. "I've got it."

Zane looked at Mr. George. "And we just walk back down the aisle?"

"That's right," Mr. George replied.

"Seems boring," Zane said.

Eli knew his brother well enough to know his brother was brewing up trouble for Mr. George.

Zane leaned down and swept Wendy up into his arms. She squealed in delight and wrapped her arms around his neck. He then carried her down the aisle to the laughter of everyone except Mr. George, whose lips tightened as he shook his head.

Eli walked to the center of the front of the room to meet Wendy's twin sister Risa, the matron-of-honor.

"We have to outdo them," Risa whispered, and then winked.

Eli grinned. This was the first time he'd met Wendy's sister, but he loved she wanted to try and show up Zane and Wendy. "I agree. Trust me and hang on."

He picked up Risa and threw her over his shoulder in a fireman's carry. Her laughter made her bounce up and down on his shoulder as he walked toward his brother and soon-to-be-sister-in-law standing in the back row of chairs. Wendy's hand was over her mouth as she laughed.

Eli set Risa on her feet and turned in time to see the next bridesmaid, Wendy's cousin Mae, jump on the back of Trevor Mason, Risa's husband and Zane's groomsman. Trevor carried Mae to where the first four members of the bridal party stood.

The last bridesmaid, Addison, met her groomsman escort. How would they beat the first three exits? The groomsman grabbed Addison's hands and they tangoed down the aisle to join the rest of the party.

Eli's mother was laughing, as was his father and Wendy's parents. In fact, everyone was laughing or smiling, except Mr. George, who looked a little worried, like this wedding could ruin his reputation.

"Very funny and cute. Now, tomorrow, all feet will be on the ground, and no one will dance down the aisle," he said sternly, but the corners of his mouth twitched. "Questions?"

Heads shook negatively, and they were dismissed for the rehearsal dinner.

"Pretty hot tango, Ms. Treadway," Eli said as he stepped up closer to Addison.

By his calculations—and he knew he was right—he and Addison were the only single members of the bridal party. Risa, the bride's sister was married to Trevor Mason, fellow groomsman. Mae, the bride's cousin, was married to Michael Rockwell, the groomsman who'd danced down the aisle with Addison. That left only Addison and him. He wondered if his sister-in-law-to-be was playing matchmaker, or if he'd just been a very good guy and fate was rewarding him.

Addison laughed. "I have no idea how to tango, and neither does he. We've both watched too many episodes of *Dancing with the Stars* and decided to fake it."

"Convinced me." He gestured toward the dining room. "Hungry? I heard a rumor my parents went all out for the rehearsal dinner."

She grinned. "Starving."

She took his arm and they walked into the Villa. Dinner was in an elegant dining room with heavy furniture and decorative wall sconces that reflected gentle light up the wallpaper toward the ceiling. Thinking about the MREs he'd eaten on his team's last mission in Tunisia, this setting was a million miles from the mud and muck that sometimes served as the dining hall on duty.

Since the dinner party had been limited to immediate family and the bridal party, it was a small gathering. Eli made sure to find two seats together so he could sit adjacent to Addison and continue their pre-rehearsal conversation. It wasn't as if their conversation had been deep or involved sharing secrets, but he couldn't help but feel something life-changing was happening.

And yeah, the guys would totally rag him if they had any idea he had thoughts like that.

Over a meal of filet mignon and lobster, accompanied by an open bar, the rest of the world ceased to exist for Eli. His focus was on Addison, and her deadly jade-green eyes. Oh, he might have spoken to his brother or some other person during dinner, but only in response to direct questions. Otherwise, his concentration remained on the captivating Addison Treadway. Her laugh. Her smile. The sparkle in her eyes as she spoke. The way she couldn't tell a story without using her hands. The way her rich, deep auburn hair flowed over her shoulders and down her back. Everything about her held him in her thrall.

They talked about growing up—him in Montana and her in Texas. She told tale after tale of being in the same social groups and sorority as Wendy and Risa. She was a couple of years younger, but Wendy had served as her big sister in Xi Omega sorority, and they'd grown quite close.

He told her some about his years in the Navy as a SEAL. He'd like to say he'd glossed over the danger and injuries he'd endured; however, that'd be a lie. He wanted this woman to be impressed, so he might have stretched the stories every now and then. But she seemed to hang on his every word, and he wasn't one to leave a lady wanting.

The sound of a knife tapping on a glass pulled his attention away from Addison—where he wanted to be—to his brother.

"Wendy and I are very thankful for our family and friends who made this trip to the Texas coast for our wedding." Zane lifted a wine glass. "Thank you to Mr. George for finding us the perfect location and staging what I believe will be the best wedding ever."

The wedding coordinator dipped his head in thank you.

Zane looked down at his wife-to-be. "And to Wendy. A year ago, when you climbed off that private plane in high heel shoes and linen pants, I was sure you'd be gone in a week, ten days max. Instead, you planted yourself in Montana and in my life, and I'll be forever thankful."

"Aww, thank you, honey," Wendy said, standing to kiss him.

Zane's father stood. "Your mother and I know there is no better woman for you than Wendy, and I thank her mother Janet for sending Wendy to hide out at our ranch."

That brought a round a chuckles and an eyeroll from Wendy.

"But she did," Henry continued, "and Betty and I are so thrilled to welcome Wendy into our family. You know, this reminds me of when Zane was a little boy. He came running up to me saying 'Watch me, watch me. I'm going to do a dangerous trick.' Then he did a summersault over my footstool, pretending he hadn't known it was there. Well, son, get ready. You're about to do another dangerous trick. Cheers." He lifted his glass, and the rest of the room followed.

"What a sweet story," Addison said.

"Zane was full of dangerous tricks growing up," Eli said with a chuckle. "We were on first name basis with most of the emergency room staff."

The party was beginning to break up, people standing and collecting their belongings.

The Villa had originally been a mansion built by an oil tycoon during the Texas Oil Boom of the 1920s and had remained in the family until ten years ago when it was bought and developed as a destination wedding and party location. Five years ago, the owners had added Inn By the Sea, a posh, upscale boutique hotel adjacent to the Villa, perfect for housing attendees of Villa functions.

"Can I walk you back to the Inn?" Eli asked as he stood. "Maybe we can catch a nightcap in the bar."

"I came with Risa and Trevor, so she'll probably be looking for me. Give me a minute to find her and let her know I'm headed back with you. Then, we can go."

As Addison crossed the room to where Risa stood with Wendy, she couldn't help but take a quick glance over her shoulder to see if Eli was watching her. He wasn't just watching. His smoldering gaze almost lit her panties on fire.

"Why didn't you tell me Zane's brother was so hot and sexy?" Addison said.

Wendy looked at her and laughed. "Well, hello to you, too. Having fun?"

Addison fanned herself, but not before making sure Eli's gaze was elsewhere. "Damn, Wendy. You might have warned me."

Wendy and Risa exchanged a look.

"If you haven't noticed, he looks a lot like the man I'm marrying tomorrow," Wendy said.

Addison looked over at Zane, then at Eli talking to his parents, and then back to Wendy. "Those are some strong genes in that family."

Wendy chuckled. "Could have knocked me down with a feather the first time I laid eyes on Zane."

"I think I know what you mean," Addison said. "It's like being hit upside the head. Was it like that for you and Trevor?" she asked Risa.

"Trevor and I had a history before we got back together, but he can still set off the butterflies in my stomach."

Wendy cleared her throat. "Eli wants to have a nightcap in the bar, so I'm headed back with him."

"Hmm," Risa said with an arched brow. "A nightcap in the bar or is breakfast in your immediate future?"

Addison laughed, but she felt the heat as it rose to her cheeks. "A drink, for now." She shrugged. "We'll see how the night goes."

Risa put her arm around Addison's shoulders as Wendy bracketed her from the other side.

"You've had some bad months lately, and the next few won't be so much fun either. If Eli can make you happy this weekend and help you forget, then go for it," Risa advised.

"I totally agree," Wendy said, putting her arm around Addison's waist and squeezing. "You know that whatever you need, Risa and I will be there."

"My parents are wanting me to come back to Dallas for treatment." She looked at Risa. "They want you to see to my care."

"Done," Risa said. "No question. Have fun this weekend. Forget about everything else. Pretend it's Addison's weekend, instead of, you know, Wendy's."

Wendy laughed. "Just remember to show up for our girls' time tomorrow and the wedding tomorrow night."

"I'll try to remember," Addison said with a laugh. "Although I'm pretty sure I'll need a two-hour massage instead of only an hour."

"Girls' time might be more fun than what Zane has planned for tomorrow. Can I come along?"

Eli's deep, baritone voice swirled through her, wrapping around her insides and sending shivers down her back.

Wendy laughed. "I'm sure your brother will want you by his side all day."

"He's not nearly as interesting." His gaze landed on Addison. "Ready to go?"

"Yes." Addison looked at Wendy and Risa. "See you tomorrow at ten, is that right?"

"Ten," Wendy confirmed. "The Spa at the Villa Inn."

Walking along the footpath that led from the original manor back to the inn took them through lush foliage and along a thick carpet of grass. Beyond the grounds, the ocean roared, washing wave after crashing wave onto the seawall.

"Can you imagine what this place would look like in spring?" Addison asked. "I mean, the fall flowers are stunning, but just think of the trees bursting into bloom or the bulbs pushing through the soil in the bed." She looked up at him. "Sometimes, I miss Texas."

He arched a brow. "Just sometimes?"

"Don't tell anyone, but there are times when I get tired of 'the mouse,' you know?"

"Never been there, so I really don't know."

"Never been to Orlando?"

"Nope. Always been on the west coast. How did you end up in Orlando and with your own talk show?"

They'd reached the inn's main entrance. Eli pulled open the door and let her enter first.

"It's a long story. Let's grab those drinks, and we can share life stories."

"Works for me." He held out his arm. "I'd hate to lose you to those heels."

She smiled and hooked her arm through his. Honestly, she would just about do anything to extend her time with him. He only knew her as Addison

Treadway, friend to his future sister-in-law, not Addison Treadway of The Chat.

Being on television meant guys hit on her a lot. Dinner out with friends, or, heaven forbid, a drink in a bar with friends would always be interrupted by some guy wanting to chat her up. Most thought they knew her because they'd seen her show, but her public persona and television persona were not who she was. She was quieter and shier than most people realized, more introvert than extrovert. Plus, at thirty-three, she was long past the partying stage, thank goodness. There had been some poor decisions made when she'd been in her early twenties, like a marriage she'd rather forget ever happened.

She'd had some major breaks in life, starting with wealthy parents. While she wasn't foolish enough to swear off her trust fund and give it away, she nonetheless lived within her salary. Her clothes were nice, but not designer. Who paid thousands for one dress? Not her. Tonight's outfit, chosen to go with Wendy's *At the Beach* theme for the rehearsal, had been ordered online.

In the bar, Eli steered them toward a table in the corner, out of the main thoroughfare and traffic. They pulled the chairs around until they were sitting side-by-side rather than across from each other. After drinks were ordered—dirty martini for her and a beer for him—he draped his arm over the back of her chair. Addison leaned toward him, enjoying his clean, male scent. His arm dropped off the chair and onto her shoulders. She was drawn to him, physically and mentally.

For the next hour, they drank and talked about growing up—Texas for her and Montana for him—

favorite movies, books, television shows, and just any subject she could think of to keep the night going. She loved how focused Eli was on her. It was like the entire outside world didn't exist beyond this small table. For the first time in a very long time, she felt...cherished, or maybe, simply appreciated for her thoughts, for who she was—not just the pretty package she presented.

"It's getting late," he said with a glance at the time on his phone. "I don't want to keep you up."

Her heart sagged at the thought of ending tonight, but she put on her brightest smile. "Are you saying I need my beauty sleep?"

He laughed. "Not hardly. It'd be hard to improve on such perfection."

"Smooth," she replied with a roll of her eyes, which made him give her a smile that sent her heart racing and heat swirling low in her belly. "But, you're right. It is getting late."

He stood and helped pull her chair away from the table so she could rise easier. Then he extended his hand. She laced her fingers through his and stood.

"Where's your room?" he asked.

"Third floor. Room three-oh-two. Yours?"

"First floor. One-three-seven. Come on. I'll walk you up."

As a rich girl with above average looks growing up, she'd never had to make the first move on a guy. Usually, she was batting them away like annoying gnats. But tonight, she wasn't pushing him away. The minute he made the move, she'd pull him in. He would make a move, right?

"Elevator or stairs?" he asked, tilting his head toward the bank of elevators.

"With these shoes? Elevator. I might break my neck on stairs. Thank goodness tomorrow's ceremony is on the beach in the sand and we'll be barefooted."

He frowned. "I thought you were breaking in those shoes for the wedding?"

"Reception," she clarified.

"Ah," he replied as they entered an empty elevator car.

It was a short ride from the lobby bar to the third floor, but long enough that Addison knew how she wanted this night to end...with Eli in her bed. Like her friends had pointed out, she had a rough road ahead of her with cancer treatments and surgery. Making some nice memories for those long nights to come might make those evenings easier to bear.

And truth be told, she and her ex-husband hadn't had sex in months before he'd left. Doing a quick calculation in her head, she hadn't been with a man in close to eighteen months. She glanced at the gorgeous man beside her. What a way to end months of celibacy, right?

He dropped her hand as they exited and put his arm around her shoulders as they walked toward her door. When she fumbled with the magnetic key—she was a little nervous about trying to seduce this man—he took the card and held it until the lock light turned from red to green. He pulled down the handle, opened the door, and stepped back.

"Tonight has been..." he started.

"What? Great? Horrible? Boring?" she joked.

"Incredible," he finished.

She lifted her face toward him for a kiss. He lowered his head and kissed her lightly, and then lifted his gaze to look into hers. She stepped into her room and turned back.

"Good night," he said, stepping back. "I'll see you tomorrow."

Disappointment stabbed at her heart. As she opened her mouth to invite him in, he turned and strode away down the hallway. Her door clicked shut.

In frustration, she kicked off her shoes and stomped across the suite. What the hell just happened? Why hadn't he followed her into her room? He had to know she wanted him, right? She hadn't said the words outright, but surely, he was aware. What had she done wrong? She really did suck at this seduction thing.

She began stripping out of her dress and stopped. No. This would not do. This was the last weekend in her pre-breast-cancer treatment life. Her girls deserved to go out fully worshiped. And she couldn't have been the only one to feel that spark between them. No way.

After cramming her feet back into those high-hell shoes, she grabbed a couple of condoms and her room key.

With a confidence she didn't really feel, she walked to the elevator and punched the button for the first floor. Nothing ventured, nothing gained.

CHAPTER 3

E li tossed his room key and pocket change on the dresser. Walking away from Addison tonight had been the hardest thing he'd ever done. But, dammit. He really liked her—really, *really* liked her.

Since the moment they'd met, he'd felt a magnetic pull to her, one that'd been impossible to ignore. He'd never experienced anything like that in his life. He'd thought she'd felt it too, but at her room, he'd waited for her to invite him in. She hadn't and he respected her too much to assume, so he'd left. Plus, how could he realistically pursue any type of relationship when they lived on different coasts and thousands of miles apart?

And then there was his job. Who knew when he'd be shipped out and when he'd return? He wanted to show her respect by not jumping into bed within hours of meeting, but on the other hand, all he could think about was jumping into bed with her.

He flung his Hawaiian shirt over the bedroom chair and went to the sink to brush his teeth. While he was rinsing his mouth, he thought he heard a soft knock on his door. Wrapping a towel around his neck, he opened it. His heart leapt at the vision standing in the hall. Pulling all the cool he could muster, he smiled.

"Hey," he said, leaning against the door frame and holding open his door.

"Hey," Addison said. "I'm probably being too forward, but..." She paused, then whipped around to leave. "Never mind."

He grabbed her arm and stopped her, turning her toward him. "Wait a minute. I'm happy to see you."

"You are?" She nibbled on her bottom lip.

Mentally, he groaned. He wanted to nibble on that lip, and the top lip, and those luscious boobs, and, come to think of it, he wanted to kiss all her delicious curves.

"Yeah." He pulled her inside his room and let the door snick shut behind her. "I was kicking myself for leaving you a while ago."

"You were?"

Pulling her into his arms, he backed her against the door. "Oh hell, yeah." He leaned over and kissed her. Her lips were soft and full and welcoming. He ran the tip of his tongue along the seam of her lips, and she opened for him. His tongue slid alongside hers.

She tasted like heaven and his future all rolled into one kiss.

That thought should have been terrifying enough to have him running for the hills. It was scary, but at the same time, he found it calming, like jumping out of a plane, sure your parachute would bring you safely to earth.

He pulled back and looked into her deep-green eyes. "I want you in my bed so bad." He paired his confession with a trail of kisses across her cheek and down her neck.

"How convenient," she said with a low moan. "I have an ache I think only you can reach." Addison leaned her head to the side to give him better access to her neck. At the same time, her hands glided up his naked chest. Her fingers spread and she threaded them through his dark chest hair.

His pulse skyrocketed. Blood rushed from the territory above his waist to below, filling and stretching his cock in response to her presence.

His breath caught as she raked her nails toward the waistband of his slacks. He sucked in his gut, not that he had one, but a sexy woman dragging her hands down his body always produced that reaction.

"I'm confused why you didn't come into my room earlier." Her hands flattened against the muscles in his chest. She raised her gaze until she could look into his eyes. "When you walked away, I felt like I'd imagined the entire evening. I wasn't sure if you were interested or wanted to see me again."

He groaned as her hand slid across the front of his pants. "I was waiting for an invitation," he growled.

She wrinkled her nose. "My bad. I'm not used to making the first move. In fact, I can't remember ever having to make the first move."

He pressed his erection into the palm she held against him. "You're doing pretty good right now," he said with a groan. "Consider yourself invited in."

She giggled. "Maybe I'm better at this first move thing than I thought."

Eli's heart thudded as he placed his hands on her

hips and pulled her with him as he moved backwards, needing to get them both closer to the bed.

A lovely blush bloomed on her cheeks. Her emerald eyes darkened as the pupils dilated. Her breaths shortened, matching his, as they both grew more aroused. All thoughts of the coming wedding and his return to Coronado melted away under the heat of her palm as she moved it along his length. He had to have her.

Now beside the bed, he moved a hand into the vee of bare skin at the back of her dress and glided it deeper, spreading his fingers to clutch one firm buttock. He lifted the other hand to comb his fingers deep into her soft red hair to anchor her as he pressed another kiss to her mouth, taking that bottom lip she'd nibbled between his. He sucked on it, let it go, and then took her mouth, gently thrusting his tongue inside to play with hers.

When she drew on his tongue, an electric tether tugged at his groin, tightening his balls.

He withdrew his hand from her dress and pulled back. "How the hell does this thing come off?" he asked, not waiting for an answer as he clutched the skirt and drew it upward.

Without answering in words, she raised her arms, and he skimmed it over her head, tossing it to the armchair beside the bed rather than the floor, perhaps the last considerate gesture he would manage for the next while because the only undergarment she now wore was a tiny pair of bikini panties. The rosy pink satin was nearly the same shade as her nipples. Add the high heels, and his cock was ready to burst his zipper.

She swallowed hard as his gaze trailed downward to her breasts. "Damn, Addison. I've never seen tits as pretty as yours."

A short gasping laugh shook them.

"I shouldn't have called them that," he said, his voice deepening.

"Call them whatever you like," she said.

His gaze darted up to find that her lips were trembling and a hint of excess moisture gleamed in her eyes. "Am I making you uncomfortable?"

She shook her head. "No. Well, maybe a little." Her hand waved toward his body.

"Ah." He moved back and quickly toed off his shoes and socks, unbuckled his belt, and unbuttoned his slacks. When he pushed everything to the floor, he straightened, his dick standing tall in the cool air.

He was gratified to see her eyes widen and her mouth drop open as she stared.

"We even now?" he asked, keeping his tone light when what he wanted to do was growl and pounce.

Addison's mouth closed, and she slipped her thumbs into the sides of her panties and drew them down. When they puddled around her feet, she said, "Now, we are."

She was smooth below. Perfect for a feast. But first, he needed to pay homage to those firm, round perfect tits. The nipples were dimpled, the tips distended. He didn't resist their invitation, lifting a hand to cup one, and then bending to latch his mouth around the velvety areola.

When her head fell back, she swayed, so he steadied her with a hand on her ass as he sucked on the diamond-hard tip, nipped it with his teeth, then soothed it with soft glides of his tongue.

Her fingernails sank into his scalp, scraping as her back arched harder. Moving across her chest, he fingered the nipple he'd left wet while he plied his lips, tongue and teeth to the other beauty.

"Eli," she said, her voice thin and high.

Yeah, he was ready for more, too. He guided her to the mattress, sat her on the edge, then knelt between her splayed thighs. The frills of her inner lips were unique, flower-like. He was fascinated with how they protruded slightly past the outer lips, like the petals of a flower his mom had kept in a pot that rarely bloomed. Some exotic orchid, he thought. He wet a fingertip then traced the delicate edges, moving downward. Then needing to see more, he pressed his palms against her inner thighs. As she spread wider, her belly fluttered and goose bumps rose.

Glancing up, he met her gaze which was fixed on him. Her hands kneaded her beautiful breasts while her dark gaze didn't so much as blink, like she didn't want to miss seeing what he'd do next.

Holding her gaze, he moved closer and lapped her petals, only touching the edges, moving upward to where they formed a definite triangle where both sides met. He flicked his tongue at the triangle, which caused her breath to catch. Then he flattened his tongue against it, pressing against the clit hiding inside. He felt the little knot and closed his mouth around it, sucking gently, while a low thready moan escaped her.

Pausing, he wet a finger and swirled it inside her while he continued to draw on her clit. Her hips moved, undulating upward then relaxing. He flattened his free hand against her pubic bone to hold her still and thrust his finger deeply inside her.

Her head thrashed on the mattress; her breaths broke apart. He continued, pulling more strongly now and slipping a second finger inside her then hooking them upward, rubbing inside her channel until she let go a ragged gasp. Suddenly, she cried out and her muscles tightened around his fingers; her legs moved restlessly, caressing his shoulders. When she fell quiet and still, he rose and lifted her body to carry it to the center of the bed. Resting on an elbow beside her, he waited until her eyelids blinked open.

"Wow," she whispered.

A smile pulled at one side of his mouth. "There's more."

Her small hand pressed against his belly and glided downward. Her fingers spread and captured his shaft. "It's my turn," she said.

Eli chuckled and placed his hand against hers. "I'm sure he'd be happy to have you go down on him, but he's not going to last long."

She waggled her eyebrows and slid her hand down to encircled the base of his cock. "He'll last just long enough." Her gaze darted downward. "Although looking at him, I'm a little daunted."

"You don't have to deepthroat him to make him happy."

"Good to know. I haven't learned that trick—and he's not little."

They shared smiles as he rolled to his back and placed both of his hands behind his head, surrendering to her.

Addison had never felt as empowered as she did at this moment. With her body still warm and tingling after the best oral sex of her life, she couldn't wait to explore him as thoroughly as he had her.

She climbed over him, straddling him mid-thigh. Then she leaned over him, bracing herself on one hand. She pulled her hair over one shoulder and held the end of one thick lock. Then she used the curl to swirl around one flat brown nipple.

Eli's breath hissed inward. "Sensitive much?" She glanced up and did it again. When his eyes narrowed, she swirled it around the other nipple, loving how quickly the tiny centers hardened.

Then downward she moved, licking and nipping at the soft skin stretched over steel-rope muscles. She let her hair fall forward to hide her actions and to drag against his prickling skin. Scooting down her legs, she couldn't help but note the way his erect cock lifted from his belly. Deciding to tease him some more, she wagged her head over him, letting her long hair brush his length. By the way his dick twitched, he liked it. So, emboldened, she took another thick bundle of hair and slowly rapped it around his shaft. While holding it around him, she opened her mouth and used the flat of her tongue to swirl on the soft, steamy cap. Pre-ejaculate oozed from his tiny slit. Pointing her tongue, she dipped in to lick it out, darting a glance up at his face. She froze there, her tongue extended, because of the tightness of his expression and chest. His breaths were coming like harsh little pants.

Addison let go of her hair and swept it back, then bent over him again, letting him see everything as she took his cock into her mouth and sank as deeply as she could. Suctioning on him, working her lips and tongue around his shaft, she began lifting and sinking, one hand going to his balls to gently massage and pull, the other going to the base of his cock to hold it as tightly as she could because he wasn't coming yet. Not until she let him.

She came up again, this time letting her teeth lightly scrape his shaft, then once she held only his thick cap between her lips, she teethed the softer tissue while she stroked him with her free hand.

His fingers sank into her hair and tugged. When she gave a soft grunt of refusal, he tugged harder and forced her to abandon his cock to move up his body. Then with a quick roll, he moved over her.

"Fuck, Addison," he hissed. "That was so fucking sexy."

Her lips stretched into a grin. "Have a condom?"

He cleared his throat. "Glad one of us is thinking." He rolled away and off the bed, swiped his trousers from the floor and quickly pulled out his wallet. When he held the condom packet high, she clapped, smiling.

Eli tore the plastic, extracted the condom, then gave a grimace as he smoothed it down his length. Ringing himself at the base, he shook his head. "Not sure how long I'll hold out."

Addison lifted her legs and let them fall open. Then she used two fingers to draw moisture from her center and rub it over her hardened clit. She liked that his gaze was locked on what her fingers were doing to herself. Liked even better the expression he wore as he stomped back to the bed, climbed over the edge, and then braced his body on one hand over her.

Reaching downward she wrapped her fingers around him and guided the tip to her entrance. Then she reached farther and drew his hand from around the base of his cock. "I won't last long," she whispered. "Fuck me, Eli. *Please*."

The next morning, Addison snuggled into the warm, soft sheets, not wanting to get up just yet. A smile stretched her mouth as she thought about last night.

"You're smiling. I hope that's a good thing."

She rolled over in bed and looked up at Eli propped on his forearm looking down at her. The muscles in his arm were firm and well-defined and made her want to drool. Damn. So not fair. He was hot and sexy even first thing in the morning, and she probably appeared more raccoon than human.

His glossy hair looked as if he'd just run his fingers through the top and each strand knew where to land. The dark shadow of a morning beard covered the firm planes of his face. His blue eyes sparkled while a sensual smile pulled up at the corner of his full mouth.

Her immediate reaction was to want to rush to the bathroom to smooth her hair, which she was sure was sticking out in every direction. Plus, even though she had no mirror to see her face, she'd bet good money that her eyeliner had moved from her eyelids to the top of her cheeks.

She licked her lips.

"Are you watching me sleep? That's creepy, you know."

He chuckled. "It was your snoring," he joked. "Woke me up hours ago."

She laughed. "Yeah, well, I had to do something to drown out yours."

Eli threw his head back with a loud laugh. It was a

fully-involved belly laugh that not only made her happy, but also sent curls of pleasure coursing through her.

When he leaned forward to kiss her, she held him off. "Morning breath," she said, sure her face was red with embarrassment.

"I love morning breath," Eli said, and pulled her against him. "There is nothing I don't like about you. Morning breath. Wild, crazy, sleep hair. Funky makeup. I love it all."

He kissed her, his tongue slipping between her lips. She let out a quiet moan and closed her lips around his tongue to suck.

Before she knew it, his body covered hers. Her legs opened without any thought from her, knees rising, hips tilting to receive him. Just as instinctively, he found her center and entered her with a single straight thrust.

Once connected, they began to move more slowly, bodies undulating together and apart. "You are a blessed, blessed man," she said, luxuriating in the way his thickness filled her so completely.

"I completely agree. I'm fucking you," he murmured.

She smiled, happier than she'd been in a long, long while. Tonight was like a dream: a handsome, attentive lover, sex so good she knew she'd savor the details over the difficult months ahead. She was making memories she'd cherish.

The sweet sensual movements gave way to a more feverish joining as their bodies heated. He rolled again, leaving her on top. Leaning on his elbows, he lifted his head and shoulders to burrow at her breasts, drawing on the tips so hard she felt it all the way to her core. She rose and fell, feeling as though she was the sexiest woman alive the way he paid homage to her breasts, and toward the end, when she was nearly breathless, near tears over the beauty of the moment, he moved her off him then came behind her, where she was free to let the tears fall as he cupped her breasts and entered her again.

They came swiftly. First, her. Then him, with fast pounding that created so much heat inside her that she came again. When they fell to the bed, he spooned against her back.

Addison cupped her hand over his, where he still held her breast, and let the tears roll away into the pillow. She wasn't despairing. She felt joy and gratitude. Truly blessed for the gift she'd been given this night.

Eli flopped back onto his pillow with a sigh. "I'd rather stay here with you than whatever my brother has planned for today."

Addison's nose wrinkled. "Shoot, I'd rather go with the guys today, if it weren't for the ninety-minute massage I'm having in place of a facial."

He leaned up on his elbow. "Do you know what my brother has planned for today? Zane might have told me, but I've long since forgotten."

"I think I heard something about jet skis and beer."

"Oh goody. Just what I want to do, water activities."

She laughed. "Busman's holiday."

"Oh, and let me add, there is absolutely nothing wrong with your face. A facial for you is a waste of money."

Her stomach butterflies launched and flittered at

his statement. "Aww. Aren't you sweet?" She leaned forward until she could kiss him.

"I'm not sweet. I'm a tough SEAL," he growled as he jerked her toward him.

She laughed. "Sorry. Right. Rough, tough, alpha guy. Got it. But you can have my facial appointment if you want it."

He snarled, which made her laugh harder. Rolling onto his back, he lifted her on top of him. She wiggled as she settled between his thighs. The look of pain on his face as she ground against him made her chuckle.

"Well, I'd better go," she said and tried to move her legs.

"Oh, hell, no," he said and wrapped his legs around hers holding her in place. "You implied I might need a facial. That's gonna cost you."

She shimmied down his body, which was much like sliding over a hard rock, which was also an accurate description of his cock as it poked into her stomach.

"Let me see if I can convince you to let me leave," she said and licked along the slit in the head of his dick, the salty tang coating the tip of her tongue.

His head pushed back into his pillow as he groaned. "Yeah, that's not much of an encouragement to let you leave. Hold on." He shifted in the bed until he was sitting against the headboard. "If you're going to suck me off, I at least want to watch again."

His words sent arousal dripping onto her thighs. She loved to give blow jobs. She loved the power it gave her over men, not to mention, how much having Eli in her mouth turned her on.

She sucked him into her mouth and gently rasped

her teeth along his rigid flesh. Then she nibbled along the thick, pulsing vein back down to the base.

"Not helping your case for leaving," he said through gritted teeth. "But watching my cock going in and out of your mouth is so fucking sexy. Keep that up and I might not let you leave this bed until the wedding tonight."

What a fucking good idea. Today would be so much more fun if they could stay right where they were. Who needed a facial and massage when she had a Navy SEAL under her control with just her tongue?

Licking her way to the tip and back to the base, she then worked her way back up, using her hands to twist and squeeze his rigid flesh. When she took him deep inside her mouth, his hips bucked up from the mattress.

"You're fucking killing me," he said with a groan. He thrust his hips, driving his cock deeper in her mouth until he hit the back of her throat. "Don't stop."

She sucked and pulled back, exposing his dick glistening with her saliva. She glanced up at her powerful SEAL. His eyes were dark with lust. His chest heaved. The vein in his neck throbbed visibly.

"I'm not going to last," he warned. "You're too fucking good at this. I want to come inside you."

But that's not what she wanted. She wanted to taste his essence when she swallowed. She shook her head and sucked harder.

He threw his head back with a loud groan. "Honey, I can't hold off much longer. I'm going to come if you keep this up. Please, keep this up."

And she didn't want him to hold off. She wanted to give him a blow job he'd smile about years from now when he remembered her and this weekend.

She sucked harder and moved him in and out of her

mouth faster. His hips pumped against her mouth until he came with a low growl and moan. "Damn, babe. I'm going to spend the whole day just thinking about tonight."

She swallowed. He tasted every bit as good as she thought he would. Looking up, she smiled. "My room. Tonight. As soon as the cake is cut."

"If I can't get you alone sooner. I'll be checking out every nook and cranny for places I can fuck you during the reception. I don't think I'll be able to wait until the reception ends." He gave her a devious grin. "No panties under your bridesmaid dress. I'll make it worth your while."

Sliding off the bed, she studied the man. Muscular. Lean. Swoon-worthy, if only she had the time. She didn't want him to know how turned on she was at his no-panties suggestion.

"I'll think about it. I've got to go." She leaned over and kissed him. "As it is, I'll barely make it back to the room to get ready." With a shake of her head, she said, "Until tonight."

For the women, the day passed with deep massages, facials, pedicures, manicures, and a long lunch with mimosas. For Addison, the day passed with her thinking about her panties. Would she? Could she?

The guys were treated to a day of riding jet skis on the ocean and ice-cold beer. By the time Eli made it back to his room to shower and dress, there were only a couple of hours before the start of the wedding. The men were meeting back in the groom's suite for an early dinner. Eli decided the wedding planner was a genius.

Food would go far in diluting the volume of beer that'd been ingested that day.

Although Eli enjoyed being with his brother, his dad, the bride's dad, and the groomsmen, Addison was never far from his thoughts. The way her hair smelled like vanilla. The way her laugh tugged at his gut. The way her kisses melted the wall he'd so carefully constructed around his heart.

None of the guys mentioned Addison, or made any reference to the amount of time Eli and she had spent together during dinner and later in the bar. Either no one noticed, or his soon-to-be-sister-in-law had played matchmaker and the guys were under orders to zip their lips.

At sunset, Eli took his place alongside Zane as Best Man, his heart racing, but from what he couldn't say. Was his heart pounding with excitement and joy for his brother? Or was the cause the incredible woman who'd walked from the mansion as the first bridesmaid?

Addison glowed with happiness. Their gazes met, and her smile widened. Eli's knees grew weak as he watched her approach.

Was this what love felt like? Weak knees and whirling stomach? How could he fall so quickly for a woman he'd just met? His team would tell him he was thinking with his dick and not his brain, but it didn't feel that way.

He chanced a glance at his brother. Zane wore a smile, but it was more a polite expression than the look of a man in love. Eli frowned. Was his brother making a mistake? Had he and Wendy moved too fast? Should they have waited to marry until they knew each other better?

One by one, the bridesmaids filed out onto the porch, down the stairs, and found their places in the sand on the beach. And with each one, Zane became twitchier beside Eli. Should he say something to Zane? Make sure this wedding was what he really wanted?

Then, with her father escorting her, Zane's bride, Wendy, walked through the mansion's French doors and onto the porch. Beside him, Zane's face lit up like fireworks. His smile stretched as wide as possible, even as Eli could see tears sparkling in his brother's eyes.

"She's beautiful," Eli whispered.

"And she's mine. Damn. How did I get so lucky?" Zane whispered back.

There were a few tears during the ceremony, along with some chuckles and tons of grins. To the relief of the wedding planner, the exit of the bride and groom, followed by the attendants, consisted of all feet on the ground and no tangos.

Eli maneuvered seating arrangements until he secured the seat next to Addison for the dinner, not that he tasted any of the food that entered his mouth. He could still taste Addison on his lips, and that was how he liked it.

When dinner was over, Zane and Wendy proceeded directly to the cutting of the cake. Eli had no time to whisk Addison off to a deserted room and fuck her like he'd wanted since she'd walked out onto the mansion porch.

The reception music started, and Zane led his bride onto the floor.

Eli brushed his chest against Addison's back and whispered, "Finally. Cake's cut and the groom has his bride on the dance floor. I found the perfect room we can escape to."

She smiled over her shoulder at him. "I've been thinking..."

His heart dropped. Had she changed her mind about tonight?

"Yeah? What about?"

"I'm wondering, since you are the best man and I'm a bridesmaid, how long do we have to be here before we can leave for good without insulting the bride and groom?"

"Wow. Great minds think alike." He nuzzled his nose behind her ear. "I don't think we'll be missed by anyone."

"Your parents, perhaps?"

He glanced over at his parents, who stood with the bride's parents. All four adults looked like birds who'd swallowed canaries. His mother was laughing at something Wendy's dad said.

"Nope. My folks won't miss us at all."

"Grab a bottle of champagne?"

"Not for me. I have a nice bourbon in my room. I can get champagne for you, though."

"Bring the bourbon. I'll meet you in my room."

Eli grabbed her hand, and they rushed from the reception room. At the elevator, he pushed the up button. After a quick glance around for anyone from the wedding, and seeing none, he pulled her into his arms.

"Tell me you don't have on panties." His lips found hers in a deep kiss.

The elevator dinged, and the doors slid open.

Addison stepped into the empty car and lifted her

dress. The hem climbed up her thigh until her nude hip was exposed. She leaned over and said, "Don't be late. I don't want to have to start without you."

The doors closed and Eli swallowed the lump of lust lodged in his throat. Holy fuck. She'd done as he'd asked.

Start without him? Hell, no.

He raced down the stairs to his room to get the bourbon and climbed up the three flights of stairs like the Taliban was on his ass. He wasn't even short of breath when he reached her door...props to his team leader, Bear, for working his tail off every day.

The door was slightly ajar.

"Honey," he called. "I'm home."

Her giggle came from the bathroom. "I thought I would lose some of this makeup, if you don't mind. The gal who did our faces put it on heavy for the pictures. And I'd love to take a shower. I feel hot and sweaty."

He closed the door behind him. "Fine with me. You don't need all that crap anyway. As far as hot and sweaty, you'll just get hot and sweaty again, or that's my plan for tonight."

She opened the door a crack. "Thank you. Why are you still dressed?"

He laughed.

"Oh, I called room service and ordered ice water, a bucket of extra ice, and a can of whipped cream." Her grin was evil, and he fucking loved it.

"Sounds kinky. God, I hope you're thinking kinky."

She winked. "I'm thinking of how even more delicious your cock will be in my mouth after I've covered it in whipped cream." She closed the door.

His hand covered his heart. He was seriously falling in love with this woman. Fucking in love.

Her room phone rang as the shower began to run.

"Probably room service," she said through a crack in the door. "Can you grab it?"

"Sure." He reached for the desk phone. "Hello?"

"Who's this?" a male voice demanded.

"Who are you looking for?"

"Addison, my wife. What the fuck is a man doing in my wife's room?"

Eli's chest constricted at the man's words. Addison was married? He'd been with another man's wife?

Nausea roiled in his stomach as his gastric juices sloshed and ate at the lining. His vision blurred as fury exploded.

A rich, spoiled woman who thought she'd have a fling while her husband wasn't there. He felt sick, like he might throw up.

Since he'd joined the Navy, and especially since he'd joined the SEALs, there'd been plenty of women who'd wanted to share his bed. Some had. Some hadn't. But he'd never, ever, knowingly slept with another man's wife. It went against every fiber of his being. It violated every moral code in his personal beliefs.

"Nothing. Nothing at all. I'm with room service, and I'm just leaving."

Eli left the bourbon sitting on the desk, went back to his room, tossed everything into his travel duffle and left. In the cab on the way to the airport, he left voice messages for his parents and Zane explaining that he'd been called back unexpectedly and had to leave in a hurry.

Addison Treadway may be the closest he'd ever

come to loving. He sure as shit would never want to feel what her poor husband would feel when, and if, he discovered his spouse was unfaithful.

Eli hated himself and Addison, and he feared he always would.

CHAPTER 4

"What are you doing here?" Addison asked, tugging the tiny towel tighter across her breasts.

Eli's heart slammed against his chest wall. He was unable to control his gaze that dropped to her bare feet, up a pair of trim legs, passed the exposed thigh, to her hands gripping the edges of the damp towel as though her life depended on it, to settle on her irate face. The memory of her long hair draping across his chest drew all the breath from his lungs. Tonight, however, her hair was wrapped in a towel on her head. Obviously, she'd just stepped from his shower.

What the hell?

"Did you hear me?" she demanded. "What are you doing here?"

"What am *I* doing here? What are *you* doing here?" Eli sputtered, his mind whirling with confusion.

"I live here, or rather, I'm staying here."

With a dismissive snort, he shook his head. "I don't think so. This is my apartment."

Without taking her gaze off him, she reached back into the bathroom and pulled her cell phone to her ear.

"Hey. Sorry to wake you, but can you come get your brother-in-law out of my kitchen? Thanks." She ended the call and pointed to the floor. "While we're waiting for *you* to be removed from *my* apartment, think you can clean up your mess? In the meantime, I'm going to put on some clothes."

He glanced down at the beer bottle lying on its side, beer trickling onto the floor. Tossing a sneer toward her, he said. "Don't get dressed on my account. I've already seen all your goodies." He rubbed his chin. "On second thought, seen them and don't really want to see them again."

With a scathing glare, she stepped into the bedroom and slammed the door. The pictures on the adjoining living room wall rattled.

At the same time, the apartment front door opened and Zane and Wendy rushed in.

"Eli," Wendy said as she wrapped her arms around his neck. "We didn't expect you until August."

"I caught a tailwind," Eli joked. "Good to see you, man," he said to Zane, holding out his hand.

His brother ignored his hand and pulled him into a back-slapping hug. "Dad and Mom are going to be so surprised that you're here two weeks early."

"Don't wake them up," Eli said. "I can surprise them in the morning."

"You're home!" his mother cried from the door, his father right behind her. She hurried over to give Eli a tight embrace. Then she slugged his arm. "You should have told me you were coming tonight."

"Too late," Zane said to Eli with a grin. "Wendy called them."

"And it's a good thing," his mother said. She caught his face between her hands. "You shouldn't be here for another couple of weeks." She kissed his cheek. "But I'm so glad to see you." She kissed his other cheek. "Although I ought to spank you for ruining all my plans I had for you."

Eli wasn't sure he wanted to know about his mom's plans. Usually those involved fixing him and Zack up with single women. Now that Zack was married, his mom would fixate like a laser on Eli's marital state, something he wasn't looking forward to.

"I wanted to surprise you," Eli said. "Surprise! Hi, Dad."

"Welcome home, son," his dad said, and pulled him into a tight hug.

"Come on over to the house, and I'll make coffee," his mother said. "I want to hear about your drive."

"Oh, no," Eli protested. "It's too late. You guys go back to bed. We can visit tomorrow."

His mother linked her arm through his and squeezed. "Absolutely not. Let's go."

"Bro, you know mom. Might as well go with her if you want to get to bed any time before the alarm goes off in..." Zane checked his phone. "Five hours."

As the party of five began to file out, Eli's mom turned back. "You come, too, Addison."

Dressed in a pair of shorts and a T-shirt, Addison had rejoined the group a couple of minutes ago. Of course, Eli had been aware of her presence the second she'd walked back in. It'd been like a spark had flashed in the corner of his eye.

Addison smiled, but shook her head. "Oh, thank you, Betty. but I'll pass. I had a long day and need to get some sleep, but y'all have a nice visit."

Eli hadn't forgotten they were in *his* kitchen, which was currently being occupied by a woman he'd thought he'd never see again, which would have been fine with him. Instead, she was shooting hatred glares at him from the bedroom door.

As his mother led the troops out of the barn, he glanced over his shoulder in time to see Addison close the apartment door. She didn't slam the door shut, but if her expression was any indication, she'd wanted to crash it hard.

What did she have to be all pissy about? Sure, they'd hooked up at Zane and Wendy's wedding, but he'd been the one who'd been lied to and made a fool of. Even thinking of that weekend made him cringe with shame and regret.

At the Miller house, Eli, Zane and his dad sat at the old kitchen table. Wendy sliced a chocolate cake that'd been on the counter as his mother brewed a pot of coffee. Within minutes, the five adults were gathered around the table, the sound of coffee sips and forks clinking on glass filled his parents' kitchen.

"Mom, I don't need more coffee," Eli protested. "I've got enough caffeine running through my system as it is."

"This is decaf," she said, nudging the mug by his cake. "Now, tell me how you got home two weeks early and why. Did the Navy get mad that you were leaving and kick you out?"

Eli laughed and skirted the mission the team had

been on that got them time off, which was why he was able to get away. He left his explanation with a simple, "I had vacation time coming, so I headed home."

When he asked about Addison, everyone paused as though waiting for someone else to speak.

"She's here to see me," Wendy said. "And I wanted her close so we could visit."

And the topic was quickly changed to the proposed new storage barn Zane wanted to build on the Haney property.

After thirty minutes, Eli saw Wendy hide her yawn behind her hand. He faked a wide-mouthed, noisy yawn. "Let's call it a night. I swear I'm home for good, and we will have lots of time to talk." He fake-yawned again. "I don't know about you guys, but I could use some shuteye."

The reality was, he doubted he'd get much sleep tonight. Between the caffeine and the shock of seeing Addison Treadway, his mind was wheeling and his stomach churning with acid.

His dad stood. "I agree, Eli. Come on, Betty. He'll still be here tomorrow for you to hug."

Standing, his mother swatted her husband and then kissed Eli's cheek. "I'm so glad you're home."

"Us, too," Zane said. "Russ and I are looking forward to putting your skinny ass to work."

Eli laughed. "That's why I'm home."

Zane and Wendy walked out of the house and drove away in a large, white SUV. His parents headed for their room upstairs, and Eli followed. On the upper level, they turned left for their room and he turned right. It'd been well over five years since he'd been home and slept in his old room. Luckily, all his high school memorabilia were long gone, and the room had been redecorated as a guest room. Bad enough he was a thirty-six-year-old man sleeping in his boyhood room. If all his trophies and ribbons had still been on display, he might have opted to sleep in his truck.

As he laid down, he groaned. The family had changed the subject so fast when he'd brought up Addison that he'd forgotten to ask about moving her out of his apartment. There was no way he was going to set up house in his childhood bedroom in his parents' house like some loser. That was his last thought before dropping off.

Bright sun streaming through the window blinds woke him. It took a minute to realize where he was. His brain was fuzzy from all the dreams he'd had, most of them involving a red-headed hellion with a deep, Texas accent.

With a snarl, he climbed out of bed and got ready to face the dragon in his apartment. He didn't care where she moved, but he was a mature man who was not going to sleep in his childhood bedroom indefinitely.

Since he'd forgotten to grab his duffle on the way out of the barn apartment last night, he slid into the same pair of jeans he'd been wearing since he'd left California. He found an old T-shirt in the dresser, so he was able to retire his dirty shirt. There was a new toothbrush in the bathroom along with a small tube of toothpaste, probably from his mother's last dental appointment. She always liked to keep the guest room, aka his old bedroom, ready for guests, so the bath and bedroom were fully supplied with motel-size shampoo, conditioner, soap, and lotion. All of that came in handy as he got ready for the day. Once he retrieved his clothes, he'd find another set of fresh clothing, but for now, what he wore would certainly do.

He bounded down the stairs, expecting to find some member of his family still in the kitchen, but the room was empty. The house was quiet, the only sounds being his feet on the creaky stairs.

He poured a large mug of black coffee and took a seat at the kitchen table. The microwave clock read eight. He couldn't remember sleeping this late in years, but the last two weeks, combined with the long drive, had finally convinced his body to shut down. Now, he felt rested and restless to get on with moving Addison somewhere other than the apartment his parents had promised him. Maybe one of the rental cabins Zane had about a mile away was available.

The back door opened, and his mother came in, her arms full of freshly cut flowers.

"Oh, Eli, honey, can you get the glass vase down from the cabinet over the microwave for me?"

Eli hopped up and got the vase. "Beautiful flowers, Mom."

"We are having a wonderful growing season. Wendy is behind me with more flowers, so grab another vase."

Sure enough, his sister-in-law came through the door, her hands wrapped around flower stems.

"Good morning, Eli," she said. "Sleep good?"

"Exhausted, so yes." He frowned as he watched the two women arranging flowers into vases. "What are you doing with those?"

"We like to put fresh flowers into the rental cabins when we have new renters checking in. I thought it was a nice way to welcome them. Plus, I wanted to take some to Addison for her living room. I thought it'd brighten up the place." Wendy pushed roses into a small vase she'd retrieved from the pantry.

"Speaking of the apartment..." Eli turned to his mother. "I thought you and Dad had agreed to let me live there while I worked on something more permanent. I was a little more than surprised to find out someone else is living there."

His mother shook her head. "In all the excitement of having you home, I forgot to tell you we moved you."

He lifted an eyebrow. "You moved me?"

His mother laughed. "Upgrade, I swear. Cowboy Russ and Lori moved into the old Haney place. She's pregnant again, and they needed more room."

"I'd forgotten Zane had bought the Haney's ranch."

"Right, so their place is empty. Your dad and I, and of course Zane, thought you'd be more comfortable there. Their old house is much bigger than the barn apartment. Go over and take a look this morning. I was going to order furniture for you, but your surprise arrival last night kind of messed that up."

"Not to mention, you're a grown man who needs to pick out his own furniture," Wendy added.

His mother chuckled. "Well, yes, that too. Wendy has been reminding me on a regular basis that you aren't the eighteen-year-old kid who left here. And I wondered what you'd be bringing back from California. For all I knew, a delivery truck would show up with a full load of furniture. So, will there be one?"

Eli shook his head. "Nope. Sold almost everything before I left. There'll be a truck bringing a table a friend made for me, but that's about it. Came home with my Harley, my kitchen essentials, and my clothes. I've learned to travel light."

His mom made shooing motions. "Go look at the place. All that's been done since Russ and Lori moved out was a deep cleaning. I'm sure you'll want to put your own touches on the place."

"Going now," he said. He brushed a kiss on his mom's cheek. "Thanks."

Cowboy Russ and Lori had lived in a two-bedroom house attached to the original barn. It was older than the guest apartment he'd expected to occupy, but it definitely had more square footage. The last time he'd been in there had been right before he'd left for the Navy, so seventeen years ago. He hoped the place wasn't falling down.

Since the original ranch had been established by his great-grandmother after the death of her husband, and because this ranch had been started on a shoestring budget, the initial footprint for the ranch was small. The original log house had always been occupied. The logs had been well maintained and a second level added sometime in the past. The final addition to the house had been a laundry room, which abutted the barn. This was the house Russ and his wife had occupied through their courtship, marriage, and the birth of their first child.

Eli carried his coffee with him as he walked along the gravel drive toward the original horse barn. His path took him directly past the supply barn and the apartment where Addison was staying. The idea that she had the nerve to be on his family ranch after what she'd done had his stomach tied in knots and his anger flaring again.

He thought about stopping for the duffle he'd left in her laundry room, but walked on, hoping to get his ire under control before he saw her again.

The supply barn and the stable barn were located only a few yards apart, the gap between them providing a breathtaking view of the rolling Yellowstone River. This morning, the sun was bright and bouncing off the rapids in the fast-running water. Typically, the area rafting companies did a bang-up business taking tourists on rides down the rapids. He didn't see any rafts at the moment, but it was early. There would be screams and laughs rising up from the boats a little later in the day.

As his gaze shifted to the left, his heart leapt into his throat when he saw a person sitting in a deck chair on the patio behind the supply barn apartment. The person faced the river, the back of the chair toward the buildings. Addison. It had to be, even if her long, red hair was covered with a headscarf. He was charging across the open space toward her before he realized what he was doing.

He stomped onto the flagstone patio. She momentarily paused her knitting to look up at him.

With a shrug, she dismissed him, and her needles began moving again.

"What do you want, Eli?"

"I want to know what you're doing at my family's ranch. There are lots of places you could be. Hell, there are forty-nine other states you could haunt. Why here?" He walked around in front of her, deliberately blocking the view of the water. He stood with his legs spread and his fists on his hips.

"Why shouldn't I be here? Zane and Wendy offered the apartment to me for a visit, and I took it. What difference does it make to you?"

He decided to get to the point. "Where's your husband, Addison?"

"I don't have a husband."

"What? Did he find out you're a philandering, unfaithful wife?" His words were harsh and rough, just like he felt. He snorted his disgust at her actions from a year ago. "Well, did he?"

Abruptly, Addison stood, forcing him to take a step back. "I don't know who the hell you think you are or why you think you have the right to speak to me like that, but fuck you, Eli Miller."

She hugged the knitted yarn to her chest. "Just stay the fuck away from me." With that, she wheeled around and marched back into her apartment, albeit at a slow, careful pace.

Eli crossed his arms over his chest and watched her walk along the side of the supply barn until she turned and went out of view. Hell, he and her ex-husband were the injured parties...Well, the ex-husband more than him. But still, sleeping with a married woman violated every moral inch of his soul. Infidelity was unforgivable.

He turned toward his new house, looked over his shoulder at what he now thought of as "Addison's Barn." Before he could decide which place to head—his place or hers—he saw his mother and Wendy headed across the back yard from his parents' house to where he stood.

"Eli," his mother chastised. "I told you to leave

Addison alone, and then the next thing I see is you standing like the Hulk lording over her and shouting."

"I wasn't shouting."

His mother waved off his comment. "I am so disappointed in you. I raised you better than this, and I know the Navy instilled even more and better manners." She shook her head. "You don't understand."

Eli fisted his hands on his hips. "Then explain it."

Betty exchanged looks with his sister-in-law, and then shook her head. "It's not my story to tell. Addison will tell you if she decides to, but until then, leave the poor girl alone. She's had a horrible year."

I bet, he thought to himself. His past year hadn't been so great either, what with losing a fellow SEAL on a mission and leaving the Navy without a great life plan. Not for the first time, he wondered if leaving the SEALs and joining the Air Force reserves to finish out his twenty-year commitment was the right path.

"Eli." Wendy touched his arm. "Addison is a dear, dear friend. She's here at my invitation. Your parents were kind enough to let her stay. Back off, please."

Dammit. Wendy had used her nice, understanding, calm, doctor-voice. That always worked.

"Fine. You have my word."

The women headed back toward the main ranch house, and Eli walked between the two barns, and thus, between his new place and Addison's place. Might as well pick up his duffle bag while he was close. He wouldn't bother Addison. In and out and gone.

Except, when he walked in and picked up his bag, he heard Addison's sniffles through the apartment door. Dammit. He hated women's tears. In war, he had the misfortune of seeing too many women crying over dead husbands and children and elderly parents. A woman's tears had a way of getting inside him and activating his male protective gene.

With a long sigh, and an apology forming on his lips, he knocked on her door.

CHAPTER 5

A ddison sniffed and blew her nose. Her allergies were going to be the death of her. Sadly, spring and summer pollen had become more of a problem in the last couple of years. Living in Florida hadn't help at all. She'd hoped Montana would be better, but not so far.

She put another row of stitches into the socks she was knitting, her eyes watering from being outside. The view of the rushing Yellowstone River from the patio was simply too incredible to not enjoy, allergies be damned.

Sniff.

Blow.

A heavy knock at her door made her sigh. There was no doubt in her mind who'd be standing there.

"Come in," she called and braced herself for another round. "It's open."

Eli stepped through the door, and she immediately hated herself for the flips her tummy did when she looked at him. It wasn't fair that he could look like that when she looked, well, like what she was...a patient recovering from major surgery.

"Eli." She didn't stand. "What now?"

"I'm sorry, Addison. I feel awful about what just happened. I shouldn't have let my temper get away from me and made you cry. That isn't like me. I went out of my mind when your husband called your hotel room, and I was standing there with my dick in my hand. I was embarrassed and angry and—"

Addison held up her hand for him to stop talking. "Stop." She pointed to the sofa. "Sit. I'm confused. First, I'm not crying. Allergies are killing me, and second, my husband called you?"

"Not me, you. Last fall at the hotel. You'd ordered room service and stepped into the bathroom to freshen up. The phone rang, and I thought it was room service calling back for some clarification on the order, so I answered it. The man said he was your husband and asked to speak with you."

She dropped heavily against the back of her chair, her stomach in knots at the mention of her ex. "Ah, Denis. The boil on my butt that never stops giving." With a sigh, she set her knitting aside. "Denis *was* my husband, but we'd separated and divorced before that weekend. He found a woman with more money than I had and wanted to tie those purse strings down, so he left me for her. Then..."

She paused, unsure if she should tell the whole story. But then again, why-the-hell-not? His opinion of her couldn't get much lower.

"Let me finish," she said when Eli opened his mouth. "When Denis left, we had to undergo court ordered mediation, and it was during that time I was diagnosed with breast cancer."

His expression froze. He reached out to touch her hand. "Oh, fuck, Addison. I'm so sorry about the cancer. I didn't know."

Jerking her hand away, she shook her head. "Don't feel sorry for me," she snapped at him. Then, she blew out a long sigh. "It's life. I'm actually luckier than a lot of women. The tests found the cancer so early it was still small and confined. Most women my age aren't fortunate enough to get a mammogram and have it covered by insurance, or in my case, by my television station. Insurance usually begins paying for them when women are about forty or have some high-risk condition or family history. I had none of the qualifiers for an insurance-paid mammogram."

"Why did you get one? Some sort of premonition?"

She chuckled. "Nope. I was filming a segment for my show. I did the scan in August with the segment that showed my mammogram scheduled to run in October since that's breast cancer awareness month. The plan was to show how easy and painless a mammogram is and encourage women to get theirs done." She blew out a breath. "Not the outcome I'd expected."

She studied her fingernails, which had only recently begun to grow back after losing them, her toenails, and all her hair from the chemotherapy treatments.

"Don't leave me hanging," he said, his voice roughening. "What happened?"

"I had a cancer type called triple negative breast cancer, which means the cancer cells can't be controlled with hormones. I had six months of chemotherapy..."

she paused to draw a deep breath, then blurted, "and then a bilateral mastectomy."

She feared she'd see the disgust on his face at the mention of her mastectomy. Many men were repulsed by the idea that a woman not only had had cancer, but now, didn't have her breasts either. Plus, she remembered how much he'd loved her breasts. He was definitely a breast man.

She flicked a glance up at him. He raked his hand through his hair. She saw concern on his face, and then she saw the underlying pity.

"Don't," she snapped out.

"Don't what?" His brow wrinkled in confusion. "I didn't do anything."

"Your face is full of all kinds of pity. I don't want that from anyone."

With a nod, he said, "Yeah, it probably was, but it wasn't pity about the cancer. It was empathy for the surgery. If I tell you something, you have to promise not to tell mom."

She snorted. "You keep secrets from your mom?"

"Hell, yes. If she'd known about this, she'd have flown to Germany and then home with me to California."

"Fine." She pretend-zipped her lips.

"I was shot a few years ago on a mission. It was pretty bad." He lifted his shirt. On his chest were seven scars. He twisted on the sofa until she could see his back. The scars there were puckered and obvious. "Shot more than once, actually. I hated recovering from surgery, and I suspect you did, too."

"Not *did*, but do. I'm still recovering."

He lowered his shirt. "Ah. Got it."

"Anyway, back to Denis. He told the court that he refused to be married to a woman without her tits, as he put it, and wanted out. The court granted his divorce petition, but didn't give him the alimony he requested." She chuckled. "He was not happy. Oh, the rich, older woman booted him out too. I assume he was calling that weekend to ask me for money, like I'd given him a penny. I'd been a faithful wife. He was an unfaithful husband, and sad to say, on more than one occasion." She sighed. "I hated going through the divorce. It's like a public announcement that you've failed spectacularly at something, but in my case, I was embarrassed that all the world knew my husband was a cheater. At the same time, I was glad to have him gone."

Eli leaned forward, his forearms resting on his thighs and blew out a breath. "I am so sorry, more than words can express. I've never been divorced, but I think I can understand where you're coming from. Your ex is a fool for letting you go, obviously a loser lacking any sense at all."

She rolled her eyes and quirked up the corner of her mouth. "I should have suspected he wasn't right when I found out he legally changed the spelling of his name from d-e-n-n-i-s to d-e-n-i-s. Kind of pretentious, right? D-e-n-i-s?"

His lips twitched. "Can't argue that point."

"So, I'm sorry you were dragged unknowingly into all the drama with my ex, but at least, now I understand why you disappeared that night."

"Is he still bothering you?"

"Not here, he's not. That's one of the many reasons I came here. I changed my cell phone number, and he hasn't figured out how to contact me, but he will." She sighed. "Unless I get lucky and he latches onto another woman who can pay for the lifestyle to which he'd like to become accustomed to."

"Fingers crossed then. How are you doing otherwise?"

She shrugged. "Okay. Tired mostly. I sleep a lot. Brain's still a little foggy, but Wendy assures me that will clear with time."

"Whew. I hear chemo is rough."

"Oh yeah." She removed the scarf from her head. Her long, red hair had been replaced with spiky, platinum blonde. The length was about one inch all over. "Lost all my hair and my nails." She wiggled her fingers. "The nails are starting to come back. The hair, too. You like the color?"

"It's definitely an eye-catcher."

She laughed, and he responded with a grin.

"On you, it's very sexy. Don't get me wrong, I loved your long hair, but this short cut looks great on you."

Now, realizing all she'd been through since they'd last seen each other, he felt like an ass for jumping down her throat, which only added to how horrible he felt about walking out eight months ago.

It might have been nice if his brother had clued him in. Yeah, he put having a long talk with his brother and the rest of his closed-mouthed family high on his to-do list.

"Listen, I really have to apologize for walking out last November. What I did, walking out and ghosting you, is unforgivable. I know that. I'm ashamed of how I reacted. Ashamed, embarrassed, and furious with myself. I've thought about that weekend almost nonstop. I know the cancer made the past year incredibly difficult, and my being an ass then and this morning didn't help. You have to know that's not me." He ran his hand down his face. "Let me try to make it up to you. What can I do? How can I help?"

"While I appreciate your apology, you hurt me deeply. You have to know that."

His head drooped, and then he looked up at her. "I'm sorry. I really didn't know about your ex. I don't think we spent that much time talking." His voice was so sincere, it was hard to hold on to the grudge she'd carried around.

She chuckled. "Nope. We couldn't keep our hands off each other."

He grinned. "You were the sexiest woman I'd ever laid my eyes on." His eyes grew serious. "And I am so very sorry. How can I make up for my past bad actions?"

"Honestly, there's nothing I need. I'm doing great. Wendy is an excellent surgeon, and my incisions are healing nicely."

"Wait. Wendy? That's why you're here? Wendy did your surgery?"

"Well, Risa, her sister, is a big deal breast cancer doctor and researcher in Dallas. Did you know that?"

He shook his head. His brain whirled from all the new, and surprising, information he was trying to absorb. Cancer. Mastectomy. A bastard of an ex. Now, his sister-in-law did Addison's surgery? He was surprised the top of his head didn't fly off. His brother had a lot of explaining to do.

"I was lucky that Risa squeezed me into her schedule and served as my primary cancer physician, coordinating my chemotherapy with an oncologist as well as doing my mastectomy. I had a plastic surgeon lined up to do the reconstruction, but—you're never going to believe this—his wife shot him for having an affair with his nurse."

"You have got to be kidding."

"I'm not. She didn't kill him, and last I heard, they were trying to work out their differences, but trust me when I say, the last thing I needed was more drama in my life."

He rolled his eyes with a snort. "Work out their differences? Yikes. Sorry, but if my wife shot me, that would be a bridge too far."

She grinned. "Me, too. Anyway, Risa called Wendy and twisted her arm to do my breast reconstruction. I don't know if Zane mentioned it, but Wendy was one of the most respected plastics reconstruction surgeons in Dallas."

"I didn't know that. I mean, sure, I knew she was a doctor, but Zane never mentioned what kind, and I didn't ask." He rubbed the back of his neck. "I was in my own little world out there in California. I'm glad she was able to help you."

"So, that's how my year has been."

"File it under memorable, but let's not repeat?"

"Exactly."

"So, I'll ask again. What can I do to help you or make amends for adding to your personal drama?"

Her gaze was steady. "Honestly, treat me normal. As much as you pissed me off out there on the patio, that's the first time anyone hasn't treated me with kid gloves." She smiled. "I miss being normal."

He nodded, his expression solemn. "Normal, it is then. I hate I wasn't there for you this past year as a friend, as support." He shook his head. "Again, I am so sorry. I handled the whole situation horribly."

"That's Denis's fault, not yours." She squinted at him. "On the other hand, if you'd just talked to me..."

Holding up his hands in surrender, he said, "I know, I know. I can't put the toothpaste back in the tube, but can we start over? Put that night behind us?"

"I think so. I know I'd like to."

"Great." He stood and turned to leave, but then looked at her again. "Want to walk over to my new place and see what has to be done to make it livable?"

She stood. "Only if I get to help buy furniture and spend your money."

"This is going to cost me, isn't it?"

"Maybe," she replied with a laugh.

Eli grabbed his duffel bag out of Addison's laundry room as they passed. He was still a little rattled at seeing her again. Damn. Breast cancer, chemo, and surgery. She'd had a horrible year, and his ghosting her had been shitty on his part. Of course, he'd believed he'd had a solid reason; however, did anyone really have a good reason for being an asshole? He should've let her know what happened long before today. That was on his head. She couldn't have made things right on her own. After all, who would call someone who'd ghosted them as blatantly as he had her?

He glanced over at her shocking platinum-blonde hair. He'd loved her long, red hair last fall, but damn if she didn't look scorching hot with the new short hair. Since none of her hair appeared to be much longer than an inch or two, the style emphasized her long neck.

He had a vivid flashback of nibbling her neck and the cock-raising moans she'd made. Visions of her long hair draped over his chest and wrapped teasingly around his cock filled his mind. His body responded, rushing blood below his waist.

He cleared his throat and his mind. This was not the place nor the time to spring a raging hardon.

They stepped from the hall that led to her small apartment and into the storage barn that held the feed, saddles, and bridles for the owners who boarded their horses at Grizzly Bitterroot Ranch.

Addison drew in a deep breath and exhaled. "I love the smell of leather and horse feed in here, don't you?"

"Yeah. I've forgotten how much I loved some of the scents around the ranch. Of course, I could live the rest of my life without the smells that mucking out stalls stirs up."

She wrinkled her nose and laughed. "Agreed."

"Have you spent much time on a ranch or around horses?"

"I have actually. My grandparents had a small farm with a couple of horses when I was a kid, so I learned to ride by the time I was seven or eight. Then I went a number of years without riding. When I went to college, I met Wendy and Risa. They grew up on a cattle ranch in Texas with a lot of horses. I took advantage of every invitation to visit and rode their horses every chance I got. I was fortunate to spent a lot of time there."

"So, where's your cowgirl hat?"

With a chuckle, she replied, "Long gone, I'm afraid. Gosh, I guess it's been at least eight years since I've ridden."

He made a mental note to order her a Stetson as a *sorry-I-was-an-ass* gift.

They walked out of the supply barn toward the original barn built by his grandparents. The original homestead house was attached to this barn, and this was the house his parents were giving him. He hadn't been inside in years, maybe as long as a decade. The permanent ranch hand, Russ, and his wife, Lori, had lived here most of the time Eli had been in the Navy. What he remembered of the place was that it was nice when they'd lived there. Since they'd moved to the old Haney place months ago, he worried about the amount of work that'd be required to make it inhabitable.

As they crossed the open space between the two barns, Eli nodded his head toward the opening.

"You spend a lot of time on the patio?"

"I do. But gosh, I really thought Montana would be better on my allergies than it's been."

"Lots of the trees around here drop pollen, and it can be horrible in the spring. Probably worse than it is now."

"Heaven help me if I were here in the spring."

"When did you get here?"

"Late April. Once Wendy agreed to do my surgery, I didn't waste any time getting up here." She chuckled. "I was afraid she would change her mind."

"She's really that good?"

"She's that good. Plus, I wanted something other than silicone or saline implant replacements. I wanted autologous breast reconstruction. That involves using my own tissue to build the breasts. It's a little more involved and complicated, and I know you don't know what that all means, but trust me, Wendy is fabulous."

He nudged her shoulder with his. "And you wanted only the best."

"Who doesn't want the best when they are going under the knife?"

They stepped onto the porch of the log house.

"Well, here's the test," Eli joked.

"I think you're going to be surprised," Addison said. "Your mom and Lori have been over here working on the place. From what she told me, Lori left it in pretty good shape."

Eli opened the door and smiled with relief. The floors were solid hardwood as he remembered, and today, they gleamed in the morning sun pouring through the large windows. The ceiling had been constructed from the same hardwoods while the walls were drywalled.

"The walls could use a coat of paint," he observed and dropped his duffel to the floor.

"True, but that's easy to do, especially since there's no carpet or furniture to deal with." She frowned. "Speaking of furniture, you mentioned shopping. Does that mean you shipped nothing home from California?"

He walked toward the kitchen to check out the appliances. "Just my kitchen stuff and a large table a friend built for me."

"How come? Was it too expensive to ship?"

"No, nothing like that. I hosted a lot of our team parties, so my living room furniture took more than its fair share of abuse from the guys. I ended up selling all the furniture, other than my big table, to a new SEAL just starting out." He chuckled. "Thank goodness furniture can't talk."

She grinned. "Oh yeah? Like it would know some serious blackmail material?"

"Maybe, and that's all I'm going to say about that."

They both laughed.

He glanced around, assessing the dated kitchen. "Looks like I need to do some serious updates in this kitchen. Maybe I'll take out this wall and open up the downstairs so it's one big living-dining-kitchen area. I should've brought a piece of paper to take some notes."

"I can run back to my place and grab a tablet."

"Nah, that's okay." He pulled out his phone. "I have an app for that."

She shook her head. "There's an app for everything."

He clicked on his recorder, making verbal notes about appliances as well as removing the wall between the kitchen and living room. Walking through the kitchen, he opened the door to the laundry room.

"Well, this is something I bet you'd see only on a ranch."

"What's that?" she asked, wiggling her way past him and into the room. "Well, that's clever."

The laundry room backed up to the main barn. A door allowed entrance to the laundry room from the barn. A shower had been built into the corner of the room.

"Yep," he said. "Drop your nasty work clothes in the laundry room and take a shower before you enter the house. Leave that mud and poop smell here."

"Better yet, drop those clothes directly into the washer and get it going," Addison suggested.

"Good point. Okay, I need a washer and dryer for here." He made a verbal reminder in his phone. "That's done. Let's finish checking out the downstairs before we head up. I never ventured upstairs while Russ and Lori lived here."

The rest of the downstairs tour revealed a half-bath, small bedroom, and small office. Then they headed up the stairs and stopped on the doorless landing. Addison gasped as Eli whistled.

"Wow," Addison said. "Why do I think this wasn't part of the original house built by your great-grandparents?"

He chuckled. "The original house was the downstairs area, minus the laundry room. This was the attic. I always wondered what Russ had done with this area."

To the left was a bedroom, now empty. The area was large, at least twenty feet by twenty feet in his estimation. It was certainly large enough to easily hold a complete king-sized bedroom suite with every piece of furniture he wanted to use.

"This is huge," she said. "Over there?" She pointed. "You could have a nice seating area for reading or whatever. And over there..." She gestured toward a wall. "A television or big dresser. Heck, this might be larger than some Manhattan apartments."

He nodded. "Yep. Dresser, chest of drawers...Hell, whatever I want to put in here will fit."

She rubbed her hands together. "I can't wait to see what furniture we can find."

"So, you were serious about helping me fill this place up with stuff?" he asked.

"You bet. Spending someone else's money is always fun. Let's take a peek at the bathroom."

The master bath was directly above the kitchen/laundry room area. It held a large walk-in shower, a single sink, a toilet closet, and a large walk-in clothes closet. The flooring was vinyl, which was fine for Eli. At least it didn't have carpet.

"Tell you what," Addison said, giving him a sly look. "You seem to really want my place, so let's trade."

He laughed. "No deal. What's on your schedule for tomorrow?"

She thought for a minute. "Finish knitting a pair of socks. That's about it. Why?"

"Shopping, of course, if you're serious about going."

"Oh, I'm serious." She rubbed her hands together. "I do love to shop."

With a groan, he said, "What have I done?"

"Hee, hee, hee," she replied.

"How about we head to Bozeman after breakfast?"

"Is that cowboy breakfast time, which is, from what I can tell, about dawn, or is that normal people time?"

"What is normal people time?" He grinned. "And I'm pretty sure cowboy time and SEAL time are about the same."

She groaned. "Normal people. Eight or nine."

"I'll pick you up at eight. We'll have breakfast on the way so I know you'll be fueled up and ready to shop."

"Oh, silly man. I'm always ready to spend someone else's money."

CHAPTER 6

E li spent the rest of the day researching furniture stores, reviews of furniture brands, and finding a good place to eat lunch in Bozeman. He compiled a list of all the various sheets, towels, and other linens he'd need.

Truth was, while he was extremely picky when it came to food, he wasn't so particular about kitchen and bath towels. If they were absorbent enough to dry, they were good enough. And sheets? Any sheet, no matter the thread count, beat some of the places he'd slept. Heck, having a bed could be a luxury at times when you're a SEAL.

Tossing and turning like a chicken on a spit would best describe his night. When he did sleep, a beautiful, platinum blonde infiltrated every dream. When he woke, he lay in bed thinking about his dreams, the wedding weekend with Addison that felt so long ago, and the anger and hurt he'd carried like a huge chip on his shoulder for the past year.

Now, his irritation was focused on himself. If only

he'd taken the time to talk to Addison that night, or anytime later. Things might've been different. But she'd been through so much cancer crap that the last thing he would do was to give her any stress, and that included any relationship bull. She was here to recover under the watchful eye of his sister-in-law, and then she'd go back to her regular life.

Hmm...how much longer would she be here? If her television show was as popular as his mom intimated, then surely her station was anxious to get her back. Once she was home in Florida, then they were back to basically living on different sides of the country.

Until she went home, the least he could do was be a friend, something he could have been doing for months, if only he weren't such a miserable bastard.

The next morning, before knocking on Addison's door for their shopping trip, he allotted himself an hour to clean out his truck. There were more snack food wrappers and soda bottles than he wanted to admit to. Plus, after the long drive from California, the truck needed a bath and vacuuming.

He'd sorely underestimated his guesstimate for cleaning. By the time he was done with the truck, grabbed a shower, and dressed, the clock had rolled to eight-fifteen. He hadn't been out of the Navy for a week, and he was already slacking off. That would never do. He still had a seven-year commitment with the Air Force Reserves, and while he didn't expect the Air Force to be as grueling as the Navy SEAL program, he figured he'd still have to be on his game.

He chuckled to himself as he thought about all the hell his team had given him when they'd found out about the Air Force Reserves, calling it the Chair Force

Reserves and Keyboard Warriors. At his age, Chair Force sounded perfect.

"So, the Navy *doesn't* run a tight ship, and allows you to come and go on your own schedule?"

The sound of Addison's voice brought a broad grin to his face. He turned toward her. "You ought to thank me. I spent an hour this morning cleaning up this truck just for you."

She fanned her face with her hand. "Why, I'm flattered, sir," she said in a thick, southern drawl.

He laughed as he opened the passenger door. "Your clean chariot awaits. I hope you don't mind waiting until we get to Bozeman to eat. I read about a place there named *Jellies*. The menu was interesting, and all the reviews were raves. I thought it might be fun to try it."

"An hour? You want me to wait an hour for coffee? Be right back."

Addison wheeled around and jogged back into her apartment, leaving Eli standing beside the open passenger door. Within three minutes, she racewalked out carrying two travel mugs.

"One for me and one for you, or two for me if you don't want coffee."

He snatched the travel mug from her outstretched hand. "Seriously? I never turn down coffee. Never."

"Great." She wrapped her fingers about the truck's grab handle and hoisted herself into his truck. "What? You couldn't get one higher off the ground?"

With a chuckle, he closed her door and walked around the truck. "I guess I could get one of those truck suspensions that raises the truck an additional five feet off the road," he said, sliding behind the wheel.

"Aren't lifted trucks illegal?"

"Yep, in most states, but nobody enforces that."

"Still, I'm going with *no* on that idea. But..." She turned to look at him. "I do love sitting high off the road. I feel like I have a better field of vision to see all the other cars around me. In my car, I'm almost on the ground."

He drove down the long drive toward the highway. "Really? I haven't seen some low-slung car here. What are you driving?"

"Your mom gave me her Jeep to use."

He nodded. "Sure. I should've thought of that. She used to drive it in bad winter weather, and then drive her Lexus the rest of the year. Now that they go to Florida for the winter, I guess the Jeep isn't getting driven that often. What do you usually drive, and where is it?"

Her face flushed. He wondered what he'd asked her that would cause her embarrassment.

"What?" he asked. "What'd I say?"

She gave a nervous chuckle. "It's just that...well, my car causes people to judge me."

He lifted one hand off his steering wheel. "I promise not to judge. Besides, the Navy trusts me to keep a secret, and you can, too."

"Apparently so," she said dryly. "You didn't tell me for almost nine months that you spoke with my jerk ex-husband."

He winced as his stomach twisted. "Yeah. I still feel horrible about that."

She laughed. "I'm pulling your chain, frogman, but I do have a super cool car. I have a metallic blue Ferrari 812 Superfast."

His mouth gaped, and he whipped his head to look at her. "Are you freaking kidding? I looked at one of those in California. That baby was over three-hundred-k."

"True, but I got a deal on mine. Remember, living in Orlando and being kind of well-known, what I drove around town brought a lot of attention, to me and to my show, and, frankly, to the dealer's name on the license plate. So, I promised to keep the dealer information on the car as promo, and he gave me a smokin' hot deal."

"Smart girl. You miss it? And where is it now?"

"Do I miss Elvira? I do, so much, but she would not like these Montana sideroads! She'd be fine on most of the highways in the summer, but can you imagine how bad she'd do in the winter?" Addison laughed. "Elvira is a summer car, for sure. She was perfect for Florida."

"Elvira, huh? Mistress of the dark?"

"Yep."

"Why Elvira?"

"Because when I drive her the way she deserves to be driven, all you'll see is a dark-blue streak."

He laughed. "Where is Elvira now?"

"In Texas in my parents' garage. They've promised to drive her a couple of times a week." She snickered. "I heard from one of my friends back there that my parents have been taking Elvira everywhere."

"When do you go home?' He wasn't sure what he wanted to hear. On one hand, he wanted the reminder of how poorly he'd treated her gone from sight. On the other, he wanted her to stay so he could make it up to her.

She shrugged. "Not sure. Maybe September."

He responded with only a nod, again not sure what response he wanted to feel.

For the rest of the hourlong drive to Bozeman, the conversation stayed light, talking about all the cars they'd driven, whether cars and trucks should have male or female pronouns—surprisingly they agreed on female—and other topics of no real consequence. It was as though they'd each decided to keep everything light. No digging into their pasts, or her current cancer situation.

The map on his phone directed them to *Jellies*. The restaurant was located in a red brick building on the main drag of Bozeman. Finding a place to park proved to be a challenge, but being that it was a Thursday, he lucked into a spot down the street. The long line inside *Jellies* made him wonder if getting a table on the weekends would be impossible.

"What a crowd," Addison said under her breath. "I bet Saturdays and Sundays are nuts."

Eli chuckled. "Great minds think alike."

Luckily for them, most of the people were picking up takeout orders, so they were seated within ten minutes. They each picked up the menu and began to read.

"I think I'll have the left side of the menu," she said with a grin. "Everything sounds so good. I think it was a rookie mistake to come here starving."

"Sorry about that," he said with a laugh. "I'm having pancakes. I think I'll do that trio where I can try three different ones. What about you?"

"I want crepes. I love them and haven't had any in months."

"Shoot, girl. I'll make you some crepes that'll make you cry from delight."

She lifted an eyebrow. "I don't believe you."

"Fine, then. Once my kitchen is together, breakfast at my place. And when you sob and beg me for my recipe, I'll just turn away and say no."

She laughed. "You're on. I'll believe it when I taste it."

The waitress came by, and they placed their pancake and crepe orders, adding cups of coffee and glasses of orange juice.

Once she'd walked away, Addison placed her elbows on the table and leaned in. "Seriously, Eli? You can cook?"

He shrugged. "Yeah. I'm comfortable with a gun or a spatula in my hand, both serving different purposes," he said with a laugh.

"That's so cool. How'd you learn to cook?"

"I joined the Navy right out of high school, so I had the tastebuds of a teen. Burgers, pizzas, doughnuts, and anything fried. I was in heaven, until morning PT. I had to run off all those calories, and let me tell you, those calories add up to a lot of long runs. I realized after about a year that fast food couldn't be my future.

"There was a SEAL instructor who befriended me while I was in BUD/S. His name was Benjamin Blackwell. He'd been on teams for years before he married and took an instructor position. His wife, Holly, was an excellent cook. They had some of the guys over for meals, and I spent some time talking with Holly. She offered to show me some simple things, like spaghetti and chili. I took her up on the offer. Found I love the aromas that cooking food produces. I took a few cooking classes after that. So, that's how I ended up cooking all the time. What about you? Love to cook?"

"Oh, heavens no," she replied with a laugh. "I love to eat. I don't mind cleaning up after a meal, but I hate cooking. What spice should go in this pot? How do I tone this sauce up or down? Not for me." She shook her head. "My show always had a cooking segment, my least favorite time, trust me. Most of the cooks who appeared were pretentious and snobby, and what they prepared never sounded good to me, nor easy to make."

"Why did you book them, then?"

"I didn't. My producer did. The segments were popular with my viewers." She shrugged. "I was the outlier, so I went with the flow." With a dramatic shiver, she continued. "The last chef I had on smelled horrible. He swore it was the spice he was using, but to me the odor was unwashed human."

Eli chuckled. "It probably was the spice like he said. Cumin can smell like body odor before it's cooked. And trust me when I say, I've been around some very rank-smelling guys. I'll take cumin over SEALs who haven't showered in seven days."

"Wow, I'll trust you on that and not go sniffing ripe SEALs."

Their food arrived and both dug in with gusto. Addison's sighs and moans with each bite had his cock taking notice and getting semi-hard. This was not what he wanted to happen. He would be a good friend to Addison, and that was it. Nothing more.

There was a slight tussle over the bill with Addison wanting to pay her half, but Eli firmly refused.

"After all," he said, "I'm using you to help me shop. It's only fair I provide your fuel."

"Fair enough, I suppose. Where to first?"

"I know there's a store here where all the furniture is built to specs, but I'd rather find a furniture store where I can see it, sit on it, and have it delivered. Built to spec will take forever, and I don't want to wait."

"Okay. I'm assuming big pieces in leather, or am I projecting because you're a guy?"

"Hell, yeah, I'm a guy. Leather and comfortable are my requirements. The first place I want to check out is within walking distance. Are you strong enough for that?"

"I'll try to keep up," she said, matching his long stride down the sidewalk.

He glanced over at her and slowed. "I looked up chemo side effects last night," he said with a shrug and a gentle smile. "Overwhelming exhaustion was one of them. I don't want you to overdo today. Promise?"

She blinked in surprise. "Wow, Eli. I appreciate your looking out for me. Chemo was finished in February, so I'm getting stronger." Apparently, his face reflected his skepticism because she added defensively, "I am. Really. You don't have to worry about me."

"Hmm," he said with an arched eyebrow. "My reading said it takes months to regain all your strength, so promise me you'll let me know if you get tired. We aren't under any kind of schedule. We'll get done what we can today, and what we don't can wait until another day. So, you'll tell me if this gets to be too much?'

She smiled. "I promise.

Taking her hand, they walked a couple of blocks to *Ricky's Fine Furniture* and entered.

A salesman greeted them with, "Can I help you find something?"

"We're looking for living room furniture," Addison said. "Sofa, chairs, tables, and so forth. The furniture has to be leather and comfortable."

The salesman grinned at Eli. "I see you let the little lady make all the decisions."

Eli's ire flamed at the salesman's obvious sexism. He glared at the man with a tight jaw.

The man coughed nervously. "This way. I'm sure I have just what you are looking for."

"Don't scare the nice salesman," Addison whispered.

"Why are some guys such assholes when it comes to women?" Eli replied. "So what if I did let my wife—if I had one—pick out furniture? Little lady." He scoffed. "This shit better be perfect or we are out of here."

To Eli's displeasure—only because he would've loved to walk out—the salesman led them to exactly the type of living room set Eli wanted. A four-cushion-couch in deep-brown leather. The side tables were hardwood with leather tops. The set also contained a matching chair-and-a-half with a leather ottoman.

"There's a recliner that isn't part of this grouping, but would work well with the color of the leather, if you're looking for something like that," the salesman said, making sure to address Eli.

Addison snickered, and Eli bit the inside of his cheek to keep from grinning in response. The sound of her snicker made him ridiculously happy.

"Yes, I'd like to see it. What do you think, Addy?"

It was the first time he'd let his nickname for her slip out, and a smile bloomed on her face. His heart swelled with an emotion he wasn't ready to put a name to.

She dropped onto the middle cushion of the sofa and stroked the leather. "Seriously, yummy." Pulling her feet up onto the couch, she stretched out full length. "What is this? Six-feet?" she asked the salesman.

"Actually, it's six-feet, five-inches. It's one of our longest sofas."

She wiggled on the leather as though settling in for a long nap, and Eli's heart began to race. She looked like she belonged on that couch. A feeling of destiny swept through him, as though he was seeing something from the future...his future...their future.

"I like it," Addison announced, as she continued to caress the leather. "Soft, but supportive, you know?"

Eli found himself jealous of all the strokes the leather was receiving, strokes he wanted to feel on his skin. "No kidding. Want me to give you some private time with it?"

She snuggled, and then sighed. "I guess I need to see how else I can spend your money." She stood. "Lead on to this magical recliner."

The recliner was name-brand with a leather that would blend with the living room suite. This time, Eli sat and moaned. "Holy hell. I've died and gone to heaven. How do I put my feet up?"

The salesman pushed a button on the side, and Eli's feet rose and his back reclined.

"I'm never getting out of this chair. I might have to load it onto my truck today and take it home."

The salesman's eyes lit with the understanding Eli and Addison weren't lookie-loos but were serious buyers. "I can do that, sir," the salesman said.

Eli laughed. "I was kidding...or was I? How much is this sucker?"

Addison rolled her eyes with a snort and shook her head.

"It's only three-thousand-four-hundred-and ninety-nine," the salesman said with a flourish. "And, if you buy the living room suite, I'll give you ten percent off the price of all of it."

"Twenty-five percent, and you have a deal. Free delivery, right?"

The salesman's face fell. "I'll have to get with my manager about any discount above ten-percent."

"Go do that," Eli said. "Addy and I will sit here until you get back."

"Where is this to be delivered?"

"I have a ranch about thirty minutes this side of Gardiner, so it's maybe forty-five to sixty minutes from here."

"Okay. Let me get all the numbers for you, and I'll be right back."

Addison took the chair next to him. "You know how much that living room set was, right? Like ten grand for all those pieces, and then you add the recliner? Eli, you're talking about spending fifteen thousand dollars."

He arched an eyebrow. "You sound pretty shocked about prices for a gal with a three-hundred-thousand-dollar car."

"I told you. I got a deal."

"And I'll get a deal here. You just wait and see."

"You really think they'll give you one-fourth off?"

"Nope. I figure they'll come back at fifteen, I'll say twenty-two, and we'll settle at twenty."

In a short time, the salesman came back with an older woman at his side. "This is Mrs. Randolph, the store's owner."

Eli stood and extended his hand. "Hello, Mrs. Randolph. Nice to meet you. I'm Eli Miller, and this is Addison Treadway."

Addison nodded from her seat but didn't stand. Was she getting tired? Was the walk here and then around the store too much? He'd hate himself if he did anything to cause a setback on her recovery.

"Nice to meet you both. Mr. Wales has relayed your request, and I'm sorry I can't do that. I have to make some money off my sales," she said with a charming smile. "I'm sure you understand."

Eli nodded, fully aware that the furniture was marked up at least two-hundred percent over cost, if not more. And Mr. Wales would have to get his commission for the sales, and that amount would need to be factored into the final price.

"And I appreciate that. I really do," Eli said. "I like to do business with family-owned stores like this. Hmm, well, I do need a mattress and bedroom furniture also. What if I find something here, and you make me an incredible deal for all of it?"

Mrs. Randolph smiled. "Okay. Let's take a look."

An hour later after some bargaining, Eli left *Ricky's Fine Furniture* with a thirty percent discount on a full house of furniture. Being a retired Navy SEAL had worked in his favor. The store's namesake, Ricky, was Mrs. Randolph's son, or had been her son. He'd died in the early phase of the war in Afghanistan. The deal on the furniture hadn't taken the full hour, but Eli and Addison had visited with Mrs. Randolph and talked about her son.

Later, as Eli and Addison walked toward his truck, he took Addison's arm in his, pleased when she didn't pull away. The touch of her flesh against his added fuel to the fire burning inside him for her. He hated himself for lusting after a woman he'd promised to be friends with, but his heart wanted what it wanted. Too bad he was a grown-ass man who'd been trained to be true to his word. He would not pursue her romantically. He would be her friend.

"I can't believe you bought all the furniture," she said as he helped her into his truck.

"What can I say? I needed it. Let's pick up the recliner to take home. Tomorrow, I need to buy bedsheets and towels. They don't have to be fancy, so Walmart will do."

"What about your kitchen?"

"Yeah, new appliances are on my list, too. But I think today's been enough excitement. You rest, and I'll get you home."

"I am a little tired," she confessed, "and that makes me so mad. I hate this."

He rubbed her knee before shutting her door. The palm of his hand burned at the touch. His fucking lust shot to level ten. Damn. "This too will pass," he said, not sure if he was addressing her fatigue or his own feelings for her.

Once he had the recliner secured in his truck, he drove through a coffee hut and bought lattes for both of them. Even with that caffeine jolt, Addison was asleep twenty minutes into the drive home.

He couldn't help but continue to glance over at her as he drove. Her ex-husband had to be blind and stupid. Addison was fucking gorgeous. She was smart, clever, and funny. And she drove a car that would give any man an erection.

But then, he pretty much kept semi-hard around her, even when he'd been so mad the first night and yesterday on the patio.

He was not a man with many regrets.

Leaving her was definitely one of them.

CHAPTER 7

E li got Addison to go on into her apartment and not try to help him unload the recliner.

"That's what an older brother is for," he'd told her.

Once she was settled in her apartment, Eli phoned Zane.

"Yelp, what's up, Little Bro?"

"I need help unloading a chair from my truck."

"Can do, but I need to finish what I'm doing. Be there in fifteen."

Eli spent that time drawing out his downstairs and deciding where everything should go. Of course, it made logical sense to do any construction and painting before his furniture arrived, but he was impatient to get settled. Maybe he could work around stuff using sheets and drop cloths. He made a mental note to ask his mom for old sheets he could use for painting. But what color should he paint the downstairs walls?

"I'm here," Zane announced through the door.

"Thanks. It's the recliner in the truck."

"Lucky for my back I brought Russ along. I bet

when that chair's stretched out, it's as long as California."

Eli laughed. "Almost."

The three men manhandled the chair from the truck bed to the living room in record time. Zane dropped into the chair immediately.

"Ah. Heaven. I need one of these."

"Get your nasty ass out of my new chair," Eli growled.

"Make me."

Eli grinned. How many times had he heard those words from his older brother?

"You know, I'm not that skinny kid you used to beat up when we were younger. I'm pretty sure I can kick your ass now."

Zane laughed but stood.

"Man, this was a great place to live," Russ said, his head turning to take in the space. "I kind of miss it, you know? Getting to work was as easy as walking out the door."

"Really?" Eli said. "I can move to the Haney house and let you have this back."

Russ laughed. "I'd be a divorced man in a month. We need all of the bedrooms there. Umm..." He rubbed his neck. "We haven't told anyone yet, but, hell, you two can keep a secret, right?"

Eli pointed to himself. "Navy SEAL. Keeper of *lots* of secrets." He pointed to Zane. "He tells Wendy everything. He leaks like a sieve."

"Hey," Zane protested. "I can keep secrets...most of the time."

Russ shook his head. "Don't let Lori know I told you, but we're having twins."

"You're having twins," a female voice cried from the door. "That's wonderful."

Eli and Zane groaned. Their mother loved nothing more than being on the front end of news and being the one to tell everyone else.

"Oh, shit," Russ muttered. "Hello, Ms. Betty. You cannot tell anyone about Lori. It's a secret."

Betty Miller hurried across the living room, twisting an imaginary key in an imaginary lock on her lips. "Sealed. I swear, but I have to tell Henry, but he won't tell anyone."

"See?" Eli said. "That's where Zane gets it. He tells Wendy everything."

"You will too, honey, once you find that perfect woman," his mother said, rubbing his back.

Eli thought he'd found his perfect woman in Addison, and then he'd gone and wrecked the whole thing. And now, Addison was in no condition for him to pursue. Her health was so much more important than his lust.

He sighed. "Doubtful, but..." He looked at Russ. "I have no one to tell, so your secret is safe with me. And twins. Holy cow. That's going to be fun."

Russ scratched his beard. "Yeah. We need the money Lori makes working here and with the vacation rentals, but I don't see how she can continue to work with three kids under three."

Betty wrapped her arm around Russ. His mom had treated Russ like one of her sons since the day he'd been hired. "Don't you worry about it, Russ. We'll figure it out. I promise." She bounced on her toes. "I'm so excited. I'm going to be a sort of grandma to twins. I can't wait to tell Phyllis. She's always bragging on her grandkids and making all of us at Criterion Club look at baby pictures. Ha-ha. With the twins and Zane and Wendy's baby, I'll have so many pictures and stories, she'll never get a word in edgewise."

"It's a secret for now," Russ warned.

"I know, I know." Betty rubbed her hands together. "I'm just making plans. Oh, we have to have a shower for Lori. She's going to need double everything."

She walked out of the house, making a list of all the women she would invite.

"Hey, man. Sorry," Eli said.

"Me, too. Guess I'll have to confess to Lori tonight."

"Take her out to dinner," Zane suggested. "That always puts Wendy in a good mood for bad news. Leave Rose with us tonight. Wendy and I will enjoy playing with her."

"Right, right," Russ said. "Dinner out. Good plan." He pulled his cell phone from his pocket and punched in a number. "Lori, honey. Let's go out to dinner tonight. No cooking. No dishes. Zane and Wendy said they'd keep Rose."

He listened, and his eyes shut. "What? I didn't do anything wrong. I just thought my beautiful wife could use a night off from the kitchen."

He listened again. "Exactly." He clicked off the phone.

"Well?" Eli asked.

"She asked what I'd done that merited dinner out and promised not to kill me."

"Perfect," Zane said. "You've got this in the bag."

Eli laughed. "I'm so glad I'm not married."

But watching his brother and Wendy, as well as Russ and Lori, made him ache for that sort of relationship. A confidante. A lover. Someone to hold when either of them had a bad day.

"You'll be singing a different tune one day," Zane said. "And Russ and I will be here to rub it in, right?"

"Yep," Rus said with a definitive nod.

Once the guys were gone, Eli paced around his new space, restless to get something else accomplished. Some people would count dropping a few thousand on new furniture this morning as getting things accomplished, but he wasn't ready to settle down for the day. It was just three in the afternoon. SEALs would never quit so early in the day.

Plus, moving out of his parents' house and into his own meant he had lots of items to cross off his to-do list. Since the living room and bedroom furniture had been decided, what interested him more was his own kitchen. He needed to get his hands deep in kneading the perfect pastry dough or smoking a nice brisket. Hell, he'd settle for making a thick beef stew.

With that decided, he climbed back into his truck. He could be at Lowe's in Bozeman in under an hour. He didn't want to hinder Addison's recovery by pushing her too hard, so he'd go alone. Besides, nobody knew more about what he'd want in his kitchen than he did.

By seven that evening, he was back on the ranch. After parking his truck, his heart tripped and splatted in his chest when he saw Addison on the patio watching late rafters on the Yellowstone River. Her white-blond hair was spiked and glistened in the late afternoon sun. Her arms were moving rhythmically, and he assumed she was knitting. Shoving his emotions into a corner, he strode toward her.

"Those people are crazy," he said, as he joined her on the patio. Hoping she didn't notice how his breath caught at her beauty, he made himself act normal and snagged a chair to pull it closer to her. "And so are you." He waved his hand. "There are mosquitos out here."

She pointed with a knitting needle to a can by her foot. "Mosquito fogger. I'm not a fool. Now, those idiots in rafts? They're questionable."

He laughed. "Actually, rafting's a blast. I'm assuming you haven't rafted the Yellowstone?"

"Nope. Not sure I will either. Even if I wasn't recovering from surgery, I don't think I'd have the nerve to try it."

He wanted to kick himself. Of course, she was still recovering.

"Well, then, you have an excuse. However, once you're healed, I'll drag you down there. Honestly, it's so much fun."

"But I'd get wet," she said with a fake whine.

"Yep, more like soaked, but it's safe. Every raft will have a professional guide. Besides..." He patted his chest. "I'm a SEAL. I could save you."

"You *were* a SEAL. Now, you're just a cowboy."

He grabbed his chest as though he'd been shot. "You got me."

She giggled at his antics.

"You know, if you want to sit outside, but don't want to hassle with bug spray, I do have a screened porch. You're welcome to use it anytime."

"Thanks. Your mom said the same thing, but I wasn't sure how you'd feel about finding me there."

Coming home to find her on his screened porch

making herself at home would make him feel fucking fantastic.

"I'd feel fine about it," he said, with more calm than he felt. "Make it your second home, if you want to. No pressure. Feel free to spray sticky, nasty bug repellent all over you instead."

She snorted and looked up at him. "Where have you been?"

"Were you looking for me?" He flattened his hand on his chest. "I'm flattered. You missed me."

"Not really, but I saw your truck was gone. When Wendy checked on me this afternoon, she mentioned that Zane and Russ had had to help you unload that, quote, monstrosity, unquote, of a chair you bought. Her words, not mine. I think Zane wants one now."

"Correction. I know Zane wants one," he said with a laugh. "And did she really call it a monstrosity?" He laughed again. "She'll be sorry for insulting my baby. I'm calling Zane later and taking him to Bozeman to get his own chair."

"Oh, she'll love that. You'll drop out of favorite brother-in-law status."

"Not worried. My big brother will protect me."

"She's pissed because she knows Zane is going to insist on putting one in the living room."

"She shouldn't have married a heathen, then."

Addison snorted again. "I'll be sure to mention that to her."

"You do that." He turned his chair toward her. "I was restless this afternoon. I got anxious to rework that kitchen, so I drove to Lowe's and ordered appliances."

"There's a Lowe's in Gardiner?"

"Oh, God no. Gardiner isn't big enough. I drove back to Bozeman."

"Why didn't you take me?"

"You were exhausted from this morning. Sorry, but you were kind of pale when I got you home. I didn't want to overtax you. After all, I still have towels and linens and groceries to buy."

"You know, you can order sheets and towels online, right? Have them shipped right to your door?"

"Yes, I know, but I want them now, not two or three days from now. If I go to Walmart, I can do it all at one time."

"I'll point out that you don't need them now." She shook her head.

"I know, I know. Fine. You can help me pick out sheets and stuff, and I'll have them shipped. Once I get settled, I'll buy local, but I have a list a mile long of spices and staples I need, and I need to get those in Bozeman, I think."

She laughed. "Look at the tough SEAL using words like staples. I doubt many men even know what those are."

"Do you?"

"Nope. I told you I don't really cook. Are you going tomorrow?"

"No. I want to get started on the painting and kitchen renovations tomorrow. I have an old high school buddy who owns a construction company. I talked to him today while I was driving. He's coming over in the morning to look over what I want to do."

"Renovating a kitchen can get expensive and time-consuming."

"True, but I'm not planning to take out the cabinets

or anything with this round. Just making room for my new stove, fridge, and microwave. Oh, and a new sink. Got new toilets coming, too."

She rolled her eyes. "New toilets? You think your ass can't sit on what's there?"

He laughed. "Not at all. I've taken bathroom breaks in places you do not want to know about."

She held up a hand like a stop sign. "Don't need to hear about those."

"Russ mentioned that the toilet had a crack and slow leak and needed to be replaced. He'd never gotten around to doing it."

"Got it." She collected her knitting project, shoved it into a bag by her feet, and then stood. "I need to head in. It's getting late, and I'm starved."

He jumped to his feet, not ready to let her go yet. "Let me take you to dinner. I know all the best places Gardiner has to offer."

"I'm sure you do, but I'll pass." She yawned. "I want to get to bed early, but thank you for asking. Raincheck?"

Disappointment flooded his gut. "Absolutely. I'll head in and study paint colors online."

They began walking toward the front of their respective apartments. "Have fun but don't pick white."

"Yes, ma'am," he said and gave her a sharp salute.

She laughed and walked inside.

Eli got up at five with his parents, mucked out the main barn stalls, and was waiting in the drive when his high school buddy Knox McCrea's beat-up, dented, rusted, black construction truck pulled in and parked.

A sign on the driver's door read: McCrea Construction.

Knox exited with his hand extended. "Eli, you sonofabitch. How are you? It's been forever."

Eli took his hand and pulled him in for mutual backslapping. "Good, good. You still married to Nancy?"

"'Til the day I die," Knox said.

"She's too good for you," Eli said, remembering all the shenanigans he, Knox and their running buddies had gotten into back in the day.

"I know," Knox said.

"Kids?"

"Four. Three boys and one girl."

Eli flinched. "A girl, huh? Bet that'll be fun when the boys start coming around."

Knox glared. "I keep my shotgun oiled up and loaded."

Eli laughed.

"Now, what's this project you're wanting to do?"

"Follow me."

Once they were inside the house attached to the barn, Eli gestured around. "My folks are giving me this place until I can get a house built. Since I have no idea what kind of house I want, nor where I want to put it, I may be here for a while."

Knox looked around the large living room area. "Great space. You might want larger windows overlooking the river. They'd let more light in. With the wooden floors and ceilings, this place could get kind of dark."

"Good morning," a bright female voice chirped from the door.

Eli turned and smiled. His stomach might have released a flight of butterflies at the vision of the platinum-blond beauty in his doorway.

"Addison. Come in. This is my old high school buddy, Knox McCrea. Knox, this is Addison Treadway, a, um, family friend. She's staying with us for a while."

Addison stuck out her hand. "Nice to meet you, Knox. I expect you to provide lots of blackmail stories from Eli's past that can be used against him. I pay well."

Knox gave a hardy laugh. "In that case, I have a few of those."

"And I have more that Nancy probably doesn't know." Eli looked at Addison. "Nancy is his wife."

She nodded. "So, what do you think of the place, Knox?"

"Just got here, but I think the space is awesome. Eli was just walking me through what he thinks the place needs."

"I'll get out of your way then," she said.

"No, no. Stay. I'd love to have your input," Eli said.

Forty-five minutes later, they had a plan. Take out the wall separating the kitchen from the dining/living room area. Replace the kitchen cabinets—Knox's suggestion—but with stock cabinets available faster than custom. Paint the kitchen cabinets in a Navy blue —a salute to Eli's history. The countertops would be replaced with a durable stainless steel. Eli loved that idea since it would give the kitchen an industrial look but in an old-fashioned log house.

The walls downstairs would all be painted in a grayish-white tone...light enough to reflect sunlight to brighten the space, but not as stark and cold as white. As per Knox's suggestion, the windows would be replaced with two sets of folding patio doors that would open to the small outdoor patio Knox would enlarge later.

Upstairs, the bedroom would get a fresh coat of bluish-white paint, as would the bathroom. The shower insert would be replaced with a tiled shower, as well as the toilet replacement that Eli had already planned. The single sink counter would be replaced with a quartz dual-sink design.

Knox agreed that the floors were in remarkable condition and would only need polishing, no sanding.

"So, what are we talking timewise?" Eli asked. "A week?"

Knox's hardy laugh boomed again. "Only if I were a magician. Realistically, maybe three to four weeks if I can get additional workers, but with you doing the painting and helping with the other items, maybe we can get out of here in fourteen to sixteen days."

"The cost?" Eli frowned and gave his friend a squinted glare. "And you're going to charge me double?"

"For a friend like you? Only triple," Knox said.

Addison said, "I can't believe you can get this done so quickly."

Knox shrugged. "The only big thing is taking down that wall and that can be done in a day, and the windows replacements—that'll take a couple of days, maybe three or four. We aren't replacing flooring or doing anything to the ceilings, so I think my guys can get it done." He looked at Eli. "When do you want to start?"

"Yesterday," Eli replied.

"Great, next month it is," Knox said.

Eli slugged Knox's arm. "When? And what's Nancy's cell phone number? I bet she doesn't know about the float trip with Delilah our senior year."

Knox snarled, and then laughed. "Fine. I'll be here first thing Monday morning with a couple of my guys. I've got another renovation project going and when it's done, I can move those guys over here. You might want to get that nice chair out of here. We'll start with that kitchen wall. When will your appliances arrive?"

"I told them I'd give them a delivery date. I'll get Zane to help me move the chair to the screened porch."

"Great. We'll know more tomorrow when we see how it goes."

After Knox left, Addison said, "Seems like a nice guy."

"He is. I trust him to do this job right."

"Can you get the paint in Gardiner?"

"Nope. Requires a trip to Lowe's in Bozeman."

"Doesn't that get old?"

"Honestly, I drove that road so many times growing up that it doesn't feel that long. You want to come along?"

"Yes. I'd love to get out." She wrinkled her nose. "The walls are closing in on me."

"We can do lunch while we're out, if you want."

"You're asking if I want food? Me and food? What do you think?"

He grinned. "Like I said, we'll grab lunch."

One of the things he loved about Addison was her unabashed love of food. She wasn't a salad-with-no-dressing kind of gal, or she'd never been when with him. She'd eaten like a death row inmate at Zane's wedding, and had ordered mini-cinnamon rolls to go with her crepes at breakfast yesterday. Still, her figure was thin. Was that due to her genetic makeup or from the cancer treatments?

Man, he hated the thought her slim figure might be due to chemotherapy.

She hurried off to get dressed to go, but he didn't see a thing wrong with the shorts and shirt she was already wearing. Her butt looked sexy and luscious in those shorts. Of course, she would make any outfit look like designer couture.

Well, now that he thought about that, he was wrong. Addison Treadway's beauty would outshine any clothing, regardless of designer name or style.

He'd left his work boots on the porch when he and Knox had entered. Now, he pushed his feet back into them and walked back to his parents' place to change out of his mud-splattered jeans into a clean pair.

The drive to Bozeman passed quickly, with Addison telling him about the guests she'd had on her show. She made him laugh and groan with varied tales...from dogs lifting their legs on live television to a chef who'd set his dish towel on fire by accident.

"You know, when I look at you, I see..." she said and then paused.

"What? What do you see?"

With a shrug, she said, "A Navy SEAL."

He chuckled. "Well, what do Navy SEALs look like?"

"On all the romance novels, they're broad-shouldered and hulky. You are broad-shouldered and not so bulky. I guess the shoulders come from all the swimming."

He nodded. "Most of us spend a lot of time in the

water doing laps, or on land running. I worked out with weights, but I focused on my shoulders and arms to be able to pull myself through water with as much ease as possible."

"What about your legs?"

"I have a pair," he joked.

"Har, har. No, I mean, did you use weights to build up the muscles there?"

"Can't help but build muscles in your calves and thighs. Kicking in the resistance that water provides does that, but I did some work with leg weights. So, you were starting to say that you can't see me as what?"

"A chef."

"That's only because you haven't tasted one of my fabulous meals."

She twisted in her seat to face him. "Give me an example of a meal you made for your team."

He thought about that. "Man, there were so many. Sometimes, they didn't want fancy. They'd ask me to fix something that reminded them of Sunday meals with the family. One of the dishes they loved was mashed-potato-stuffed-meatloaf, with yeast rolls, green beans with blanched almonds and bacon, and fried corn-on-the-cob."

"That sounds delicious." She pressed her hand into her stomach. "You made my stomach growl. Tell me a fancy one."

"Hmm, let's see. A fancy one. Well, I'd start with some appetizers. Maybe goat cheese crostini with red onion marmalade and woodfired roasted pork belly."

"What's a crostini?"

"You know what bruschetta is?"

"Yep."

"Well, crostini is a sort of cousin to bruschetta. Where bruschetta is whole slices of rustic Italian bread or sourdough, crostini is made from finer-textured bread like a white baguette. The baguette is sliced into small rounds of bread and then toasted."

"I've eaten those," she said with a chuckle. "I just had no idea that's what they were called. Okay, what else?"

She pulled her knees into her seat and leaned toward him as though enthralled with what he was saying. He had to admit, his ego enjoyed her attention.

"Well, if I wanted a second appetizer, I could do bacon-wrapped dates with whipped feta cheese or maybe seared scallops in hazelnut butter with mascarpone."

"My mouth is drooling. Main course," she demanded. "What's the main course?"

He chuckled. "The team loved my pork chops with a cherry port reduction, potatoes au gratin with a grilled romaine lettuce salad. And before you ask, dessert was a lemon souffle with raspberry crème anglaise."

"I wouldn't believe you could make all these, but you have to have, otherwise you'd never know all these dishes. It's not something most guys could roll off the tongue. And you have to cook for me. It doesn't have to be something fancy at all. I just want to sample something you can make."

"I'd love to cook for you. How about tomorrow night I make us three-way spaghetti?"

"Do I want to know what makes it three-way?"

"Nope. You just have to trust me."

She grinned. "Always."

The way she sounded when she said *always* make his heart swell.

At Lowe's, they went directly to the paint department and divided up. She went to one paint sample display and he to another. Then they regathered and share the samples they'd pulled. He was amazed at how close some of the gray-white shades were. The differences were subtle and only noticeable if he studied them.

They narrowed their choices down to two grays for the living room and kitchen, a dark-Navy blue for the cabinets, and the perfect shade for the bedroom and bathroom. After a vigorous back-and-forth over the grays, he ended up going with the one Addison had chosen. First, she was probably right. And second, it was less expensive than the one he'd chosen.

While the Lowe's employee mixed their order, they wandered down the tile aisle. Even though he wasn't there for shower tile, they found exactly what he wanted. In addition, Addison pointed out some sheet tiles that would make an excellent backsplash for the kitchen. Even though he hadn't planned on doing a tiled backsplash in the kitchen, he knew tiling that area would take no time at all, given its small size.

He bought a piece of the backsplash tile and some tile pieces for the shower with the gallons of paint. When he was ready for the tile, Lowe's would deliver the rest.

As they settled back into his truck, Eli said, "I would ask if you were hungry, but I've come to realize that's a dumb question. What would you like for lunch?"

"Your three-way? Is it a heavy dish?"

"Yeah, pretty filling."

"So, let's get something light. Sandwiches or soup or salad."

He chuckled.

"Why are you laughing?"

"I was thinking earlier that you never eat salad."

"I do, just not every day. Too boring. Hold on. I'll pull up restaurants on my phone and find one."

Fifteen minutes later, Eli was parking in front of the *Three S Shop*, i.e., soups, salads, and sandwiches.

Over a leisurely lunch of half-hoagie sandwiches and bowls of soup—broccoli-cheese for him and chicken won-ton for her—she peppered him with questions about his military service. He told her stories, filtering out the highly classified ones. They compared hospital stories, hers with cancer and his with gunshot wounds, but only after she agreed again to not tell his mother. She'd promised to keep his secret, but she'd laughed and joked about him still being scared of his mother.

He didn't mind. Her laughs and smiles made his day brighter.

He dropped her off at his apartment, sad to see their time together end for now.

Unloading the cans of paint—he refused to let her carry any of them because of their weight—he set the cans into their assigned rooms.

Tomorrow, the real work would begin.

Tonight, he had a date with Addison and her kitchen. While he was eager to be cooking again, he was more excited to spend time with Addison.

As a friend, he reminded himself.

CHAPTER 8

A ddison fluffed her short hair with her fingertips. The white-blond coloring had been a surprise when the hair grew back. Growing up, she'd always had red tones in her auburn hair. As an adult, she'd "helped" the red tones become more pronounced, and she'd enjoyed the highlights around her face. But she didn't miss the time it took to do the hair color, nor the expense. The platinum was fun.

However, short hair was a new world to her and she struggled to style it. Many days she missed her long hair. Taking care of that mop had been so easy. Pull it into a ponytail when she didn't want to fuss with it. Wrap the hair into a bun on her head. Braid it when she felt spunky. Now?

She studied herself in the bathroom mirror. Her face looked sickly and sallow, and the dingy yellow bathroom lights didn't help. Was she that pale, or was her white hair doing that to her skin tone? She brushed on a little more blush. Lipstick? A tube of deep red sat in the bottom of her makeup bag. She tried to remember the last time she'd worn makeup and lipstick. It had to be months ago.

She didn't want to look like she was trying too hard for tonight's dinner. She and Eli had become friends. This was a dinner with a friend, not a potential lover, even if he'd given her the most incredible and unforgettable night of her life. Even if her tummy squeezed and her heart leapt and raced every time she saw him. Even if his deep voice made breathing almost impossible.

He'd put her firmly in the friend category. She had to find a way to do the same.

This was a simple dinner, nothing fancy, but she didn't want to look like a recovering cancer patient or someone fresh from surgery.

People who knew about her cancer always gave her pity eyes and she hated those. That was one of the major reasons she'd left her talk show. With the help of wigs and a professional makeup artist, she could have continued working much longer than she had. However, she couldn't abide the looks the crew gave her or how everyone treated her as though she'd break like fine china.

Her October report on mammograms, followed by her own cancer detection had punched ratings through the roof. She took her viewers along as she did follow-up ultrasounds, the biopsy and even the genetic counseling. The only time she didn't allow a camera was for the MRI of the breasts and when she met with a medical oncologist. She hadn't liked the man, nor his attitude. He'd been almost flippant about everything.

She'd reached out to her friend, Dr. Wendy McCool, who called her twin sister, Dr. Risa McCool-Mason, who was a renowned breast cancer surgeon and researcher in Dallas. At first, Risa had suggested Addison do her treatments in Orlando, but with Addison's insistence that she wanted Risa involved, she'd put Addison in touch with a medical oncologist on her staff who'd agreed to do her chemotherapy treatments on Fridays.

Following her show on Thursday mornings, Addison would fly to Dallas, do chemotherapy on Fridays, rest at her parents' house until Sunday, and then fly back to Orlando and do her daily show Monday through Thursday, when the process would repeat.

The first chemotherapy treatment in November had been ten days after meeting Eli, the Friday after Thanksgiving.

The Monday morning after her third treatment, she was drinking coffee and reading the Orlando Sentinel to see what news she might have missed while she was in Dallas. Saundra, the station's hairstylist was busy brushing and fashioning Addison's long hair for that day's broadcast, when she let out a gasp. Addison stilled and looked into the mirror. Saundra was holding a hank of long, red hair from Addison's head.

"I'm so sorry," Saundra said. "I barely touched it."

Addison sighed and nodded. She'd known the day was coming when she'd lose her hair, but knowing it was coming in the future was not the same as facing the reality of it happening today. Tears filled her eyes before she could hold them off.

Saundra thrust a box of tissues toward her. "I can fix this for today."

Addison heard what Saundra didn't say. She could fix Addison's hair today, but no promises for the future.

"Thank you, Saundra."

Addison lived with her thinning hair until Wednesday. When she'd showered that morning, long strands of red hair washed down her body with the soap suds. Reality sucked sometimes, and without a doubt, this December would be one of those times.

She'd used the same hairstylist for highlights and cuts for years. They had a great relationship, so when Addison called that afternoon, her hair stylist agreed to shave the rest of the hair off. Since Addison was so well known in Orlando, her friend met her in the closed salon Wednesday evening to protect Addison's privacy. She'd shared so much of her cancer journey with her viewers, but she just couldn't bring herself to appear on-air with a bald head. She didn't like to think herself vain, but she supposed everyone had a streak in them. Shaving her head hadn't hurt physically, but emotionally, it'd been devastating.

Thursday morning, she'd done her show wearing a wig for the first, and only, time. It'd been Christmas Eve Day and her show was scheduled for reruns until the end of the year when she would return in January with all new programming.

Except, she said her goodbyes that day.

Her inbox filled with well-wishes and holiday greetings. And, as hard as it was to believe, trolls found her social media sites and blasted her with nasty comments about her wig and how she should die. She shut down all her social media accounts that afternoon.

Christmas Day, she packed her bags. The next day, she shipped her clothes to her parents' house, packed as much as she could into her Ferrari, locked her condo door, and drove home to Texas. For the first time in a very long time, she needed the care and comfort only her mother could provide.

A heavy knock at her door jerked her from those memories. She'd made it through all that, plus two surgeries. She was strong. She was a survivor. She could do anything she put her mind to, even if that meant only being friends with Eli and nothing more.

However, she would have to be gone before he started dating, or fell in love with someone else. She might not be able to survive that.

"Come on in," she called from the bathroom as she hurriedly ran her fingers through her hair, making it spike. "Do you need a hand?"

A paper grocery bag clunked on her recently cleared and cleaned kitchen counter. "Nope. I've got it."

He was unloading meat, fresh spices, and various cans of who-knew-what from the bag when she walked out of the bathroom.

He glanced up at her, smiled, and went back to emptying the bag. "You look amazing," he said. "But then, you always do."

Her heart fluttered and her hand reflexively touched her hair. "You like this?"

Eli stilled and looked at her. "I thought your long, red hair was the sexiest thing I'd ever seen. But now, I love this style, too. It shows off your long neck." He shrugged. "Maybe it's just that you look great no matter what your hairstyle."

Then, as if he hadn't just blown her away, he disappeared below her counter. Pans rattled in her cabinet, or maybe that was her heart rattling against her ribs.

She was far, far from an innocent virgin. But the

number of men she'd allowed in her bed could be counted on one hand, and have a couple of fingers left over. In the past few months, she'd asked herself if she hadn't been facing cancer and the loss of her breasts, would she have pursued Eli with such dogged determination at Zane and Wendy's wedding or would she have slept alone?

One thing she knew for sure was she didn't regret their time together. She'd thought she'd made love before, but he showed her how a lady should be treated in the bedroom and out.

Denis certainly hadn't made her feel like she was treasured and her high school boyfriend had been as clueless as she. Eli made her feel beautiful and strong and sexy...until he hadn't.

When she'd walked out of that bathroom and he was gone, but his bottle of bourbon was sitting on the desk, she'd assumed he'd run to his room for something. She'd been sure he'd be back, so she'd spent a few minutes fluffing pillows and straightening her room.

But thirty minutes passed, then an hour and she knew he wasn't coming back. When Denis finally reached her the next day, he hadn't mentioned the call the night before, so until Eli told her, she'd had no idea Denis and Eli had spoken.

"Addison." Eli tapped a metal spatula in the frying pan.

Her heart jumped at the loud sound. She whirled around to face him. "What?"

He laughed softly. "Where'd you go?"

"Just thinking."

"About?"

"Um, how your furniture is going to look with that

wall color," she lied. "I can't wait to see it all come together."

He eyed her as though he didn't quite buy what she was selling, but he didn't question her further.

"I asked if you would like some wine before dinner?" He held up two bottles.

"Sounds great. Red. What can I do to help?"

"Sit there and talk to me." He gestured with a wine glass to a bar stool on the other side of the counter.

"Now, there's a cooking assignment I can do."

Her gaze soaked in the pop of his biceps when he carried the heavy pot of water from the sink to the stove. Setting it on a back burner, he let the water come to boiling before adding the dry pasta. Her mouth watered at the muscle definition in his forearms as he stirred or opened lids. His movements were smooth and unhurried as he browned hamburger meat, opened chili beans, and added spices Her mind filled with visions of how luscious his well-defined, washboard abs would look just standing there.

She was watching a master at work.

She took a sip of wine as a distraction, but that didn't help. Balancing her head on her hands, she stared, entranced at his every movement.

Some chefs on her show's cooking segments struggled to talk while they worked, complaining later that having to talk distracted them. So, she filled the silence on the set with explanations of what the chef was doing, having prepared by studying the recipes ahead of time.

But that didn't describe Eli in the least. He chatted and stirred and strained without missing a beat. One thing he'd been right about tonight's meal. Three-way spaghetti didn't take long to prepare.

"I'd like to let the chili sauce cook a while before we eat," Eli explained. "I want the spices to mingle with the meat and tomato sauce long enough that we can't tell where one begins and the other ends."

She nodded, not that she really grasped that concept. As she said, she wasn't much of a cook. "Okay. Want to move to the living room while we wait?"

Eli laughed. The living room was an area three feet behind her. The apartment's entire living area was comprised of a tiny living room with a counter bar and stools that served to separate the living room from the tiny kitchen.

"I don't know, Addy. That living room is a long way off."

She picked up the wine bottle and refilled their glasses. "Since neither of us has to drive tonight..."

"True. I can easily stumble home from here."

She rolled her eyes. "What would your mom say? Actually, what did your parents do if you or Zane came home drunk?"

He picked up his glass and gestured for her to follow him to the sofa.

"Well, since I'd have been underage when it happened—and I'm not saying it did or it didn't—dad would have banged on my bedroom door about four or four-thirty, insisting he needed help on the ranch. The day would be spent doing the worst things you can imagine when you're hungover. Mucking stalls. Riding boarding horses. Hauling hay from the loft in one barn to another. Brutal stuff."

"Riding horses doesn't sound like punishment."

"Are you kidding? Imagine being queasy, your head spinning, and your stomach wanting to show you its contents. Now imagine all that happening on a horse whose trot is as jarring as a pogo stick. He made sure we were assigned only the worst horses to ride."

She giggled. "Poor baby. Bet that stopped those Friday night keggers."

"Yeah, well, you'd lose that bet. You'd think after Zane went through that hell I would learn from his example, but no. It's true that you only learn from your own mistakes."

"How long do we have to let the sauce simmer?" Her stomach growled as the delicious aroma from the spicy concoction filled the room.

"At least an hour. Got a favorite movie to watch?"

She stifled her groan of starvation. "I've got the new *Fast and Furious Fourteen*, if you're interested in fast car chases."

"You've been holding out on me. Load that puppy."

They sat on her small two-cushion sofa, sitting so close, it was impossible not to bump shoulders. After the second time, he put his arm along the back of the couch behind her, his hand lightly touching her. The temptation to curl into his side and sniff the delicious testosterone rolling off him was almost unbearable. Luckily, she'd already watched the movie because she couldn't concentrate on anything but his heat and scent.

About halfway through the movie, they'd taken a break so Eli could check on the sauce. He surprised her with goat cheese crostini with red onion marmalade wrapped in bacon strips as an appetizer.

She embarrassed herself with moans and sighs as she noshed on their goodness. From the strained look on Eli's face, she must have embarrassed him, too.

At the end of the movie, he pronounced the sauce ready.

"Do you like onions?"

She raised an eyebrow. "You just fed me onion marmalade."

"I know, but marmalade isn't the same as chopped onions."

"Bring on the onions, but only if you're having them also."

"I have to. Otherwise, your onion breath will be too much for me."

She bopped him on the head with a loose roll of paper towels as he laughed.

He prepared both plates and set them on the counter. Then he came around and took the second stool beside her.

"Tell me what I'm eating."

"Angel hair pasta topped with spicy chili sauce, chili beans, sharp cheddar cheese, and sweet, red onions. I sprinkled a little parmesan cheese over the top." He snapped his fingers. "Hold on. I forgot the crackers."

He pulled a tray of warmed saltine crackers from the oven, and put them in a bowl. Beside those, he added a stick of soft butter.

"Warmed crackers and butter?" she asked.

"Oh, yeah. Trust me."

Following his directions, she smeared the soft butter over the warm cracker and took a bite. Her taste buds danced in delight to the salty, fatty, yumminess.

Dinner was everything he promised and more. If only she'd had someone like him on her show back in Florida. A handsome, sexy SEAL doing live cooking exhibitions? The ladies would have gone nuts. Her ratings would have crashed through the roof. She chuckled at the thought.

"What are you laughing about?" he asked.

"Just thinking about my show in Florida."

"Are you going back? Are they holding that slot for you?"

"Funny you should ask. I talked to my producer just the other day. They replaced me with some young, fresh-faced baby wannabe and the ratings are in the basement."

"So, you're going back?"

"Honestly, I don't know. I'd been restless for a while. Even bored with my own segments. I'm not sure what I'm going to do next." She snapped her fingers. "Hey! Wait a minute. I just remembered something I read today. Hold on."

She slid from the stool and hurried to her bedroom. That flyer she'd picked up in town about the Beer and Buffalo Meat Challenge Event had to be in here somewhere. She'd been reading it last night, and there it was, on the floor under her bed. She grabbed the paper and headed back to Eli.

Thrusting the glossy flyer toward him, she said, "Look at this."

He took it, read it, and handed it back. "Okay. You want to go? I'll take you."

"No, you goose." She gave his shoulder a slap with the floppy paper. "I think you should enter the buffalo chili contest." She pointed to the print. "Look. There's a thousand-dollar prize."

He smiled. "You're sweet to think my chili is good enough to win, but there will be people who enter and do these contests all the time. Contest pros. I'm not that."

"No, but you could be. You could pay for your house renovations." When he replied with a raised eyebrow, she added, "Okay, you can pay for your tile. But if you don't want to do chili, there're other meat divisions. Tenderloin, butt, ribs, and brisket."

He laughed. "I think the proper term for the butt is buffalo round."

His laugh was deep and full and did funny things to her insides...like melting them into a gooey blob.

Last November, she'd told herself she was having a wedding weekend fling. She hadn't mentioned that to him, so maybe him ghosting her was partly her fault.

Now, she questioned if a fling with this sexy man was what she'd really wanted, or had they connected on a level recognized by their souls, if not by their minds.

"Whatever," she said. "You need those winnings."

"I hear you saying I could have chosen a less expensive tile."

She giggled. "Not really. What you picked is beautiful. But seriously, Eli, I think you should enter this. The festival is in the middle of August. With no real holidays that month to celebrate or draw people here, it appears Gardiner decided to invent a festival to give visitors another reason to visit Montana and Yellowstone. You have plenty of time to get ready. It'd be fun."

"Hmm, I've never cooked buffalo. I'd have to do some research." He lifted an eyebrow. "Are you going to help?"

"I was thinking I might have a booth at the festival selling all the knitting pieces I've made."

"I noticed you knitting on the patio. How long have you done that?"

"Oh, forever. My grandmother taught me when I was about twelve, so twenty years, give or take a few years. There were periods where I didn't pick up my needles, but then I'd get stressed and the knitting helped. Granny said the knitting motion of her fingers helped keep her arthritis under control. Her fingers weren't as stiff."

His brow furrowed. "Do you have many pieces to sell? I only remember seeing a pair of socks."

"Tons of socks and scarves. I knitted during my day-long chemotherapy, and while I've been recovering, so I've built up quite the stash." She grinned. "My family is a little tired of all my projects ending up as their gifts. Anyway, I thought I'd display the sweaters and vests and take orders if anyone was interested."

"If I tell you I'll think about it, can we put the topic to the side and have dessert?"

Addison clapped and may have wiggled with happiness on her stool. She did have a voracious sweet tooth. "Yes! What's for dessert?"

With a laugh, he said, "Don't get too excited. I didn't have time to make much. I was kind of busy today."

"But you made me something, right?"

"I have something." He lifted a baggie from a paper sack and set it on the counter. From her freezer, he pulled out a carton of vanilla ice cream. "I have turtle brownies with pecans and caramel. I thought we could heat them and put a scoop of ice cream on top." He pulled a jar of caramel sauce and a jar of chocolate sauce from the sack. Last, he got a can of whipped cream from her refrigerator. "I cheated on the whipped cream and the sauces. Usually, I prefer to make my own, but time got away from me. So, store bought will have to do."

"I have no idea what you are rambling on about," she said. "I heard nothing after turtle brownies."

He snorted. "Sit. I'll heat us each a brownie. Big piece or little?"

With a tilt of her head, she gave him an exaggerated scoff. "Seriously?"

"Got it." He put two large turtle brownies on small plates, heating one plate and then the other. "Caramel or chocolate fudge?"

"Yes."

With a grin, he plopped a big scoop of ice cream atop each brownie and followed with caramel and chocolate fudge sauces. Without asking, he squirted a mountain of whipped cream on top.

"Hey," she protested. "You didn't ask if I wanted whipped cream!"

"Oh. Sorry. Do you want whipped cream?"

"Yes, thank you." She laughed.

"As if there was ever any question," he said, setting the plate in front of her.

She moaned with her first bite. "Damn. I'd weigh a thousand pounds if I let you cook for me on a regular basis."

As she said that, she realized that she might not mind him cooking for her every day.

"Not to worry," he assured her. "You couldn't possibly afford me."

"Really?" She arched a brow. "What is the going rate for a sexy ex-SEAL who is a gourmet chef?"

His face lit with pleasure. "You think I'm sexy?"

"Please. I know all about frog hogs. I bet those women were all over you all the time."

He shrugged and took a bite of his brownie. "You learn early on to stay away from them, else you find yourself a father before you're ready."

Everything froze inside her. Had that happened to him?

"You got quiet all of a sudden," he said.

"Did that happen to you?"

"Oh, hell, no. Remember that SEAL instructor I told you about? Benjamin? Well, it was his wife who got me into cooking. He'd been around teams for a long time. He drilled the risk of an unplanned SEAL baby into our heads, not to mention all kinds of other things."

"Like what? STDs?"

"Sure, but also, spies. You can't be too careful with governmental secrets. While most of these women probably just wanted a SEAL notch on her bedpost, it was just as likely she could be a spy out to learn what she could learn."

"Pillow talk," Addison said.

"That, and snooping around your house, or car or even your official backpack."

"Wow. That's scary."

He gave a nonchalant shrug. "It happens. There are all kinds of female, and male, operatives out there looking for intel. One of our tasks was to make sure they didn't get it from one of us."

"Worst thing I had to fear was a rival television personality trying to get my job by sleeping with the producer."

"Did that happen?"

"Not to me personally. Liza, my producer, wasn't like that, but it sure happened to people I know."

Eli's phone dinged. He pulled it out and read the message. He typed a reply and returned the phone to his pocket.

"Everything okay?"

"Yep. That was Knox confirming that he and his crew would be here at seven a.m. on Monday to get started."

"Early bird gets the worm."

"I'll settle for a large mug of coffee."

She laughed.

"Seriously, I should help you clean up this kitchen and get going. To be honest, I hadn't realized how late it'd gotten."

"You cooked. I'll clean."

"In most situations, I would agree, but you're still recovering from surgery."

"Stop it," she demanded. "I'd rather you hate me and yell at me than to be nice because I've been sick."

"It's not—"

"Yes, it is." She stood and picked up her plate and his. "You can help me clean, or you can leave it all to me, but it's my kitchen. I'll be cleaning it up."

"Yes, ma'am. You load the dishwasher and I'll handle putting away the leftovers. Deal?"

"Deal."

When they were done and he was leaving, her heart raced when she thought he was going to kiss her. They were in her tiny kitchen. He folded a kitchen towel and hung it over the rim of the sink. She'd leaned over to put soap in the dishwasher and start it. She straightened and found them almost nose to nose. His eyes dilated and his chest heaved. Leaning in ever-so-slightly, she waited for his kiss, but he took a step back, and then another.

Her spirit plummeted to the floor, along with her heart.

"This was fun," Eli said. "Let's do it again soon."

"Absolutely," she agreed and straighten her spine, praying he hadn't noticed when she'd gone in expecting a kiss.

As the door closed behind him, her shoulders sagged with kiss disappointment. The rational side chastised her emotional side. The last thing she needed was to get involved with her best friend's brother-in-law when Addison was sure she'd be leaving Montana soon and never see Eli again.

CHAPTER 9

Since Eli was fairly certain his time would be consumed over the next couple of weeks with renovation projects, he threw himself into helping Zane and Russ with the multitude of chores that running a horse ranch entailed. Saturday and Sunday passed in a haze of horse manure, fence repairs, and any other nasty job his brother could think of. Zig's question about Eli's ability to go back to being a cowboy after so many years away had planted in his brain, but the weekend proved he'd forgotten little. The days started early and finished late and Eli was exhausted at the end of the day. However, it was a good fatigue...one that satisfied the work ethic he'd developed in the military.

Both days, he kept his eyes peeled for Addison, even if only a glance, but he didn't see her. Sunday afternoon, he approached his brother.

"Have you seen Addison this weekend? I haven't and I'm a little worried. Is she okay?"

Zane studied him for a minute. "Well, I probably shouldn't tell you this. Wendy's been all over me about doctor-patient confidentiality, but since you asked, she was worn out from going to Bozeman both days. Wendy insisted Addison stay inside and rest all weekend. Since she didn't get any argument about her stay-home-and-rest orders, Wendy told me she was sure Addison had exhausted herself."

Eli wanted to kick his own ass. "Fuck. I should have known I was pushing her too hard."

Zane scoffed. "Nobody pushes Addison to do anything she doesn't want. I've learned that in the months she's been here. If she hadn't wanted to go, she wouldn't have. Still, she's been to hell and back in the last year. Her divorce was tough. Wendy tells me her ex was a complete asshole. The cancer was the cherry on her shit sundae. She puts up a good front, but sometimes the rest of us have to make her stop even when she doesn't want to. You might want to remember that."

Eli nodded. "I'll do that."

"Especially if you care about her." Zane stopped Eli's response with a head shake. "I'm not asking. Gotta head home. Wendy promised me meatloaf if I got home early."

Eli grinned. "Remind me to give her my bacon-wrapped-cheese-mashed-potato-stuffed-meatloaf recipe."

Zane waved. "Will do. See you in the morning."

"Remember renovation starts tomorrow."

Zane didn't respond; he just climbed on the ATV and headed toward his house, giving Eli a wave over his head.

· · ·

Monday morning, Eli found himself still in the foul mood he'd been in all weekend. He was ready to get going on the renovations, but for the last forty-eight hours, no matter how nasty the task Zane had assigned, he'd done the work while reliving his Friday night dinner date with Addison. Had he made a mistake in how he'd ended the evening?

He'd wanted to kiss her Friday night more than he'd wanted his next breath. It'd taken every ounce of determination not to kiss Addison's luscious lips that night. He'd lost count of the number of times she'd moaned and crooned while she'd eaten his food. Lost count of how many times her tongue had flicked out to wet her lips. And then, he'd damned near lost his mind when she'd licked the caramel and chocolate off her spoon. The vision had sent his cock into overdrive, pushing against his zipper like it was trying to break free. He'd been surprised there hadn't been a zipper pattern on his flesh when he'd finally taken off his pants.

During his time in teams, he'd gotten used to operating on only a few hours of sleep, or no sleep at all. Friday night had definitely fallen into the no-sleep-at-all category, and he'd been a bear all weekend.

He hadn't been kept awake by pain, or PTSD, or anything other than a nagging picture of the woman he couldn't pursue. He'd handled, so to speak, the raging erection he'd brought home, but even that hadn't given him the complete release he'd needed. He wasn't sure how long he could pretend that his only interest was in being a supportive friend.

Still, he knew a friend was what she needed, not a lover. Hadn't his own brother and sister-in-law told him that?

Knox McCrea and his crew rolled down the drive a little before seven. Eli was glad to see the construction trucks. He was ready to get busy. Of course, he wanted to get the house done, but just as importantly, they'd be taking down a wall today, and he could take out his frustrations with a sledgehammer on that drywall.

"Morning," he called to Knox. "Are you ready to rumble?"

Knox laughed. "Ready-to-rumble" had been their football team's locker room cry before taking the field for a home game.

"I'm ready," Knox said. "I'm not as good as I once was in high school, but I'm as good once as I ever was. Let's take down a wall."

Eli laughed and the heavy chip on his shoulder lightened. There really was nothing like old friends to help you shake off a funk.

"Eli. This is my son, Jason. He's a junior at Gardiner High School and working for me this summer. This here is Frank Keller and Bubba Keller. They've been with me...how long now?"

"'Bout fourteen years," Frank said.

"Frank and Bubba are brothers," Knox explained. "I'll have a few more guys on the job later this week. My other team is finishing up a project. I may have to run over there today and check on their progress, but Frank and Bubba know what they're doing, so you won't even miss me."

"Good morning, everyone," Eli said, nodding. "And Knox, how can you have a kid in high school? We aren't that old."

"Yeah, we are, bud."

Eli answered with a groan. Time had flown so quickly.

Eli led the construction guys into his house. Once there, he pointed to the offending wall between his kitchen and living room. "That one. Gone."

Knox nodded. "We're good to go on that." He looked at his son and the two construction workers. "Not weight-bearing, so taking it down should be a breeze. Some minor electrical to deal with, but that's it."

"One thing before we start," Eli said. "I really need to work out some issues. Think I could take the first whacks with the hammer?"

Knox laughed. "Sure thing. Jason, get that heavy sledgehammer from the truck and let Eli take a few swings."

"Sure."

Quickly, Jason was back. He passed the tool over to Eli.

"Thanks."

Eli was beginning his backswing when Knox stopped him. "Yeah, that was a test. Jason, you never, ever use something like this without a hard hat and safety glasses. I'll be damned if I let the person paying the bills get hurt on one of my job sites, and then try to live off the insurance."

Eli chuckled.

"Sorry, Dad. You're right. I totally forgot. I'll get them from the truck."

Jason left, and Knox looked at Eli with a shake of his head. "Damn boy had a first date with some gal he's been chasing since ninth grade. I suspect that's all that'll be on his mind all day."

Eli grinned. "I remember those days," he said, as if there wouldn't be a gal on his mind all day, too.

Knox returned his grin. "Those were some good times." As Jason hurried back in, Knox said, "Put on the hard hat and safety glasses, and then you can beat that wall to your heart's content."

Appropriately attired, Eli took his first swing, expecting to crash through the drywall and make a huge hole. Instead, the hammer head hit the wall and promptly got stuck. When he jerked it out, a tiny chunk of plaster came with it and tumbled to the floor.

"Yeah, I meant to do that," he said with a grin.

Knox laughed. His son snickered. The other two guys looked at the ceiling, but Eli could see they wanted to laugh.

Eli drew back and swung again. He connected firmly with the plaster and a huge hole appeared.

A whistle and clapping from the entry caught his attention. He looked over in time to see Addison put her fingers between her lips. When she blew, an ear-splitting whistle echoed through the room.

"Very impressive, Miller," she said. "At that rate, the wall should be down by Labor Day."

This time, all the guys joined in the laughter.

"As much as a beautiful woman brightens up our work area, you shouldn't be in here without a hard hat and safety glasses. I'd hate to have something fall on you," Knox said.

Addison nodded. "Good point. Okay if I look through the door from time to time to see the progress?" She held up a camera. "I thought I'd take some pictures, before and after shots. Is that okay?"

Eli nodded. "Actually, a great idea. Thanks."

She snapped a few pictures of the hole in the wall, and the guys as they posed beside it. "Okay. I'm headed outside for a while."

"Knitting?" Eli asked.

"Of course. If I want to have a large selection of items to sell at the festival, I have to keep working."

"You talking about the Buffalo and Beer Event weekend?" Knox asked.

"I am," Addison said brightly. "Eli's going to enter the buffalo chili cook-off."

"You are?" Knox looked at Eli.

Eli rubbed the back of his neck. "I don't know. Addison thinks we'd have fun entering. I don't expect to win, or anything like that."

"But you would," Addison said. She looked at Knox. "His chili will knock your socks off."

"I think it'd be cool, man," Jason said. "Dad's entering, right?"

Eli swung his gaze to Knox. "You're entering the chili event?"

"Nope. I'm in the microbrew beer event. I can't cook worth a crap, but I make the best beer in Montana."

"See, Eli?" Addison said. "You have to enter. I bet a bunch of your old buddies will be there."

She smiled at him brightly, an attempt to sweet talk him into agreeing. Looking at her sparkling eyes and beautiful face, his heart rolled over. She could probably talk him into just about anything, he feared.

"Maybe. How long do I have to decide?"

Knox shrugged. "I don't know. I filled out my entry last week. Good thing you aren't trying to enter the microbrew competition."

"Why? Afraid I might kick your butt?"

Knox laughed. "Not in the slightest. It's full, so there's no spots left. But as importantly, I'd kick your ass and then you'd be pissed and fire me from this job."

Eli snorted. "Okay, then. We need to get back to work. Thanks for taking progress pictures, Addy."

"I can take a hint. I'm gone." Addison waved and walked out.

"Okay, men," Knox said. "Let's get going. We should have this down by lunch."

The five guys tackled the wall, knocking out the drywall, followed by cutting the wall boards. There had been some electrical wiring for one wall plug, but Knox was able to handle that without a problem.

Addison stuck her camera through the door for random pictures, but Eli was busy and wasn't sure what shots she'd gotten.

At noon, Jason hauled out the last of the boards and stacked them beside the barn as Eli had requested. If the boards weren't fire-retardant, they'd make great fuel for an outdoor fire later this year when it got cold.

Once, Jack Marsten, one of his team members, had hauled a pickup truck full of wooden pallets over to Eli's to use for a cookout, only the wood refused to burn no matter what starter fluid they'd tried. Turned out, all the wood had been infused with a fire retardant. Luckily for the team and their dates that night, Eli was obsessive-compulsive when it came to grilling out and he'd brought charcoal as a backup.

Even though the wall was down, there was still a mess of debris that would have to be cleaned up before moving on to other projects.

"Lunch," Knox announced. "You guys be back in

forty-five. I'm going to run over to the Ransfield house and see how that's coming along."

With that, the workers headed to their trucks and headed off for lunch.

"Where did everyone go?" his mother asked as she walked up.

"Lunch break."

Her expression brightened. "Are you hungry? I've all the makings for my famous hoagie."

"Sounds wonderful, but..." Eli looked at his dusty jeans and dirty shirt. "I'm too nasty to come inside."

"Back porch then. Go wash up, and I'll meet you there."

Mentally, he laughed. Externally, he grinned. Here he was at thirty-six and his mother was still telling him to wash his hands. She probably would forever. "Yes, ma'am. I'll be over shortly."

The water and power to his barn house had been turned off for renovation, so washing for lunch would be cold water from an outside faucet, which was fine. Mother nature was pumping the heat up for July.

At his parents' house, he turned on the faucet, and cold water spurted out the end of the hose. Putting the hose between his knees, he washed his hands first then bent over to run cold water over his head. He hadn't realized how hot his head was until the first blast of icy water rolled through his sweat-drenched hair and dripped off his grimy face. He scrubbed his face with a clean hand, and then grabbed the towel he saw in his peripheral vision.

Rubbing the thick, terry material around his face, he said, "Ah. Thanks, Mom." He spoke into the towel as he dried his eyes.

"You're welcome...*son*."

He jerked the towel away from his face and looked into Addison's sparkling green eyes.

"I'm old enough to be a mom, but not quite yours," she said with a chuckle. "Your mom handed me the towel and asked me to bring it around to you."

"Thanks. I needed that head dunking. Whew. That was some dirty work."

"I just peeked in and took a picture. I like the wall gone."

"Me too. Want to join me for lunch?"

"Your mom already invited me, and yes, I am."

They walked around to the rear of the house to the screened-in porch his parents had built when Eli had been a sophomore in high school. He had hated it. Before then, he'd been able to easily sneak out of the house with his buds. However, after the screens went up, one of his favorite exit spots had been cut off.

As an adult, screening out bugs and flies seemed like an excellent idea.

When he pulled the door open, the door springs groaned out a loud squeak.

"Sounds like that door could use some grease," Addison said as they walked in.

"Supposed to sound like that," Betty said as she exited the house with two plates loaded with sandwiches and homemade potato salad.

"It is?" Addison said, her voice echoing the astonishment reflected on her face.

Betty chuckled. "Better than any alarm system. No one's going to break in, but I might have been aware of a couple of boys who used to sneak out from time to time. I'm not mentioning any names, of course."

Eli grinned. "It was Zane," he told Addison. "Always sneaking out and getting into trouble."

Betty swatted him with a dishtowel. "I did not have to come to the sheriff's station and pick up Zane from a kegger when he was in high school."

Addison chuckled.

"What is the statute of limitations on that, anyway?" Eli asked.

"The day I die," Betty said.

"Which I hope is far, far in the future, like decades and decades," Eli said and bussed a kiss on his mom's cheek. "Thanks for the chow."

"Chow, indeed," Addison said. "This looks and smells wonderful."

"You need to put on a few pounds," Betty said to her. "Some good meals will put color in those cheeks."

"And some fat on my hips," Addison said with a laugh.

"Ain't nothing wrong with your hips," Eli said, then ripped off a bite of his sandwich with his teeth.

"See? Now eat." Betty turned toward the door leading inside the house.

"Aren't you going to join us?" Addison asked.

"I had lunch with Henry," Betty said. "Besides, you two are old enough to eat together without a chaperone."

"But what if she throws food at me?" Eli asked, forcing his eyes wide.

His mother laughed, as did Addison.

"Well, come tell me, and I'll ground her for a week," Betty said. "Let me know if you need more."

After she left, Addison glared at him. "Throw food

at you? I'd dump my glass of water over your head, except you're already soaking wet."

Eli chuckled as he lifted the hefty sandwich off his plate. "Bon appétit!"

Addison scooped up a bite of potato salad and lifted it to her mouth. Eli couldn't take his eyes off her as she opened her lips, put the fork in, shut those luscious lips, and pulled the fork slowly from her mouth with a long moan. Immediately, visions of his cock between those lips made him grow stiff and uncomfortable.

He shifted his butt on the seat of the chair.

"What?" Addison said. She grabbed a napkin and dabbed at her mouth. "Do I have something on my face?"

"No. I was just watching you enjoying your food."

She relaxed. "Your mom is a great cook. I bet you missed that a lot when you left home."

"She is, and I did. That was one of the things that contributed to me learning to cook for myself."

"I know that SEAL's wife taught you some things, but you also mentioned some classes. Did you take many?" She put another bite into her mouth, and he stifled the groan he felt.

He exhaled and slid his fork into the potato salad. "I took classes every chance I got. Sometimes, I even got to finish them," he said with a chuckle. "I was in and out of the country so often that I'd do as much as I could, and then have to leave class assignments undone. Once, I was determined to get through the entire eight lessons, and I did, but it took almost nine months."

"The instructor stretched the class out that long?"

He shook his head. "I would join when I was in town. I think I was officially in four or five different sessions." He chuckled quietly. "The class would be on lesson four, and here I'd show up for lesson five, and they'd look at me like...*Where'd he come from? Never seen him before.* But it worked out."

"I'll say. I can't wait to taste more of your skills."

He grinned. "Baby, I've got skills in the kitchen and out."

Her fork froze on her plate, and he wanted to slap himself upside the head.

Friend, he reminded his head and his cock. *Nothing more. Drop all thoughts of beds, and sexy voices, and slick skin against slick skin.*

Addison raised her gaze from her plate to his face and cocked a brow. "You don't say?"

"Sorry. I shouldn't have said that."

With a shrug, she said, "That's okay."

Before she could say more, her cell chirp. Pulling it from her pocket with a frown, she scoffed at the read-out, and rejected the call.

"Problem?"

"The ex."

"You didn't have to reject the call because I'm here. I would have given you privacy."

She shook her head. "Don't need privacy. He has nothing to say that I want to hear. Now, changing the subject. I have a confession."

Relieved she'd let his sexual innuendo comment slide, he teased, "You don't say. You hit on Knox's teenage son today?"

She laughed, but it wasn't her usual deep sound. This one was high-pitched and reedy, like she was nervous about what she was going to tell him.

"No hitting on minors," she said. "But, I, er, might have...um...gone to the...um..."

"Spit it out, Addy. What did you do?"

"*Ienteredyouandmeinthechilicontest.*" It all came out in one long word. "Are you mad?"

He set his fork on his plate and leaned back in the chair. "You did what?"

She sighed. "I entered you and me in the chili cook-off."

"Why?"

"When Knox said all the beer slots were taken, I was afraid you'd—*we'd*—get shut out of entering the chili event. You should be glad I went today."

"Why should I be glad you went today?" He crossed his arms over his chest.

She mimicked his position. "Because..." She held up one finger. "First, today was the last day to enter." She held up a second finger. "Second, we got the last spot." She held up a third finger. "And third, because you know you want to do this."

He raised an eyebrow. "Got me all figured out, huh?"

She huffed. "Please. You like to show off those cooking skills. Wait! I just had an idea. No, no, I don't think I want to tell you yet. I need to chew it out in my head, but ohhhh..." She clapped her hands. "It's such a good idea."

He narrowed his eyes. "If it's such a great idea, go ahead and tell me."

"Nope. Not yet." Her hands rolled into fists, and she shot them in the air. "I love this. I'll tell you every-thing. I've got to go." She jumped from her chair.

"Wait a minute." He grabbed her wrist. "Sit down

and finish eating. Whatever you're cooking up in your brain can hold for the next twenty minutes."

She sat, but the Cheshire cat grin that stayed on her face made him nervous. In fact, his stomach was so shaky he could only eat two slices of his mom's key lime pie for dessert.

His afternoon was spent helping Bubba remove the toilets from the upstairs bath and the downstairs half-bath, and then tossing them into the construction bin Knox had had delivered. The fumes from the open sewer pipe had damned near killed him until Bubba stuck a rag in the opening.

With the second toilet, Eli made sure Bubba was ready with a plug. From Bubba's laughter, Eli was posi-tive he'd been pranked on the first toilet. He should've known there'd be a horrific odor, but face it: He'd never changed out a toilet, and he hadn't given it much thought. Guess he could add toilet changer to his list of skills, right behind blowing the lock on a secured door, and producing a perfect burgundy reduction.

Meanwhile, Knox, his son, and Frank continued on the kitchen, removing the sink and hardware and adding those to the construction dumpster.

By five, Eli was ready to call it a day. SEAL training had given him the stamina and strength to keep up with the professional construction workers. He was also used to being dirty and sweaty. However, Addison's Cheshire cat smile from lunch remained in the fore-front of his mind. What did that woman have up her sleeve? She'd already committed them to this chili weekend, but he was confident he wouldn't be thrilled by her brave, new idea.

Back at his folks' house, he showered and changed

into fresh shorts and a T-shirt. Then he headed over to Addison's to see what this brilliant idea was. To his surprise, she wasn't home. His mother's Jeep was gone.

"Looking for Addison?"

He turned toward his brother. "Yeah. You know where she is?"

"Wendy said Addison had a date."

"A date?" Eli's loud shout echoed inside the barn where Zane was brushing a mare. Eli shifted his stance, arms akimbo. "With who?"

Who was he going to have to kill? The woman was recovering from surgery. Didn't people—men—understand that? She didn't need the stress of dating on top of recuperation.

"It's whom, not who," his brother said with a laugh. "And really? You think you have the right to question who she sees? You think I didn't notice you making moves on Addison at my wedding? And now that you've found her here, you think you might want to pick up where you left off? I know all about you walking out and ghosting her. She told Wendy. You really screwed with her mind, you know? You did enough damage. Leave her alone."

"Who does she have a date with?" Eli asked through gritted teeth. "Tell me right now."

"What? You gonna use your super-secret SEAL fighting techniques on me if I don't spill the goods?" Zane snorted.

"Damnit, Zane, who?"

"Not that it's any of your business, but she and Wendy went by the clinic for a quick check on Addison's incision sites, and then they're going out to dinner. Sheesh, Eli."

"She shouldn't be dating," Eli said. "All that relationship stuff would put too much stress on her. She needs time to heal."

"Are you telling *me* that or *you?*"

Zane pulled off his gloves and shoved them into his rear pocket. "Let's go eat, lover boy. I hear mom's got lasagna and pie."

Eli sniffed and put his nose in the air. "Fine, but keep your opinions about me and Addison to yourself, or I'll ask Mom to give you only a tiny sliver of pie. I had the pie for lunch, so you're having leftovers."

Zane laughed. "Fine with me. Better than the peanut butter and jelly sandwich I was planning."

CHAPTER 10

E li kept forgetting to ask Addison about her great idea. He'd remember, then something would come up with the renovation, he'd get distracted, and not remember again until later that night after she'd gone back to her apartment. Since she hadn't brought it up again, he decided she'd given it additional consideration and decided that maybe it wasn't such a great idea after all, whatever it'd been.

As Knox had promised, his original team of three was joined by an additional six men on Wednesday. The entire construction team worked the rest of that week getting rid of the wallpaper in the half-bath, removing the kitchen and bath cabinets, and prepping the rooms to be painted.

Eli's plan was to paint the walls in the evenings by himself to save a little money. However, at this point, saving a couple of hundred dollars wouldn't make that much difference. But he'd do whatever he could to keep this renovation on the fast track, even working over the weekend when the McCrea crew wouldn't be there.

The main challenge was making sure he had adequate light to work.

Friday night after the construction crew left for the week, he set up a spotlight in the living room, directing the beam toward the large wall at the front of the house. The late evening sun shone through the newly installed, folding patio doors at his back, but he needed a mega-watt light to help with the shadows. Since the power was still off, he ran three one-hundred-foot, heavy-use, outdoor, electrical cords from the barn to power the temporary light.

As he was putting painter's tape around the windows overlooking his front porch, Addison walked in carrying a paper bag.

"Your mom said you were working late. I brought you chips and a sandwich. Hungry?"

"Always. Hold on. I'll be right back."

He hurried to the screened porch and grabbed the two folding chairs he'd bought on his last trip to town.

"After Knox made me move my recliner out of the way, all I had to sit on were overturned five-gallon buckets. To be honest, my ass didn't really like those, so I got chairs."

"Ohhh, fancy," she said with a laugh as he unfolded them and set them up.

"Sit," he said.

"Yes, sir." She lowered herself into one of the chairs. "What's for dinner?"

"I ran down to the Dairyaire. I have a couple of buffalo burgers and fries. Argh." She stood. "I forgot the drinks."

"You sit. I'll get them. Where are they?"

"My fridge. I have some diet drinks, beer, and

water, I think. Get whatever you want. No beer for me." She patted her shirt over her abdomen. "I don't want the empty calories. I need to get back into shape."

He rolled his eyes at her comment. Her stomach was as flat as a board.

In her apartment, he opened the fridge and pulled out two waters and two diet drinks. As he shut it, his gaze fell on a piece of mail setting on the counter. The return address was WCDA in Orlando. That was none of his business, but he couldn't help but wonder...were they trying to lure her back to work? Or maybe it was from a friend she'd worked with there? Of course, she must have had tons of friends there, and he bet they all missed her.

He remembered her comment about getting back into shape. Was she talking about trimming down? He'd always heard a television camera added ten pounds, but she certainly didn't need to lose weight. Besides, she wasn't ready to go back to Florida yet, right?

He wasn't ready for her to go either. They still had that upcoming weekend event. Plus, he wanted to spend some time showing her his old stomping grounds. He doubted she could ride a horse yet, but they had a great side-by-side ATV they could use to explore the ranch. Zane had added on acreage, and Eli hadn't had time to see all of it.

Nope. She couldn't go yet. There was still too much he wanted to show her.

She stayed for an hour after they ate, watching him paint and keeping him company. She offered to help, but he declined, telling her he was so picky about every-thing, which was of course a bold-faced lie. He couldn't care less about the paint on his walls, but he didn't want her exerting herself too much.

"Sooo," she said, dragging out the word. "Are you mad about the chili cook-off?"

"No, of course not. I wish you'd talked with me about it first, but we'll have fun. Who cares if we win or not? Right?"

"Hell, no," she said with a laugh. "If I enter a contest, I'm in it to win it, and you're the best one I could find to enter a cooking contest with. I'm only using you for your cooking skills."

He looked over his shoulder at her. "Really? So, if say, Bubba or Frank Keller were good cooks, you'd have asked one of them?"

Her cute, pert nose lifted into the air. "That's right."

Eli laughed and turned back to his work. "Sure. You tell yourself that. You're just turned on watching me cook."

Dammit. He had to stop thinking like that about her. They'd agreed on the friend zone, and he was a man of his word, or he was at least trying to be.

"Hmm, maybe I am."

He whipped his gaze toward her, but she stood before he could respond.

"I'm headed out," she said. "I've got some work I want to get done before it gets too late. See you tomorrow?"

"One more thing."

"Yes?"

"Get ready to taste batches of chili. If you're determined to win, I'll want to tweak my recipe until it's perfect. I forgot to ask. Is it buffalo meat only or do we have any options?"

"The title of the event is buffalo chili, but that's about all I remember. Sorry. I'll get the rules and specifications to you tomorrow."

He waved his paintbrush. "You know where I'll be."

A smile bloomed. "That I do. Night, Eli."

Saturday and Sunday, Addison dragged her knitting bag from her place to his and knitted while he painted. The way the needles clicked, and how her fingers flew weaving the yarn in and around the metal fascinated him. And that she could carry on a conversation at the same time was astonishing.

Her presence along with her dry sense of humor kept him entertained all weekend. The hours flew with her regaling him with stories from her years working at various television stations. All the behind-the-scene affairs. The backstabbing. The on-air mistakes.

She even confessed that once, during an interview with Orlando's mayor, her bra had come unsnapped. Luckily, she'd worn a back closure and could simply lean back against her chair to keep everything in place, so to speak. Since no one wrote letters to the station, nor made a comment on any of her social media sites, her clothing malfunction had gone unnoticed by the audience. However, her crew was another matter. It took weeks to live that incident down.

The other thing she did both days was to make sure he stopped long enough to eat. Canned soup and a sandwich she made for him was Saturday's dinner and his mom's homemade chicken and dressing filled his belly on Sunday. Without her delivering the food and eating with him, he probably would've guzzled down a soft drink and continued painting.

By Monday, he'd gotten two coats of paint on the downstairs walls. He'd opted for an off-white for the study and small bedroom, deciding to use some paint he could get locally. The time he'd spend in those rooms was probably limited, so a quick paint refresh would have to do. In the small half-bath, he went with a light blue, also a standard color available without driving to Bozeman for a custom mix.

Monday morning, McCrea's crew began parking in his drive at seven. Knox was surprised at the progress.

"You know, Eli, at this rate, I think we'll be done this week if everything goes as planned. Of course, there wasn't a ton to do. I'll get the guys going on installing the kitchen cabinets I talked you into."

Eli frowned. "Installed? I thought they'd paint them first."

Knox shook his head. "Nope. I've got the kitchen under control. Why don't you go ahead and tackle the upstairs painting?"

"Lowe's is scheduled to deliver all the appliances on Thursday."

"We'll be ready. The new countertops and sinks will be here tomorrow. We'll get the kitchen installed in the morning, and then get to the upstairs bathroom's counter and sink by tomorrow afternoon or Wednesday. Two of my guys are tackling the new shower today. They'll have all the tiling and grout work done sometime tomorrow, so the grout can cure. It's not a huge shower, and these two have put in a million of them for me, so they know what to do. I've got this."

Eli raised both eyebrows questioningly. "Furniture

on Friday?"

Knox wrinkled his nose. "I think we'll be ready, but you might want to check if the company has any flexibility in delivery dates. Depending on how the week goes, we might have to move your furniture delivery to Saturday. I'm glad you took my suggestion and moved that recliner outside on the screened porch. Bubba and Frank were debating last week who'd get to sit there for lunches."

Eli laughed. "I'd planned on sleeping in it, but staying with my folks has been okay. Oh, and I'll be taking off every day by three. With the festival only a couple of weekends away, I need to work on my chili. Buffalo chili is something new to me. Wish Addison had realized beef and buffalo meat aren't interchangeable without some tweaking." He sighed. "I'll be so sick of chili by the time the festival comes."

Knox nodded. "I know what you mean. Been sampling beer every night and, hard to believe, but I'm getting a little tired of it."

Eli smiled. "Well, any time you need a second opinion, hit me up."

"Me, too," said Knox's teenage son, a broad grin on his face.

Knox laughed. "Thanks, Eli, and no, Jason."

"Man, I never get to have any fun," Jason said.

"I'll give you some fun," Knox said. "Help Frank and Bubba carry in the new kitchen cabinets."

Eli chuckled. Jason rolled his eyes, and headed outside to do as his father requested.

That evening, after the guys had packed up for the day and left, he headed back to his folks' house to take a shower and think about buffalo chili. When he walked into his parents' house, he was surprised to find Addison, his mother, and Wendy, in the kitchen sorting through a large pile of individually wrapped packages of meat.

He put his fists on his hips. "What the heck are you doing?"

"Oh, hi, honey," his mother said. "Addison bought seventy-five pounds of ground buffalo meat for you to make sample chili. I didn't know you'd entered the chili cook-off. I'm so excited. This will be so much fun. I didn't know you could cook."

Eli turned to the instigator. "Addison? Why?"

She looked up from the white-wrapped bundles. "I figured I got you into this, the least I could do was help by getting practice meat."

Wendy snickered. "Practice meat. That's hysterical, Addison."

Addison bumped her hip against Wendy's with an audible snicker. "You know what I mean. Besides, I got it at a good price because I bought so much."

He rubbed his forehead. When had the headache started? Probably when he'd walked in and found the three women with their heads together.

He drew a deep breath. "We have two weeks before the event. How much did you say you bought?"

"Only seventy-five pounds, and I got it on sale."

"Good lord, Addy. We'll never need that much meat."

Her cheeks reddened. "Well, I might have told the event committee that we'd give away small bowls of chili for donations to help raise additional funds for the Gardiner Public Library. It's for a good cause," she hurried to add.

"Okay," he said with a long sigh. "Buffalo chili, it is. Do you remember from the rules if I can use anything other than buffalo?"

Addison shook her head. "I gave you those rules this weekend. Let me think."

She tapped her finger on her bottom lip, drawing his gaze and attention to the fullness of her mouth. Damn. He could still remember how good she'd tasted, how her mouth had fit his perfectly. With effort, he reined in his memory. He couldn't go there, at least not right now. Later, in the shower, he'd turn all those memories loose.

She blew out a long breath. "I think other meats can be used with the buffalo, but I'd have to look at the rules again. And I'll help." She held up two fingers like a scout. "I got you into this. I'll help you cook and collect the library donations. I promise."

"Zane and I can help man the booth," Wendy said. "I have to be there anyway. I'll see if I can get the medical tent placed somewhere in the area close by since I'm supposed to assist there, too. If I can, I'll be able to go back and forth between the two areas easily."

"And you know your dad and I will help," Betty said. Her face lit with a broad grin. "This is so much fun. I love having my boys back home, and having these two wonderful women, too. It's like having a couple of daughters."

Addison's face pinkened. Eli's jaw tightened. He wouldn't embarrass Addison by reminding his mother that Addison was only here temporarily and not joining the Miller clan, but he would talk privately with her later.

. . .

Addison felt the flush that rushed up her neck to her face. She adored Eli's mom. The lady had been nothing but kind and caring since the day Addison had arrived in late April. Betty had welcomed Addison with open arms. As much as Addison missed her own family, Betty's mothering had been instrumental in Addison's rapid healing. Of course, having her own mom and sister come up a few times from Texas had helped Addison immensely.

Still, she'd make sure to have a quiet word with Betty that Eli wasn't interested in her like that. He was being a good friend, but that would be the extent of it, much to Addison's disappointment. She'd been the one who'd done the pursuing the first time. She couldn't risk putting herself out there again.

"All right, everyone," Eli said, clapping his hands together. "I need some room to work. Move it, move it, move it. We've got to get all this meat stored safely. I've never worked with buffalo meat, so leave four pounds. I'll do a practice run tonight as a place to start."

Wendy piled wrapped meat packages into her arms. "Freezer?"

"I suppose so," Eli said. "I'd rather work with fresh than frozen, but it'll never stay fresh that long." He looked at Addison. "Can I put some in your freezer? Seems like it was mostly empty."

"Of course," she said. "Betty, do you have a laundry basket we could load up so I can carry them to my kitchen?"

"Sure. Let's see how many I can get in my deep freeze, then we can work on yours. And Wendy, don't you be carrying any laundry baskets full of meat to Addison's place."

Wendy groaned. "I'm pregnant, not disabled."

"Yes, well, tell that to your husband. He didn't like that you carried flowers the other day."

Wendy gave her mother-in-law an exaggerated eyeroll. "Please, who's the doctor and who's the worrywart?"

"We all know the answer to that question," Betty said, as she rearranged the shelves inside her upright freezer. "Besides, you're carrying my first grandchild, so I'm going to err on the side of caution. You can hand me packages. Addison, you know where my laundry room is. Go in there and get the green laundry baskets. There should be at least a couple. Those are for clean clothes. Let's not use the red one I set aside for the nasty ranch clothes Henry wears home after working all day in the barn."

Addison headed to a door under the stairwell. That door led to a laundry area with an outside shower. Obviously, the Millers had been ranchers long enough to know the type of stinky mess that could come home on clothes. Two empty green baskets sat on the washer, and a red basket of dirty clothes was on the floor. She grabbed the green baskets and headed back.

"Whew," Betty was saying as Addison walked back into the kitchen. "How many did we shove in there?"

"I lost count," Wendy said.

Betty moved her finger along the white ends as she counted. "There's thirty here. Eli, I don't see any way we can get forty-one pounds of buffalo in Addison's tiny refrigerator freezer."

He sighed.

"I can take some to our house," Wendy offered. "I have a huge refrigerator in the house and one in the garage. Between the two of them, I bet I can store the rest."

"Great," Eli said. "Store as many as you can at Addison's place since it's so much closer. The refrigerator freezer should be okay since the meat won't be there that long. Plus, it'll make fine chili for the free stuff."

He looked at Addison, who gave him her best beatific smile, the one that used to get her out of trouble with her folks. It must have worked because he continued to speak.

"Then. whatever is left over, Wendy can take to her house. I want to get started on tonight's chili. Addison, while you're at your apartment, can you get the rules for the chili? Just buffalo or can other meat be added? If you don't have another copy, the one you gave me is upstairs in my bedroom."

"I think I have another copy, but I've been thinking about that since you asked. I'm pretty sure the rules said buffalo had to be seventy-five percent of the meat, but I'll get the rules to make sure."

"Since all I have is buffalo meat right now, I'll make buffalo chili tonight. Mom, where are your spices? I'll need to get out tomorrow and get fresh ingredients."

"Want me to run to the Lancasters' store in Gardiner? I can get some new cans of spices," Betty said.

He shook his head. "Not tonight. This is just a practice run. I noticed a store in Bozeman that advertised fresh, whole spices. I'll make a run up tomorrow and see what they have."

Addison started loading packages of meat into a basket, checking that she could pick it up.

"Wait a minute," Wendy said. "Addison, you cannot pick up that basket. You're still recovering, and I won't have my excellent work messed up. Eli, you'll have to carry these."

Addison hung her head. "You're right, Wendy. Sorry. I've just felt so good, I forgot."

Eli turned off the burner on the stove and set aside the pan of meat. "I can do that. Besides, I left some butter at Addison's the other night. I want to brown the buffalo in butter."

He lifted a basket that had to weigh thirty-pounds as though it were empty. Betty followed her son out the door.

Addison could hear her asking, "Why did you leave butter in Addison's kitchen? Have you..." Her voice faded as they walked farther from the house.

Wendy grinned. "Why did Eli leave butter at your place?" She pumped her eyebrows. "Are you two into some kinky sex thing? As your doctor, I give you total permission to have sex, lots and lots of sex."

Addison scoffed. "I wish. He's made it plain that he wants to be my friend, but that's the extent of his interest. And for your information, Ms. Nosey, he cooked me dinner the other night. No big deal."

"That's Dr. Nosey, if you please." Her friend grabbed her hands. "*Girrrl*, did you at least get a kiss good night?"

Addison pulled her hands away. "I just told you. We're friends. Period. Now, how much of this meat can we get into your fridge?"

Wendy grinned. "Right. Friends. Famous last words."

"I'm leaving, Wendy. Remember? My plans are still

to go home. Now, whether home is Texas or Florida has yet to be determined."

"Well," Wendy said with her nose in the air. "Your doctor has to release you from medical care. Don't forget that."

Addison chuckled. "On a different note, when can I get nipples tattooed on? Hold that thought. I want to grab those rules from Eli's bedroom before I forget."

She started up the stairs and Wendy laughed, "How do you know which room is his?"

Addison stopped. "Damn. I don't, and I'm not going to stick my head in every room to find it."

Although confident she could find his bedroom by his unique male scent if she had to, she felt funny snooping around Eli's room even if she had a good reason. She stomped back down to the kitchen. "You stayed in his room when you first got here. You know which one is his. You go get it."

"Don't you want to see how Eli lives? How messy he might be?"

"Don't be ridiculous. Go get that paper before he returns."

"Chicken," her friend said as she headed up the steps.

Addison twisted her fingers together. Of course, she wanted to go into his bedroom. Hell, she might even sniff his pillow, or better yet, steal it. That way, she could bring his wonderful essence home with her.

Wendy was coming back down when the door opened to admit Eli and his mom back inside.

"Whew," Betty said. "We got twenty in there, so that's fifty. Wendy?"

"I know, I know. Let me run down to my house and rearrange my fridge as much as I can. I'll be back."

She left, and Eli said, "She'll be back with Zane in tow is my guess. He won't want her carrying anything heavy."

"Probably," Betty said. "I'll be back. I want to get a load of wash started."

And then Addison was alone with Eli, which made her palms sweat and her heart race. Surely this adolescent response would stop soon. Maybe if she simply kept exposing herself to him, she'd build up resistance, like the flu shot. Introduce a small amount of the disease, and let your body build natural antibodies.

"Here're the rules," she said, thrusting a printed sheet of paper toward him.

He took it and began to read. In the meantime, she fiddled with her camera, getting it secured on a tripod and directing the lens toward Eli.

Without looking up from the paper in his hand, Eli asked, "Why is there a camera looking at me?"

"Remember that great idea I had at lunch?"

"Uh-huh. I remember you having an idea. I don't remember us ever discussing it."

"Trust me. This is brilliant. Since we'll be cooking different meats, I thought I could film each cooking session and make notes, you know, like what meat you used, which spices, how much, and so forth. Then you'd remember."

He smiled. "I'll remember. I promise. If you want to write things down, then that's fine, but I really don't need a recording of me cooking."

She paced away from the camera and back. "Well, I sort of had another idea."

"I bet you did," he said, narrowing his eyes. "What's going on in your head, Addison?"

"Well—and I think you'll love this idea—I thought if I recorded everything, and then you win, which I totally expect you to do, Liza, my show's producer in Florida, has agreed to run the video on The Chat. It'd be my first time back in months. The station could hype my return from Montana into their homes. No one has seen me with this hair." She stroked nervously at the top. "And it would be a way to start working my way back into people's memories."

When he looked doubtful, and like he was going to protest, she put her fists on her hips. "Viewers have short memories. My show is going down the tubes with the chick they replaced me with. I worked hard to build up a healthy viewership, and I'll be damned if I'll let some twenty-something with no talent, except for giving an excellent blowjob. run it off the air." She sniffed. "At least, that's what I heard."

He laughed with a shake of his head. "Addison Treadway."

She held up her hands. "I know, I know, but hear me out. If this first video does well, think of all the fabulous cooking shows we could do online. First videos on *YouTube*, or maybe your own website. Sexy SEAL. Delicious food. Well, we'd have a million subscribers in no time. Advertisers would be beating down the doors to run ads on your platform. And I could even post quick snippets on *TikTok* to stir up interest."

"Addison..."

"I know. You need to think about this, but it's a good idea. My producer loved the idea. Totally jumped on it. We could even go live from the event. Show the people of Florida how beautiful Montana is and give them an update on my progress. Think about it, okay? Okay?"

Her heart pounded as she waited for his response. Her producer hated working with the new host, calling her a prima donna and a bitch. She wanted Addison to come back and had, in fact, pushed Addison for a return date. While Addison had been flattered—after all, who doesn't love a little ego stroke now and then?—she also wasn't completely sure she wanted to go back to Florida and morning television. It was grueling to be out of the house by four a.m. five days a week. She'd gotten a little spoiled being able to sleep in until seven.

What if he said no? Should she go ahead and broadcast live from the event anyway? After all, she hadn't given her producer a definite yes about returning. Heck, she wasn't even sure she wanted back on Florida television. She had another idea, but only time would tell if it had any legs.

Eli blew out a long sigh. "Fine. You can record, but I have to see all the videos and approve them before you can do anything with them, okay?"

"Yes! Yes, of course." She threw her arms around his neck and hugged him. "Thank you."

His scent overwhelmed her when her nose pressed into his neck. His firm body against hers felt like heaven. Her crummy bad luck continued as his mom walked in just as Addison brushed a quick kiss on his cheek.

"Don't let me interrupt," Betty said with a huge grin. "Didn't see a thing. I'll go upstairs and, well, find something else to do."

"You don't have to leave," Addison and Eli said at the same time.

Betty chuckled and walked up the stairs.

"I'll talk to her," Addison said. "Explain that there's nothing going on."

He shrugged. "You can, but she'll ignore you. She sees what she wants to see. Okay, now to work. Turn your camera on." He frowned. "Am I supposed to talk? I don't know what to say."

"I'll ask you questions. You answer them, like an interview. It'll be simple. Ready? I'm starting the camera."

He turned the burner back on to brown the meat. His mother had been thrilled to turn the kitchen over to him tonight, but he looked forward to making the barn house into his own personal space with all his equipment and tools.

Zane came through the door with Wendy, just as Eli had predicted.

"Wendy says we have to take buffalo meat home with us. Do I want to know why?"

"Nope," Eli said.

Zane's shrugged. "Okay, then." He jerked up the basket with the remaining pounds of buffalo meat and headed out.

If he had to get tired of chili, he figured he'd spread around the misery to his family. Just wait until Zane found out he'd be eating lots of chili in the coming week, chili his little brother made.

Eli's stomach twisted. He really hoped his family enjoyed his chili. His team would eat anything, literally. After MREs, everything tasted like heaven, so SEALs might not be the best food test audience.

His family? Yeah. They were the ones he wanted to impress.

CHAPTER 11

His buddy Knox pulled in his entire crew for the last week of renovation. Country music blasted from radios as workers climbed all over his house finishing up the rooms. By Friday afternoon, Eli had a home, complete with a new, bigger kitchen, freshly painted walls, a tile shower, and two new toilets. He'd moved the living room and bedroom furniture deliveries to Saturday as Knox had suggested, so Friday would be the last night in his parents' house. Saturday, he'd be watching television in his living room, sitting in his new recliner before going to sleep in his new bed with its freshly laundered sheets.

His only regret was doing all these activities solo. He wanted the companionship he saw between his brother and Wendy.

During the months leading up to his departure from the SEALs, he'd watched five of his team find the women they'd spend the rest of their lives with. Even back then, watching the couples together had made him long for that kind of relationship, and unfortunately for him at the time, the only woman who'd consumed his thoughts had been the one he'd believed had been unfaithful to her husband, something he could not abide. For months, he'd told himself he hated Addison Treadway.

Now, not only did he *not* hate Addison, he found pretexts to find her during the day to get her opinion, or show her something in the house, or simply tell her something funny that'd happened. He was pitiful. Thank goodness she never noticed his weak-assed excuses.

For example, when he'd decided to drive to Bozeman for fresh ingredients for his chili, he'd asked her to ride along to help him pick out the ground beef, ground venison, ground pork sausage, ground Italian sausage, and chicken he'd be using in his batches of sample chilis. He invited her to come along and help.

She'd laughed and rolled her eyes, but climbed into his truck anyway. They both knew he needed her help as much as the ranch dog needed a wig. And maybe he didn't need her assistance selecting meat, but he needed her company more than he wanted her to know.

Friday afternoon, the workers packed up their tools and left. Eli stood in his newly refurbished house in amazement. In two weeks, the entire place had been completely overhauled and had a fresh, new look.

"Hey," Addison called from the door. "I'm here for the final inspection."

He laughed and waved his arm in the air. "What do you think?"

Her gaze swept the room. "I think it's incredible. But, in my humble opinion, it needs a good cleaning before the furniture gets here tomorrow."

He sighed. "I know."

"And that's why I brought the team," she said, and flung her arms wide with a flourish.

Voices filled the room as his parents, Zane and Wendy, Russ and Lori, and Knox and Nancy filed through the door, bringing cleaning cloths, spray cleaners, a bucket and mop, and a vacuum still in the box.

"Hi, honey," his mom said. "Your dad and I got you a few housewarming presents." She gestured to all the cleaning supplies.

"Thanks, mom. Thanks, everyone." He ran his hand through his sweaty hair. "I don't know what to say other than thank you."

"Wow, Eli. This looks so good. Wish we'd taken down that wall when we lived here," Lori added.

Addison shoved her fingers between her lips and a loud whistle filled the space. The adults quieted.

"You have got to teach me that," Wendy said.

"Me, too," said Lori. "I'm going to need it for my brood."

"I've got everyone assigned by rooms." Addison passed out sheets of paper. "The men will clean all the windows and wash down the doors to get any dust and dirt. Lori, take Nancy and Betty and head upstairs to start cleaning the bathroom and bedroom. That's the hardest job, and I think you three will knock it out in no time. Wendy, you and I will tackle the half-bath and the two small rooms. Guys, when you've cleaned all the windows and doors, and that's inside and out by the way, can you take on the screened porch and front porch? Both need to be swept and hosed off. Be sure to wash the window screens, too. Questions?"

With a sheepish grin, Eli raised his hand. "Um, you want me with the guys or what?"

Addison smiled. "You start in your kitchen. That's your baby. Wendy and I will join you when we're done with the half-bath and cleaning the floors in the downstairs office and bedroom." She put her hands on her hips. "Why is everyone standing here? Pizza will be here in two hours. Let's get moving."

The group chuckled, grabbed whatever cleaning supplies they needed for their assigned tasks, and headed off.

Eli couldn't stop himself from placing a kiss on Addison's cheek. "Thank you. How did you know I needed this?"

She smiled. "No one remembers how dusty and dirty a new house is until they get ready to move in, and then they realize everything needs to be dusted or mopped or washed."

"Thank you. I owe you."

"I dragged you into the chili contest, and I expect you to win it for us. We'll call it even."

He winked.

"Addison," Wendy yelled from the half-bath. "Get your skinny ass in here. You drafted me. I'm not doing this by myself. I've got my own bathroom toilets that need to be cleaned."

Addison laughed. "Gotta go."

As Eli wiped down his new, stainless-steel appliances and countertops, he counted his lucky stars for his family and friends. Real friends and family would be there even when there long periods of time between visits, and today's cleaning crew had reenforced that.

. . .

Saturday morning, Eli was sitting on his porch in his folding chair waiting on the furniture from Bozeman when a large truck rolled down the drive and stopped. A heavy-set man stepped out and walked around.

Eli stood. "Can I help you?"

"Maybe. Looking for Eli Miller."

"That's me."

"Great. I've got a table and some chairs for you."

In all the excitement of his new place and the hours of hard work he'd put into getting it ready, he'd completely forgotten about his table coming from California. When the team had first started coming to his place for meals, they'd sat wherever there was an open space. However, when dates and significant others appeared on the scene and at his dinners, he'd wanted them to have a better place to sit than the floor or fireplace hearth. He'd commissioned a friend to make him a large table that would hold sixteen comfortably, and more, if people squeezed in. Originally, Eli had wanted a one-piece table, but the table maker convinced him to go with table leaves for expansion.

The table was made from heavy white oak. His friend was a craftsman when it came to building this table. Without expansion leaves, the table would sit six people comfortably. With each leaf, four more chairs could be added. The table came with three leaves. Eli had added a collection of mismatched chairs.

"Are you by yourself?" Eli asked, stepping down to the drive.

"Yep. Hoping you have some help here. This table was a heavy bastard."

Eli grinned. "I know. I'll call my dad and brother to come. In the meantime, you and I can get the chairs and table leaves out."

Twenty minutes later, Eli studied his table sitting in his house. How appropriate that his first piece of furniture in his new place was the last piece from his old life.

"Eli," Addison called from the porch. "Another truck's headed down the drive. I think the rest of your stuff is here."

By three that afternoon, Eli had a house full of furniture. His mother was upstairs with Addison putting sheets on his new bed while he and his dad carried up armloads of towels and washcloths for the bath.

All his kitchen cookware and dishes had been unpacked yesterday. Eli knew he should offer to fix dinner for his parents and Addison for their help, but he was exhausted, physically and mentally. If he'd followed through with his original plan to make test batches of chili using different meats mixed with the buffalo meat during this last week of renovation, he could have offered up those. But he hadn't. He'd decided to do those in his new kitchen, especially since Addison would be recording each preparation.

He'd agreed to her insane idea mostly because he would have those videos after she went home. If she wasn't in the shot, he'd still have her voice. But he had every intention of pulling her into the frame.

Addison, his parents, and he collapsed in his living room.

"Whew," his mom said.

"Agreed." Addison wiped her forehead. "That was a lot of work over the last two days."

Eli frowned. "It was, and you shouldn't have done it."

"You didn't want my help?" Addison asked, a tinge of hurt in her voice.

"Don't be ridiculous," he said. "Of course, I wanted your help. You were invaluable, but I worry you did too much."

"I rested this week. Wendy gave me the go-ahead, so I'm fine."

"Leave her alone, son," his dad said. "Women are gonna do what they're gonna do. Us poor men have little say."

His mother swatted her husband with a laugh. "Is that so?"

"Um, do we or do we not have a second home in Florida?" He lifted an eyebrow at his wife.

She put her nose in the air. "You wanted that house as much as I did."

He chuckled. "Sure." He looked at Eli and said in a stage whisper, "If you can, always agree. Makes life easier."

Betty and Addison laughed along with Eli.

"I wish I had food here. I'd offer dinner," Eli said. "But since I don't, let me at least buy dinner for everyone. The Old Tyme Corral should be open by now. I assume it's still super casual?"

"It is, but this old woman is going home for a long shower. I'll make something for your dad and me. Don't let us stop the two of you from going out." Betty stood. "Come on, old man. Shake a leg."

Henry followed his wife's lead and rose. "I'm with your mom, Eli. You two enjoy your dinner."

After Betty and Henry left, Addison stood and stretched. "I'm out of here, too."

Eli leapt to his feet. "What about dinner? Let me at least feed you as a thank-you for all your work."

She shook her head. "Thanks, seriously, but I'm beat."

"You need to eat," he insisted. "Let me feed you. I owe you for yesterday and today."

She shook her head again. "Thanks, but no. I'll talk to you tomorrow, and we can set up a filming schedule for your cooking. Night."

Eli dropped back into his recliner as soon as the door closed behind Addison. That was the second time she'd declined his offer to go out to dinner. A private dinner in with a friend appeared acceptable. Was a dinner in a restaurant too much like a date, and that's why she kept turning him down?

He understood terrorists better than he ever would women.

The walk from Eli's place to her place should have taken Addison only a minute or two. It took twice as long. Addison's legs ached. Her back hurt. She could barely lift her fatigued arms. But none of that touched the degree of agony in her soul.

Turning him down for dinner had taken its toll on her. Without question, she'd have loved to have gone out with Eli, but as a date, not an obligation on his part. He'd only offered to take her to dinner because he owed her. He'd been plain on that point. A friend repaying a friend. It was getting harder and harder for her to be friends with him. The longing to touch him, to slide her tongue down the ridges of his stomach, to take him deep inside her was beginning to overwhelm her. If she hadn't already pitched the recording idea, she'd bury it so deep in her mind, not even hypnosis could retrieve it.

But it'd been all her idea. She'd sold him on it, and even had a promise to run one of the videos on WCDA if her producer liked it. She would look like a flighty, bubbleheaded blonde if she backed out now. No one would respect her, including herself.

Saturday night, she ate a peanut butter and grape jelly sandwich and watched a *Lovemark* movie sure to make her cry.

Success. She bawled at the happy ending.

On Sunday, she didn't awaken until after ten a.m. She'd slept a full twelve hours, something she almost never did. However, things in her life didn't look so glum this morning, or maybe she was simply rested.

She carried her knitting and second cup of coffee outside to the patio. The sunny day was too beautiful to spend it inside. There was a light breeze, bringing the aroma of pines and evergreens across the yard. She inhaled deeply, feeling her muscles relax.

While the autologous breast reconstruction hadn't been the highlight of her life, coming to Montana might have been. The Mountain Time Zone coordinated perfectly with her natural circadian rhythm. Going to Central Time wouldn't be too bad, but the idea of adjusting to Eastern Time again had her shoulders tensing. She drew in another breath and rocked her head from side to side to loosen the muscles in her neck.

"You okay?"

She startled, throwing her cup toward the sound. Laughter bubbled up as her lukewarm coffee dripped down Eli's face. She rolled her lips between her teeth to hold in the chuckle, but it refused to be contained.

"I am so sorry," she said with a laugh. "You scared the moose crap out of me."

"That's okay." He lifted the hem of his T-shirt to wipe his face.

Acres of thick muscles rode across and down his stomach and disappeared into his shorts. Her tongue burned to trace the pair of sexy V-shaped muscles that ran from his hips and under the waist of his khaki shorts. Wendy had once told her that area was called the Adonis belt. She'd never forgotten that. Right at this moment, she badly wanted to measure that belt with her tongue.

She swallowed the drool collecting in her mouth. Better than letting it run down her chin. How could he look so damn hot all the freaking time? Even his dark morning beard looked great. She squeezed her legs together as she remembered the scratch of that beard on her inner thigh.

"You sure you're okay?" Eli asked as he lowered his shirt back into place. "Your face is a little flushed." He looked up at the sky. "Maybe too much sun?"

She coughed. "No, no. I'm fine. How did you sleep in the new bed?"

His bed. Why did she have to think about his bed? Her brain started a slideshow of Eli wrapped in sheets, Eli covered only with a top sheet riding low on his hips, Eli propped up on an arm leaning over her, Eli's head between her legs. She squeezed her thighs harder.

Hell. She was in hell.

"Slept like a baby with a full tummy. We did a good job picking out that mattress."

"Great." Her voice was a tad too cheery, like a drunk teen trying to convince the parents that, of course, she wasn't drunk...just very happy.

He gave her an odd look and shook his head. "Okay, then. We only have until Saturday to get the chili recipe we want to use decided. If you're available today, we can do a couple of batches. If not, that's fine. I mean, it's short notice, and I can do some practice batches without you. It's just that you wanted to watch...?"

The last comment came out as a question, like was she serious about recording everything.

"Heck, yeah. I'm ready. Are we going to break in the new kitchen?"

He grinned and waggled his eyebrows. "We are."

God. Surely, he wasn't thinking sex in his kitchen... like she was.

Suddenly, her lust-filled brain cleared. Sex? She couldn't have sex, unless it was with the lights off and she only undressed from the waist down. Her breasts were not the same as they'd been the last time he'd seen them, fondled them, sucked on them. Hell, most women had no feeling in their breasts after what she'd been through. Granted, some of the uber lucky ones who did the autologous reconstruction regained some of their breast sensitivity, but hers felt like dead blobs sitting on her chest. Sure, she was still healing, but she felt positive that if she were going to have some sensitivity, she'd have it by now, right? Maybe this was a conversation she needed to have with Wendy and not her brain, which knew nothing about the topic.

"Hello?" Eli said.

"Sorry. My mind drifted. What are we making today?"

His eyes softened. "I've read that chemo can really mess with your memory."

Crap. He thought she was mentally deficient because of her chemo? She wanted to yell at him, "It's not my brain giving me problems. It's my pussy," but decided maybe that wasn't the best way to handle things.

She nodded. "Be over in about ten minutes. Don't start without me. Remember, I'm recording all your work."

He nodded and gave her a damned caring look. "I understand."

She headed toward her apartment in a hurry before her mouth shouted, "Pussy, not brain," and embarrassed them both.

When she got to his house, the front door was open, so she walked in. Eli was on the phone, and while she wasn't eavesdropping on purpose, she couldn't help hearing.

"Yes, of course my life is incomplete without you." He listened and chuckled. "You could have told me you loved me before I left California." He snorted. "Fine. Love you back and see you soon."

Addison's heart flopped over. Of course, he had a girlfriend he'd left behind. Just look at the man. He was gorgeous. It was only reasonable that some woman had swooped in and collected him.

Was he planning on going back to California and the woman he'd left behind? Or was he considering moving her here? Or maybe she was coming to check out Eli's Montana home?

But most important to her, did she really want to

hang around long enough to see him with other women?

Her tripod thudded against the wall, and he whipped around.

"Gotta go," he said. "Work calls."

Great. She was work.

If she hadn't dragged him into this weekend's event, she might've headed for Texas sooner rather than later. But that wasn't an option now.

"Hey," he said. "I didn't know you had some fancy camera setup. I'm impressed."

"It'll do better than my phone," she said, not mentioning the camera and tripod were new and she'd only been practicing with them for a week. "What are your thoughts for today?" She held up her hand. "Wait. I'm starting the camera. Not sure if I'll use any of this, but it's easily erased."

His watching her set up the system made her nervous. Because of the shaking in her fingers, it took her three tries to get the camera attached to the tripod. Her stomach flopped around as though it was a fish out of water.

"Where will you be doing your work? Should I focus only on the stove?"

"Have you ever done your own videoing of your segment?" He grinned. "You seem a little nervous."

"Nope. Not nervous at all. Excited. Totally excited. I think I'll move off to the side where I can get a better shot of the stove and the closest counter."

He shrugged. "Whatever works for you. Ready?"

"Wait. Which chili are you making today?"

"We're on such a short timetable, I thought I'd make

a couple of different ones. Buffalo only and Buffalo with ground beef."

She nodded. "Sounds good. Let's do two different videos, then. Change your shirt between them so it appears we did it on different days."

"Fine, but this is a competition. Don't post these and show them to anyone else."

He winked, and she almost fainted. Damn, he was sexy.

"I won't. Ready? Wait until I point to you, and you'll know I'm recording."

She held up three fingers, two fingers, and finally one finger and pressed record.

"Today, we are with ex-Navy SEAL and chef extraordinaire Eli Miller."

He waved and smiled.

"So, Eli, what are you cooking?"

"Today, we're making a thick chili with buffalo meat and ground beef."

"Sounds delicious. Can you walk us through the steps?"

"Sure."

He started browning the ground beef first, explaining he needed to use the grease from the beef for frying up the buffalo since buffalo meat is so lean, it would stick. As he stirred the meat, he carried on a conversation with Addison, explaining exactly what he was doing.

As she'd suspected, the man was a natural. Being in front of the camera didn't shake him at all. Like the night she'd watched him in her kitchen, his movements were smooth, calm, and controlled. He exuded an air of confidence that came through the camera. Women were going to love watching him, and cooks would love getting his recipe secrets.

His discussion of the recipe and why he did what he did was so simplified anyone could follow along. Addison wrote down all the ingredients as he added them, suspecting viewers would want to know each one. She'd be able to either post the recipe at the end of the video or in the comment sections. She was starting to think his own website would be a good idea to showcase his cooking. Now, she only had to convince him.

Even if women didn't have any interest in the recipes, they'd have to be dead not to enjoy the Eli Miller show. All that brawn and muscles. Yum. And his face was a total double yum.

For the first video, he wore a pair of jeans and a dark-blue, SEAL T-shirt, which would have looked good with his eyes, even if the short sleeves hadn't hugged his biceps like ropes, which they did. Her gaze had fixed on his ropey, thick arms, barely able to keep her mind on her job.

This was a good idea, she kept telling herself. Women from all over were going to lust after him. How could they help it? Eli Miller was lust material.

The jealousy dragon that lived in her belly lifted its head and blew a jet of fire. Did she really want women longing for him like she did? Wasn't she yearning enough for the rest of the world?

And to her frustration, her lust-filled fantasies were just that...fantasies. He gave no indication of any interest in her beyond pal, buddy, and friend. Argh.

To close the first video, Eli slid a lid onto the pot. "And now, we wait. We want all those juices and spices to mix and mingle." He grinned. "Sounds like a great party going on in the pot, right? And it will be. Good things come to those who wait. For this, let it simmer for three to four hours. Serve it up with warm crackers and a sprinkle of Parmigiano Reggiano, or maybe some sharp cheddar cheese, and enjoy."

"And cut," Addison said. "That was fabulous. Are we doing the buffalo chili next?"

"Changed my mind. I want to try some chicken with the buffalo. I think it'll be okay, but nothing great. Still, let's try it."

"Sounds good. Go change your clothes."

"I will, but you need to make an appearance in the next one."

She groaned. "No. Not today." When he looked like he was going to protest, she hurried on. "I will tomorrow. I'll fix my hair and slap on a little makeup. I promise. But right now? I looked like someone who's been sleeping in a barn."

He chuckled. "You do not. You are beautiful. I don't know why you don't see that when you look in a mirror." With a sigh, he said, "Be right back. Don't touch the pot or try to move it while I'm gone. It's too heavy. I'll move it into the oven while we do the next one, and then let them both simmer this afternoon."

He left, and she headed into the kitchen to clean. She wouldn't touch his precious pot, but she could wipe down the counter and stovetop. She grouped his spices together, rinsed measuring cups and spoons, and dried them for the next take.

Eli returned wearing a pair of khaki shorts with a white T-Shirt that bore the Grizzly Bitterroot Ranch logo.

"Seriously?" she asked, eyeing his attire. "That's what you're wearing for the next video?"

"What's wrong with it? I thought the ranch could use a little promo."

"Oh, I don't care about that, but a white T-shirt while making a tomato-based chili? Are you crazy?"

"I was a Navy SEAL. Of course, I'm slightly crazy."

She laughed. "Okay, then."

"You cleaned up."

"Yep. I didn't touch your precious."

He chuckled at her *Lord of the Rings* reference. "Give me a minute, and then I'll be ready."

CHAPTER 12

There were six sample chili batches that needed to be made. Two on Sunday, two more on Monday, and the last two on Tuesday.

On Monday, she ran the first couple of videos by her old show producer. Would Liza see what Addison saw when she viewed Eli at work? Liza, long past the teenager stage, had squealed like a fourteen-year-old who'd just met her music idol.

"Addison, he's gorgeous and so sexy," Liza had gushed. "We have to have these for the show. Tell me he's agreed. I sent you those contracts for him to appear exclusively for WCDA days ago. Did you get them? Did he sign them? Why haven't I gotten them back yet? You aren't shopping this around to other stations for a better deal, are you?"

"I wouldn't do that."

"No, but your snake of an agent would."

Addison chuckled quietly. Her agent definitely would do that, if Addison had told him what she was up to, but she hadn't.

However, Addison had put herself in a tight position. First, she hadn't told Eli that she'd sent those videos from yesterday to her producer last night. Second, she hadn't told him that the station wanted to contract with him to do exclusive cooking segments with them, combined with appearances in Central Florida. And third, she didn't want to tell Liza that she hadn't even broached the subject with him yet.

Sigh. She'd really tangled things up. She'd tell him, tonight or tomorrow.

Monday, before they started cooking and videoing, Eli told her he'd invited his parents, Zane and Wendy, and Russ and Lori over for a Wednesday night taste test. They'd discussed having everyone over to taste as they went, but agreed his dad and his brother would chow down and not remember from one day to the next what the previous night's batch had tasted like.

As she'd promised, starting with Monday night's work, Addison opened each video with the camera lens on her as she introduced Eli and told what the chili meats were for that segment. To her surprise, initially she'd been slightly hesitant to appear before the camera, concerned she would look unhealthy. But Eli's encouragement and glowing praise of her appearance gave her the strength to do the scary...except, it wasn't scary at all. She fell back into her interviewer's role with an ease that amazed and thrilled her.

Each day, while Eli worked the ranch, she would review the previous night's work and make edits, not that she had to edit much. The camera lens loved him. She hadn't found a position in which he didn't look great. His grin and laugh would have women everywhere swooning.

Wednesday evening, Addison juggled bottles of champagne in her arms as she knocked on his door at six. As he opened the door, his mouth curved into a smile that lit his entire face. Dressed in jeans and a bright-green, knit polo shirt with sleeves that drew her gaze to the thick muscles in his arms and the breadth of his shoulders, Addison's knees melted, and she bobbled the bottles around in her arms.

"Hey," he said. "You're the first one here. Let me get those." He took the three bottles of champagne. "And I know you're not supposed to be lifting heavy things."

"Please. Bottles of champagne? I can carry those."

"I might have to tell your doctor," he said with a grin.

"Ha. I'm not scared of Wendy."

"I am." He chuckled. "What's the champagne for, anyway?"

"Your new house. We have to break it in right."

"Ah. Got it. That's very nice of you. Thank you."

"We're here," Wendy called from the door.

"And starved," Zane said. "I've been hearing about this blasted chili all week. It'd better be worth all the time you took away from ranch work."

Wendy patted her husband's stomach. "Be nice."

"I am nice," Zane insisted as he laced his fingers with hers.

"Hi, honey," Betty called as she and Henry entered, each of them carrying a pie. "What can I do to help?"

"Nothing, Mom," Eli said. "I've got it under control."

"The place looks great," Henry said. "Nice work."

"Thanks," Eli said. "Addison brought champagne to officially christen the place. Wander around and tell me what you think about the renovations while I open these bottles. Addison, you've been upstairs. Why don't you show that to them?"

Zane arched an eyebrow. "Has she now?"

Eli snorted. "Not like that, and don't embarrass Addison."

Wendy groaned. "Zane."

Addison laughed. "They've all been upstairs, Eli, but fine. Follow me. I'll show off the new shower and toilet."

Eli's parents grinned and followed her upstairs. Being a small space, it didn't take long and everyone was trooping back down. Eli had champagne glasses lined up on the bar, ready to fill. He began to pour.

"For Wendy, I have sparkling grape juice," Addison said. "Oh, shoot. I forgot it and left it in my fridge. I'll run and get it."

"I can have one glass of champagne," Wendy said.

"No, you can't," Zane said harshly. "That's my kid in there, and he doesn't get booze until he is twenty-one."

"What if it's a she?" Wendy said, batting her eyelashes.

"It's not," Zane said. "It's a boy. I said so."

Betty laughed and patted her oldest child on the shoulder. "If only that was how it worked."

"I've got apple cider in the fridge," Eli said.

"Why?" Wendy asked with a frown.

"We used it in one of the recipes," Addison explained.

"Ah. Okay. I'll drink a sip of that."

Once everyone had their drinks in hand, his mother

raised her glass. "Since I'm the one who pushed his eight-pound body out..."

Eli groaned. "Not the birthing story."

Undeterred, Betty said, "As I was saying, I loved you the minute I laid my eyes on your round face, even if you did pee on my chest, and I love you more today. I am so happy to be your mother and have you finally home. Cheers."

Glasses were clinked.

"My turn," Zane said.

Eli groaned again.

"Welcome home, bro. You were gone too long, and my kiddo is going to need his uncle around."

"Aww, honey. That was so sweet," Wendy said and kissed Zane's cheek.

Eli's smile was warm. Were those tears in the tough man's eyes? "Thanks, big bro."

"Hell, someone other than my wife will have to teach the kid to drive. Have you seen her behind the wheel? Terrifying."

Wendy slugged him, and everyone laughed.

"And for Addison..." Eli began. "I have a surprise."

Addison startled and looked at him, her eyes wide. "For me?"

"Yep. Stay right here."

Eli raced to the small office at the front of the house and came back with a large, round hat box with "Stetson" stamped all over it.

"Just a little something to say thank you." He handed her the box. "The renovation help, the push to enter the chili contest, and now, organizing all the cleaning. Without you, tonight would never have happened. My house would be dusty, and we wouldn't have all this chili. Thank you for pushing me."

"You didn't," she gushed. Pulling off the lid, she gasped. Inside sat a custom-made, white Stetson hat. "Oh, My. God." She whirled to face Eli. "I can't believe this. Thank you! I am so excited."

She pulled the hat from the box and placed it on her head. The fit was perfect.

"Look inside," Eli said.

She removed the hat and flipped it over. Inside, her name had been stamped into the band.

"I told you that living on a ranch meant you had to have your own cowgirl hat, remember?"

Tears filled her eyes as she nodded.

"Now, you look like you belong here."

She grinned and wrapped her arms around his neck. After a quick kiss on his cheek, she said, "You didn't have to do this, but thank you so much. It's one of the nicest things anyone has ever done for me."

Eli gestured with his champagne glass toward the large dining table. "Everyone, find a seat at the table. Addison and I will bring out the samples. She's going to give you pieces of paper. I want you to write down what you liked, or didn't like, for each one."

"What are we eating?" Henry asked.

"Chili."

His father sighed. "I know that. What kind?"

"Ah, that's the secret," Eli said. "Every batch has buffalo, but in five of them, I've added an additional meat. I don't want to tell you what meat is in each chili just yet. Make yourself notes. At the end, I'll ask you to rank them. And before you give me any lip about this, you should be aware that: First, all this chili is

Addison's fault; and second, the taste test was her idea also."

Addison wanted to die. Why didn't he just call her brash and intrusive while he was at it? Heat flushed up her neck at his words.

"I think this is a great idea and lots of fun," Betty said.

"Bring on the chow, unless you've put squirrel in there or something," Zane said.

"No squirrel, or anything strange. I promise. I just don't want to prejudice you one way or the other. Besides, I would never serve Wendy squirrel."

"But you would me?" Zane's eyebrows arched with the question.

"I refuse to answer because Mom and Dad are here."

Zane laughed. "I'm starving. I'll eat anything."

In the kitchen, Addison put small cups on a tray and Eli filled them.

"Don't tell them what's in each one," Eli said.

She snorted. "I won't. Geeze, Eli. I made up this game. I know my own rules."

He smiled. "You were right about one thing."

"Yeah? What's that?"

"Cooking all these batches of chili with you has been fun."

Addison smiled. "So, you're okay with me being pushy?"

"Pushy? Who said you were pushy?"

"I thought you did."

"Oh, hon, I didn't, and if I did, I didn't mean anything bad." He put his arm around her shoulders. "And even if you were a little pushy—and I'm not sure I said that—assertive powerful women don't scare me." He squeezed her. "They're my favorite."

"Wasting away in here," Zane yelled. "May get too weak to drive home."

Eli blew out a laughing breath. "Poor Wendy. She has to live with him."

Addison chuckled. "Better her than me."

Carrying the tray with cups of chili, she walked around the huge table and set a cup in front of each person. She'd fallen in love with Eli's table at first glance. Massively huge and heavy, all six of them could sit around it and still have room for more chairs.

Zane eyed the small cup when she set it down and looked up at her, an eyebrow lifted questioningly.

"There's plenty more," she said to Zane, patting his shoulder. "You can have all you want of the one you like the best."

"Whew," he said, pouring the first cup into his mouth. He chewed, and his face brightened. "Damn, Eli," he yelled toward the kitchen. "That's not half bad."

"Remember to write down your thoughts and opinions about this one before we go to the next."

In the kitchen, Addison's phone rang. She silenced the call, not even pulling it from her pocket. She knew who it was. Denis had his own special ringtone. That way, when she heard it, she could ignore her phone.

"I've got this if you need to take that call," Eli said, as he filled cups with a different chili mixture.

She shook her head. "No reason to. I don't want to talk to him."

"The ex?"

"Yes."

"He's still bothering you? How often does he call?"

She sighed and loaded cups onto the tray. "Every day. I'm sure he'll get the message soon and leave me alone."

"Want me to talk to him?"

"No, but thank you."

"Just let me know if I can do anything."

"I will."

Between each chili round, Eli made them drink water to clear the taste of the last chili concoction from their mouths before moving on.

With the last round of samples, Eli and Addison joined them at the table.

"Well?" Eli asked.

Addison could practically feel the anxiety coming off him in waves. He'd only made that one batch of buffalo chili a couple of weeks ago, and only he and Addison had eaten it. So, technically, he hadn't cooked for his family since coming home, and if his brother's response was any indication, they'd had no idea how good he was in the kitchen.

"They're all delicious," his mother said. "All get tens from me."

"Not helping, mom, but thank you."

"Hmm," his dad said. "One was okay but kind of chewy. I marked that I liked numbers five, six, and seven. What'd I win?"

Eli chuckled. "There is no number seven, Dad."

"Oops."

Wendy tapped her pencil on the paper. "Like your mom said, they were good, but I tried to really taste what was there. Did I taste chili powder? Was it too spicy? Too bland? None of them were bland, so that went out the window. I loved the last one the best, but was it because it was the last one or because it was the best? I'm not sure, but all of them were excellent."

"I didn't know you could really cook," Zane said. "Could've knocked me over with a piece of hay. I have to say, I'm glad the chili didn't kill me."

"Har, har," Eli said, but his grin said he knew he'd done a good job.

"Seriously, bro. Can you cook anything other than chili?"

"I have a recipe for pork chops in a burgundy reduction sauce that will make you cry."

"Hmm. Sounds fancy. Wendy and I will be over tomorrow night for that."

Wendy laughed. "No, we won't, Eli. I promise. So, Zane, which one did you like the best?" She turned to look at her husband.

The look of love on her face took Addison's breath away. When Zane looked at his wife, his face went soft as did the smile he gave her. Addison couldn't help the ting of jealousy. Her ex had never looked at her that way.

In fact, now that she really let herself remember the wedding weekend where she and Eli had met, he'd looked at her like that. No wonder she'd fallen so hard and so fast for him.

"My wife is right," Zane said. "The last one."

"Anyone need to taste another sample of any of them?"

The general consensus was to taste numbers one, three, five, and six again. That would be chili made with the buffalo meat only, the buffalo-ground beef chili, the buffalo-ground pork chili, and the buffalo-Italian sausage chili.

Addison wasn't surprised by their choices. She personally hadn't loved the buffalo-chicken, nor the buffalo-venison. Her personal favorites were the buffalo-Italian sausage and the buffalo-ground beef chili. Of those two, she loved the spiciness that the Italian sausage brought to the mix, but she stopped herself from giving an opinion. Eli wanted his family's thoughts, not hers.

The taste test continued, and in the end, the Miller clan chose number six as the winner, the buffalo-Italian sausage chili.

"Now, can we know what we ate?" his mother asked.

He went through each meat mixture, but didn't go into the varying spices and amounts. Addison feared they'd be there all night if he started that.

He brought the buffalo-Italian sausage pot out to the table, followed by large bowls and spoons.

"Help yourself. The rest of them I'll freeze and give away at the festival for the library fund-raiser."

Addison glanced around the table at the Miller family. Everyone was talking, sometimes *to* each other and sometimes *over* each other. There was some serious ribbing of Eli, followed with grins and laughter.

Suddenly, she was terribly homesick. She missed her parents and siblings, especially her sister. Born only seventeen months apart, she and Kaitlyn were as close as twins. She missed her grandparents, too.

After the festival this weekend, maybe it was time to go home. Even Wendy said her breast incisions and the tissue collection areas were pretty much healed.

She'd lost her nipples with the mastectomy, and Wendy had suggested tattooing 3-D nipples on for looks. She could do that here by Wendy, or there was an artist in Dallas who did them. She didn't have to stay here to get that done.

She wondered if her being here was interfering with Eli moving on with his life. She couldn't help but notice in the weeks Eli had been home that he hadn't gone on one date, at least she didn't think he had. However, he'd been so wrapped up in getting his place renovated and getting settled, he probably was just too tired.

Zane mentioned that the number of women wanting to board horses had risen substantially in the last month. Wendy had slapped her hand over her mouth and snorted. Even females without horses to board had stopped by to welcome him home. He always stopped working and was pleasant to them, but she'd never observed it going any further.

Was it possible having her here made Eli uncomfortable, and he was waiting for her to leave before getting involved with someone in the area?

Or could his lack of dating be related to the phone call she'd overheard and had nothing to do with being tired?

Either way, the house was done, and he was moved in. She expected to see him bring dates around or bring his girlfriend from California home to meet his family. Now that she thought about it, Eli could be uneasy about bringing his California girlfriend home out of concern she might misconstrue the situation with Addison. Or he might be concerned Addison would say something about their weekend last November, not that she ever would.

The thought made her stomach flip as the tang of nausea bit her tongue.

"Right, Addison?" Zane's voice shook her from her musings.

"Sorry. I zoned out. What were you saying?"

Zane chuckled. "I was saying that now that Eli's house is done, he can get back to helping around here and let you get back to your knitting."

She smiled and nodded. "Good point."

The ladle in the pot holding the buffalo-Italian sausage chili clanged as Eli's dad dropped it in.

"Well, that's the end of that," Henry said. "Good chili, son, but you should know Mrs. Worthy has won this chili event for the last five years. You've got your work cut out for you."

Eli grinned. "Nothing I love more than a challenge. Now, did I see a couple of mom's pies?"

On Thursday, Eli made five batches of buffalo-Italian sausage chili, each one a little different than the other...a little more oregano, a little less cumin. That evening, Addison had to try every batch. Truth be told, she was a little sick of chili by the end of the night.

As she'd tasted each batch, Eli had read over the contracts from Liza and the station. The money they offered wasn't life-altering, but they were taking a chance on an unknown.

"So, what do you think?" Addison asked.

"About?"

She scoffed. "The contract WCDA is offering."

"Not interested. I'm fine with them using a segment

204 / CYNTHIA D'ALBA

to promote the festival, but as a fulltime job?" He shook his head. "The kitchen is my refuge. Cooking for people, watching them enjoy my food makes me happy. If I make it a job, I worry I'll come to hate the whole process. Thanks, but no thanks. I'm flattered they liked the videos, but honestly, Addison, those were your doing. You got the right angle, asked the right questions, kept the video flowing at a good pace. It wasn't me. It was totally you."

Friday morning, Addison was awakened by a phone call. She slapped her hand around on the bedside table until she found her phone.

"Hello?" Her morning voice cracked. She cleared her throat. "Hello?"

"Addison. Liza. Sorry to call so early. I forget you're two hours behind us."

Addison cleared her throat again and sat up, leaning against the headboard. This was either very good news or very bad news. If it'd been average news, Liza would've shot her an email.

"Morning, Liza. What's happening?"

"I'll tell you what's happening. After your boyfriend gave us permission to run that chili recipe of his, our phones exploded." Liza chuckled. "That blonde-twit who thinks she can replace you absolutely gushed over him. Tried to act like she was the driving force behind the video. I swear, you have to come back and come back soon. I might strangle that bubblehead. Anyway, the station's phone lines exploded, my boss is strutting around here like the male peacock in a flock, and the viewers are demanding more Eli."

"Well, that's nice, and Eli's not my boyfriend."

"Nice? Hell, girl, if you aren't boinking that stud, you're out of your mind."

"No boinking, Liza. We're friends."

"I'll just say, *idiot*, and we'll move on. The show needed this bump. Blondie is screwing the pooch on ratings."

"Did anyone say anything about me? My hair? How I looked?"

"Oh, comments about your hair have been mostly positive."

"So, my trolls were out this morning...?"

Liza groaned. "Some people should get real lives. Anyway, I reached out to the Montana NBC station closest to where you are and discovered they are sending a video photographer to the festival. Their talking head's name is Ursula Ramsey, and she'll be roaming around tonight and tomorrow. They promised they'd get by Eli and your booth and do an interview, plus one live segment with you for use during our afternoon news. You know, sort of an update of what's going on with you today."

"If that's what you want...."

"It is. I want you in the shot with him, so this works best. I can't wait to see the takes. Have fun and smile."

Addison hung up and sighed. She'd known Eli would have a draw, but this might be more than he'd bargained for.

She dressed, complete with her new Stetson, and found Eli in the barn brushing a dark brown gelding.

"He's beautiful," she said, leaning over the half door.

"He is." He looked up and smiled. "Nice hat."

She preened. "Thank you. Is this guy one of yours?"

"No. A border horse. Temporary border, at that. I

think Zane said he'll be here a couple of weeks while the owners are on a cruise. What's up?"

"The Chat ran the video of you cooking chili. They used the buffalo and beef one you approved."

"Yeah? How'd it go?"

"Gangbusters, according to the show's producer. You were a hit with the ladies."

He laughed, flashing his pearly-white teeth. "Well, that's hysterical. My old team would bust their collective guts with laughs at that news."

"Not so much hysterical as interesting. The higher ups at WCDA were thrilled. A local NBC station is covering the festival, so they'll be by for an interview for WCDA."

"Live?"

"Some live, some recorded. The station's talking head should have all the deets."

Eli shrugged. "Okay, but they'll need to stay out of my way while I cook."

"I know, I know. I'll make sure once we do our interview to send the reporter on down the way to other contestants to distract them."

With a laugh, Eli scratched behind the horse's ear. "Evil plan, Ms. Treadway. I like it. What's the schedule for tonight? I know we set up our booth this afternoon, then what?"

"The gates open for contestants at noon to give us time to set up, and then they open for the general public at five. From what I remember, there's live music, don't remember who, some contests that'll involve the public, like buffalo chip throwing, some carnival games, and I don't know what else. There's a welcome ceremony, more music, and the evening ends with a laser show.

Someone told me they used to do fireworks, but the sound terrified animals and posed a serious fire risk, so they're trying lasers this year. I hope that works. Growing up, fireworks scared our poor dogs to death."

He set the curry brush on a shelf, and she stepped back to allow him to exit the stall.

"The rules say everything has to be prepared onsite, so I've got a couple of generators in the truck for the refrigeration we're using and six propane tanks to run the burners,"

"Need me to help you load your truck?"

"No lifting. I heard Wendy. I'll let you pick up the paper bowls, but that's about it."

"Honestly, I feel fine."

"That may be, but..." Eli stopped walking and turned to face her. "We haven't talked about your cancer since that first night. I know how sick you were. I asked Wendy, and she said you'd done months of chemotherapy." He put his hands on her shoulders. "You've been through so much. I wasn't there before, but I'm here now. I want you to get well and not hurt yourself. Promise me you'll take it easy."

She looked into his gaze; his eyes were dark with concern. She hated it. Hated the cancer and hated how it made people look at her. She'd fought and won. She was strong, well, getting there anyway. And of all people, she didn't want Eli's pity.

Exhaling a deep breath, she said, "Eli, I am getting stronger every day. I take care of myself. And I have my mother, your mother, and Wendy to smother me with mothering. I don't need you to do it, too." She smiled, hoping she hadn't sounded as harsh to him as she had to herself. "Got it?"

"Got it." He pulled his hands back. "But you still can't lift a heavy freezer. Besides, it's small and not all that hard to move."

"Do you know what time you'll be headed up to the Arch? I can follow in the Jeep."

"You don't have to take mom's Jeep. You can ride with me."

"Except, I think we'll need both vehicles to get everything down there. All those gallons of chili, the propane tanks, the cook stoves, paper bowls...well, you get the picture."

"Yeah. Okay, let's pack up at eleven and head out. It'll take most of that time to get there and find where we go. What time is it?"

"Time?" She looked at her phone. "About eight."

"Okay. I'll finish up what I'm doing and see you around eleven."

"Works for me," she said. "I'm going to run a quick errand, but I'll be back."

She barely got back to the ranch in time to turn around and leave again. She pulled the Jeep behind Eli's truck and followed him up the drive. Between the ranch and the festival area near the Roosevelt Arch in Gardiner, they got separated on the road, but she was comfortable with where she was headed.

As she drove through downtown Gardiner—such as it was—she was slowed by more traffic than she'd expected. She'd seen nothing like this in the months she'd been here. As she exited from the town and turned toward the Roosevelt Arch, she was surprised at all the activity that'd sprung up in the last couple of hours. Addison had run to town earlier to locate their spot and she was glad she had. In this chaos, finding his location, even with a map, would have been challenging. She'd staked helium balloons at the corners to help her when they came back. Now, trucks and SUVs crowded the space with contestants unloading important supplies.

Her phone rang. "Hello?"

"I lost you somewhere. I have the map you gave me, but crap if I can tell a thing with all the cars and trucks. Any ideas?"

She was a little way behind him and wasn't exactly sure where he was in this melee.

"Do you see any star-shaped helium balloons?"

"Star balloons? Hold on."

"Balloons...balloons...where are they?" she heard him mumble, then say, "I see four star-shaped balloons. Are we near those?"

She chuckled. "We are those. I came down this morning and staked out our spot."

"You're brilliant. See you there."

When she backed in alongside Eli's black truck, she waved out her driver's door window.

"Good. You found it," Eli said, hurrying up to her door. "Can you believe all the people? There aren't this many people who live around here."

Climbing from the Jeep, she laughed. "Your parents told me that because of Yellowstone, this event draws visitors from all over." He followed her to the back and she popped the hatch. "This is a lot of paper products. I'm wondering if we can unload them in the morning."

"Why not? We don't need them today. Help me get the booth set up, okay? But no heavy lifting. I mean it, Addy."

She rolled her eyes and followed him to the

assigned area. He'd begun setting up eight-foot tables across the front and the sides. She was under one table, taping down the paper covering, when she heard a sultry female voice say, "You must be Eli Miller."

"I am. Have we met?"

"We haven't, but I was told to look for the most handsome guy, and here you are!"

He chuckled.

"I'm Ursula Ramsey, from KCBM, but everyone calls me LaLa. Nice to meet you."

Under the table and out of sight, Addison rolled her eyes. *Call me LaLa*, indeed. Jesus. She was dying to pop up alongside Eli and see this woman, but she didn't. Eli didn't belong to her, nor were they in any type of relationship beyond friends. She didn't have the right to pop up as though she were claiming her man.

The paper hanging down the front was long enough to hide her, but short enough that she could see the woman's boots, a pair of very expensive Lucchese. At least she had good taste in footwear.

"Nice to meet you, LaLa," Eli said, his voice sounding like he was smiling, and Addison would bet her left boob, if she had one, that he was.

"I watched your video last night."

"Yeah? Did you like it?"

Addison wanted to scoff. Seriously? The only thing that might have made a video of Eli hotter would have been Eli shirtless, not that she would ever suggest such a thing. That'd be degrading, right? Her brain said, yes. Her libido told her brain to shut the "F" up.

"I did. You were a natural in front of the camera. Are you planning on making a career of this?"

Eli's feet shuffled as he changed his stance. "Not

really. I was mostly helping out a friend. I'm working on my family's ranch for the time being."

A friend.

Yeah, that would be her, his good, good pal and buddy.

Oh no, they weren't anything other than friends.

Well, he hadn't actually said that, but the subtext was clear.

"Oh yes. You must mean the woman in the video with you." The tips of the Lucchese boots slid under the table as Ursula—she refused to think of the reporter as LaLa—stepped closer. "You'd be so much better on screen without her. That white hair was so distracting and really, she added nothing."

Addison looked at the scissors in her hand. She was close enough that stabbing the bitch's left boot would hardly require moving. Ursula was lucky Addison was so controlled.

Eli chuckled again. "I don't think so, but thanks again for enjoying the video."

"I'll be back tonight for an interview, but maybe after that, I can buy you a drink?"

"I'm not sure I can leave the booth unattended, but I appreciate the invite."

"I'll see you later. You work on getting someone to cover, okay?" The boots moved further under the table as the woman shuffled forward. "I have orders to include that blonde for one of the interviews, but I think an intimate chat with just you is something my viewers would enjoy."

Addison picked up her scissors with the sharp point down. It wouldn't take much to leave a nice scratch down the leather.

"Thanks, Ursula. We'll see," he murmured.

"LaLa, and I'll see you later. *Ciao.*"

The boot toes disappeared. Addison waited until she was confident the woman was gone before she climbed out.

"Seems like you've got a fangirl."

Eli rolled his eyes. "Let's get back to work."

CHAPTER 13

E li was relieved when Ursula didn't come back to his booth until close to four. By then, their area was staged and ready for the next day. Addison had a hankering for a corndog and lemonade and was gone when the reporter and her video photographer showed up. His plan was to get this over with and the reporter gone before Addison got back.

Eli might have enjoyed Addison's snide comments about the station reporter, and her sneers when she saw the woman walking around, a little more than he should. And he'd enjoyed the flair of jealousy he'd heard in her comments. Of course, the envy could be because she missed being in front of the camera, or maybe she was coveting the reporter's long, auburn hair, but he wanted to believe Addison's reactions were because of him. She was jealous because another woman had flirted with him.

If only he could know that for sure, but there was no way to test his theory. If he asked Addison and she denied it, their now friendly relationship could be strained.

After all she'd been through, including crappy treatment from him, was it possible she was willing to give him another chance? Did he stand a chance of being more than a friend? Another question he couldn't ask her outright. However, this was where his SEAL observation skills could come in handy.

He watched Addison make her way along the carnival games row. She licked an ice cream cone as she walked. Holy hell. His jeans got tight as his cock responded to the vision, not to mention the memories of her licking him from base to tip.

He turned away, not wanting to frighten small children with the bulge behind his zipper. At the rear of the area, Addison had set up the burners, and he made himself examine each hose, each connection until he could get himself under control.

"Great set up, little bro."

Eli counted to ten and turned around, his hard cock sort of under control. Zane stood with his arm over Wendy's shoulders. His mom beamed at him.

"Where's Dad?" Eli asked.

"Oh, you know your father," his mother said. "He saw some new tractors on display and he stopped to look. Ran into Stan Fielder, and you know how that man talks. Who knows when he'll get away."

Eli nodded, not sure if his father was the talker or Stan flourished the gift of gab. He also had no clue who Stan Fielder was, but he knew his father could talk about tractors for hours. "No problem. Dad does love his tractors."

"I'm calling him," Betty said, pulling out her phone from the purse slung over her shoulder.

"That's okay, Mom. Let him enjoy himself. Nothing's happening here right now anyway."

"Is this your family?"

Eli looked over Wendy's head. Ursula Ramsey stood with her video photographer. She smiled brightly at him.

"I thought we were done with my interview," Eli said.

"Well, nothing like a family to really bring a face to the man, you know?" She stuck out her hand to Zane. "You must be a brother. You're as handsome as Eli."

Wendy's eyes narrowed, and Eli bit the inside of his cheek to keep from laughing.

"I'm his wife," Wendy said, thrusting out her hand. "Dr. Miller."

Ursula didn't blink an eye. She shook Wendy's hand and turned to his mom. "And this beautiful woman is your sister?"

Betty giggled.

Eli shut his eyes long enough to roll them unseen under the lids.

"Oh, thank you," Betty said. "Eli is my son, as is Zane."

"Wow. You must have been a child bride."

Betty touched her hair with another giggle.

Wendy caught Eli's gaze. She rolled her eyes and pretended to gag.

Eli cleared his throat. "What can I do for you, Ursula?"

"LaLa," she corrected. "I saw the group and thought I'd stop and say hi."

"LaLa," her video photographer yelled. "We go live in two minutes."

"Oh." Ursula's eyes popped wide as though surprised. "You don't mind if I shoot from here, right?"

Eli waved his hand. "Have at it."

"Thank you." She leaned closer, but her voice carried well enough anyone in the area could hear. "I'll see you later for drinks and dancing. *Ciao*."

She turned toward the camera, adjusted the top of her shirt, meaning she pulled the vee a little lower, and put on a smile.

"Hello." Pause. "Yes, it's a beautiful day to be in Gardiner for the Buffalo and Beer Festival." Pause. A little laugh. "That's true, but I'm going to pass on the buffalo chip tossing. I'm all about the food." She continued on to talk about the weekend's events and tonight's laser show.

Food. Her? Her ass was so tiny, she'd be like screwing a skeleton, not that he had any interest in going down that rabbit hole.

As Addison neared their booth, her eyes narrowed and her lips tightened. Her gaze met Eli's, and she lifted a questioning brow.

He had no idea what she was asking, so, he shrugged, hoping he'd correctly answered her nonverbal question

"And that's it from Gardiner for now. I'll see you at nine. Ursula Ramsey reporting." She stood still with a bright smile until her photographer signaled the live feed was gone. Her shoulders relaxed, and she turned back to the Miller clan who'd stood off to the right during her broadcast.

"So nice to meet all of you. I'm sure I'll be seeing you around." She looked at Eli. "See you later."

She headed off, her photographer at her heels.

"What a nice woman," his mother said. "I've seen her on television before. She's so much prettier in person, don't you think so?"

She didn't direct the question to anyone in particular, but Zane—not being a total fool—shrugged.

"She's okay, I guess."

Wendy grinned up at him. "Nice save, cowboy." She put her hand on her barely-there stomach pouch. "Coyote's hungry."

"Coyote? You're naming your kid Coyote?" Eli's brow furrowed with confusion.

Wendy laughed. "Of course not, silly. But since we don't know if we're having a girl or a boy, he or she is 'Coyote' for now."

"But Coyote?" Eli grimaced.

"Long story," Zane said. "I'll explain later." He pulled his wife in for a tight hug. "And it's a boy. I said so."

Wendy sighed. "I'm starved." She looked at Eli. "Need anything from us tonight?"

He shook his head. "Nope. Enjoy your night."

"You are getting out to see everything, right?" Betty asked, a worried look on her face. "You can't just sit here all evening."

"Don't worry about me. There's Dad," he said, pointing off to the left. His distractionary tactic worked.

"Oh, there he is," Betty said. "You and Addison have some fun tonight."

Addison stood watching the activity around the

booth until everyone was gone. Only then did she return.

"You missed all the fun," he said as a greeting.

"Yeah, I saw *LaLa* chatting up the fam."

He laughed. "What do you want to do for dinner?"

"Oh, I ate while I was gone. There's a southern barbeque place down that way toward the parking lot. It's really good."

"You ate without me?"

That kind of pissed him off. He didn't mind eating alone, but he enjoyed meals with her much more. After all the time they'd spent together in the last month, all the meals they'd shared, all the movies they'd watched in the evenings, and now she's putting up a wall?

"You looked a little busy. Anyway, I'll stay here with all the equipment if you want."

He didn't want. He wanted her company.

With a frown, he said, "I'm not thrilled you ate alone, and you're making me do the same."

Her eyes widened in surprise, maybe because of how harsh his tone was. "I'm sorry. I thought you might want some time for yourself."

"Next time, let *me* decide what I want."

She nodded.

"Now, I'm going to get something to eat and bring it back here. You want anything?"

Her smile was almost shy. "A funnel cake, please?"

One side of his mouth quirked up. "See? How hard was that?"

Before he walked away, Addison's phone rang. She muttered a cuss word and silenced it.

"You're going to have to talk to him at some point." Eli frowned. "I don't think he's giving up. Like I said, hand me the phone next time and I'll let him know he's not welcome to call again."

"I know, I know," she said with a loud exhale. "I'll handle it."

The rest of their evening went smoothly, especially since he'd bumped into Ursula on his dinner run and explained that he wouldn't be around later, but he'd see her tomorrow.

The Miller clan came by at nine, calling it a night, which left him and Addison alone...well, with a few hundred other people.

"You headed home?" he asked.

"Are you?"

With a head shake, he said, "No. I have what I need to stay the night. I want to get an early start tomorrow. The chili tasting is at one, and I need all that time to let the competition batch simmer. I figure everyone else will be doing the same."

"Then I'll stay, too."

His heart skipped a beat. Of course, he wanted her to stay the night. He enjoyed no one's company as much as he did Addison's. However, he worried she would overdo or not sleep well and have no strength reserves left. Tomorrow would be a grueling day, and he wanted her by his side.

"You don't have to," he said, giving her the easy out.

"I know, but I want to get the whole experience. Fair food. Lights. Sleeping in my truck."

He laughed. "It'll get hot in the Jeep."

"Where are you sleeping? It'll be hot in your truck, too."

"Blow up mattress in the bed of my truck."

"But the mosquitos will eat you alive. Better warm than scratching myself silly."

He smirked. "You are such a city girl."

"Yep," she replied with a grin. "I probably should have that tattooed on my forehead. City girl. Proceed with caution."

With a snort of laughter, he shook his head. "I have a truck tent, too."

"A what?"

"It's a tent made to set up in the truck bed. Came in the other day, so it'll be the first time I get to use it. I plan to do some camping now that I'm home, and you gave me the best excuse to buy the tent now instead of later."

"Great. Glad to be of help. I'm sleeping with you." As she said the words, her face flushed. "I mean…"

He bit back a chuckle, but he couldn't stop his wide grin. "Hmm? That's an interesting offer. Sleep with me, you say?"

He told his cock to shut it down. She hadn't meant sleeping together in that sense, or at least he didn't think so. When her face reddened deeper and she dipped her head to look at the ground, he added, "I know what you meant, and that's fine," he said softly. "There's enough room for both of us." And if there wasn't, he'd sleep in the backseat of his truck and let her have the tent.

He swallowed hard before asking. "Do you have what you need to stay? Toothbrush? Fresh clothes?"

"I've got a bag in the backseat of the Jeep." She shrugged. "I wasn't sure."

"You're all ready then."

"I was born ready."

He laughed, put his arm around her shoulders, and pulled her in. "City girl. Totally."

She smelled like heaven and was as hot as hell. This might be the longest night of his life, even longer than the night in Tunisia when he'd been shot and had to wait for rescue.

After the laser show, Addison helped him set up the truck tent. It was larger than he'd anticipated and perfect for his needs. He'd been serious about doing some camping now that he was home. Montana had some fabulous spots where he could get away and fish.

"This is nice," she said, checking it from all sides. "And so smart."

"Yeah, I'm pleased."

She laughed and bumped his shoulder with hers. "It's okay to be excited, you know."

He grinned, put his arm around her shoulders, and squeezed. "I'm excited. I didn't exactly know what I was ordering. I mean, I saw pictures, but you don't know until you have it all set up, you know?"

Snaking her arm around his waist, she said, "I want to hear all about those camping trips."

"Hang around long enough, and maybe, I'll take you on one. Campfires, sleeping in a tent, hot coffee in the morning while watching the sun rise, fishing for our dinner..." He sighed. "How does that sound?"

"Heavenly, but where will I plug in my hairdryer?"

She laughed as he rolled his eyes.

"Now to get the new mattress inflated and in there."

Rubbing her hands together, she said, "Can't wait."

They were unfolding the uninflated mattress into the tent when Addison's phone rang. She looked at the caller id and swore under her breath. Eli wasn't a snoop, but he couldn't help but see the name Denis on the screen, not to mention he'd heard that ringtone too many times over the past weeks.

"You want me to handle that?" he asked, his hand extended to take the phone.

"No," she said with a long sigh. "I'll deal with him. Excuse me."

As she walked away, he could hear her whispered voice. Not the words specifically, but the hot, angry tone. She went to the Jeep and sat in the driver's seat while she talked. Shortly, she slammed the door and stomped back to the event area where he'd moved to give her privacy.

"Everything okay?" he asked, sure the answer was no.

"Fine," she said, her lips tight across her mouth. "Just fucking fine. Asshole."

The last was muttered under her breath, but his hearing was excellent. He was fairly sure he wasn't the asshole in question, at least, he hoped not. Plus, as a guy, he knew that when a woman said "Fine" in the tone of voice Addison had just used, it wasn't fine.

A smart guy would run. Not Eli. He held out a cold bottle. "Want a beer?"

She shook her head. "Nope. Would you mind if I crawled into the tent and laid down?"

"No, of course not. I wasn't thinking. You must be tired."

"More pissed off than tired." She gave him a sad

smile. "I'm mad, and I need to pout for a couple of minutes."

He grinned. "Make your pouting self at home."

He followed her as she stomped back to his truck. Taking a long swallow of his cold beer, he let himself enjoy the view of her firm, heart-shaped ass as she climbed in. Before he could turn away, she climbed back out.

"Already done?" he called. "That was some fast pouting."

"Nope. Getting my bag from the Jeep."

She retrieved a small bag from the Jeep, and then shoved it, and herself, back into his tent.

"Sulking, now," she called out. "Give me ten more minutes."

He chuckled. He decided his best course of action was to leave her alone...for now. "Going for a walk. I'll be back."

"Have fun," she called back.

He walked down the row of chili contestants, introducing himself, and shaking a lot of hands. He was surprised at the number of people he knew, or rather, remembered from his youth. When he got to Mrs. Worthy's booth, there was no one to be seen, but the cooking area was ready.

He ventured over to the craft beers section, not surprised to find Knox and his family in the area.

"Eli," Knox's wife said, with a broad smile. Nancy came around the tables to meet him in the aisle and wrapped her arms around him. "I'm so glad you're home." Pulling back until she could see into his eyes, she said, "I know Knox is thrilled, but I'm going to have to watch you two, aren't I?"

Eli hugged her while he chuckled. "Hey, I was a total angel growing up. Any trouble we got into was all Knox's doings."

"You are such a liar," Knox said with a laugh.

"Hey, Jason. Good to see you," Eli said to Knox's oldest child. "Did you get a chance to taste your dad's beer?"

"No," Nancy said at the same time Jason said, "Yep."

"What?" Nancy said, and shot a glare toward Knox.

He shrugged. "I needed an expert opinion."

Eli laughed while Nancy narrowed her eyes at her husband.

"I'm headed back to my spot. Good luck tomorrow," Eli said.

"You, too," Knox said. "Addison here with you?"

"Yep. Come by and say hi. I know she'd enjoy that. Bring Nancy."

"Will do," Knox said.

"Don't be a stranger. Come to dinner soon," Nancy said.

"I'd love to. Drop by and meet Addison." He kissed Nancy's cheek and left.

Festival visitors were supposed to leave at eleven when the music stopped. Only contestants were supposed to be in the park after that time. As he walked back, he noticed the number of people milling around was significantly smaller. He passed a couple of security guards patrolling the area. Not that he expected any trouble, but he liked knowing help was around if he needed it.

As he neared his area, he wondered if he'd be bothering Addison. She'd sounded pretty glum earlier after the call from her ex. He'd planned on sleeping in the truck bed, but he could sleep in the backseat if she was still upset.

After making sure everything was secure in his area, he went to his truck.

"Addison," he whispered, not wanting to wake her up if she was asleep.

"I'm awake. You want me to move to the Jeep so you can sleep here?"

"No. You okay if we both sleep here? I can sleep in the backseat if you want to be alone."

"No." Her voice was adamant. "This is your truck. I should be the one to go."

He climbed inside the tent. "It's big enough for the two of us. How's the pouting going?"

She chuckled, which made him smile. "Better."

"Want to talk about it?" He settled onto the soft mattress. There was some, but not much light inside, and sometimes darkness gave people the courage to talk about sensitive things, like ex-husbands. He was in no hurry. He could wait until she found her voice. In the meantime, he leaned against the side of the tent enjoying the aroma of pine and smoke filtering through the small screen window from the contestants who'd already begun their cooking for tomorrow.

With a sigh, she said, "You already know it was Denis. Someone told him about the video. He found it on the station's newsfeed and was furious to find out I was in Montana, and not Florida, as he'd assumed. I think he'd been driving around Orlando looking for me."

He hated that her ex still had enough influence over Addison to upset her. Hadn't he done enough to Addison's ego with his nasty comments about her cancer and mastectomy?

His jaw tightened. His teeth ground together. "You want to talk about it?"

"Not tonight." She sighed. "We will, but tonight, I don't want to think about him."

He patted her knee, which he realized was no longer covered by her jeans. His heart jumped. He dropped his gaze from her face to her leg, which bent at the knee and tucked under her other leg. Moving his gaze up, he saw she wore shorts. He was disappointed and relieved simultaneously.

"I'll just say, there are ways to get rid of a body so it's never found," he growled.

She laughed, and clutched his bicep. "God, thank you. I needed to hear that. While I don't require your services at this time, I'll keep that information handy."

Her fingers burned his flesh. When she removed her hand, he resisted the urge to see if she'd left an imprint. Even without a physical scar, he suspected he'd bear the scar on his heart from this woman for the rest of his life.

After she'd wormed her way under his skin last fall, he'd spent the past eight months working her out of his system, or he thought he had. But since coming home and spending so much time with her, his feelings for her had grown so much deeper and solid.

At Zane's wedding, his emotions toward her had been lust and fire.

Now, he knew Addison in a completely different way. She was kind and funny and sexy as hell. She cared about people. She'd taken care of him during the long days and nights he'd worked on his place. She'd been ready to do anything that would assist him as he made batch after batch of chili.

Her fool of an ex-husband had made a grave error, which he seemed to have realized since he kept calling her. Addison had enough to deal with. She didn't need that stress from her ex, nor the stress of Eli wanting more than the friendship they'd built. She'd told him on more than one occasion how much she enjoyed being friends.

They hadn't talked about when she was leaving. He hadn't asked because he feared he wouldn't like her answer, especially if she mentioned a specific date. What concerned him was her reaching out to her old station. To him, that suggested she was making plans to leave, even if she hadn't told him.

He hated that thought as much as he despised repairing fencing, and he abhorred that ranch chore.

When he'd returned to California following Zane's wedding, his dating life, which had never been that active, had dropped to dead. Starting a new relationship knowing he'd be leaving California for Montana wouldn't have been fair to him nor the woman. Besides, as much as he hated to admit it, his heart and feelings had been a little bruised that weekend. But the non-working weekends had been a little lonely.

In the months prior to his leaving, he'd watched his fellow SEAL team members meet the women they wanted to spend their lives with. Now, he observed the relationships between his brother with Wendy and Cowboy Russ with Lori. What he'd come to realize was he didn't want to spend the rest of his life like he'd spent the earlier months of this year...alone. The couples had shown him what living with a life partner could be, and he wanted that. Someone to be there on days when things didn't go as planned. Someone to hold. Someone to love. He wanted all that and more.

No, he *needed* all that.

To his regret, Addison had let him know she wasn't available for that kind of relationship. She simply didn't see him that way. Okay with being friends, but anything beyond that wasn't on her radar.

It wasn't as if there weren't single women in his area. There were plenty, but he didn't have the motivation to meet any of them. Maybe once Addison was physically out of his life, he could move on, but as long as he had her, he lacked the desire to meet another woman. Until she cut him out, he would go on enjoying having her with him, in whatever manner she allowed. His life with her was so much better than his life without her.

"You got quiet," she said. "I was just kidding about killing Denis, not that I would shed many tears at his funeral."

He chuckled. "I'm here. I was mentally reviewing local dumping ground laws."

With a chuckle, she bumped his shoulder. "Where'd you go?"

"While you were sulking?"

"Pouting, but yes."

"Nowhere, really. Met my competition. Ran into Knox and his family. Just walked the event grounds."

"What time are we getting started in the morning?"

"Early. I need to have time for simmering. I figure the first rays of light will wake me, but if for some reason they don't, I set my phone alarm for five as a backup."

She groaned. "I do not miss those early wakeup calls," she said as she scooted her hips down the mattress and stretched out. She sat up on her forearm. "You sure this is okay?"

He followed her lead and laid down. "It's fine. I promise to keep my hands to myself and on my side of the truck."

"If you insist," she muttered under her breath. "Night." She fluffed her pillow—the woman had brought a feather pillow—and rolled to her side.

What had she meant by that muttered comment? Well, that'd keep him up all night trying to figure it out.

Women. Fuck. Their brains were so different from men's. He would most likely spend the rest of his life in woman-talk confusion.

Sometime around one in the morning, Addison moaned. The sound was quiet and would have gone unnoticed if Eli had been asleep. But he wasn't. Instead, he'd been lying there looking at the stars through the netting of the tent windows. The night had been peaceful. A light breeze had carried the scent of live pine and hickory smoke to swirl around his truck.

Late Friday night, many of the contestants for the other buffalo meat categories had begun the process of smoking the meat for Saturday's judging. Next year, if he entered, he'd love to do brisket. Buffalo brisket would be a challenge to get tender and moist, given its lean texture. But he had a year to work on it, something he'd enjoy.

But that wasn't what kept him awake. Nor was he bothered by the chirp of crickets or the occasional coyote howl.

His problem was one-hundred percent the woman

beside him. As soon as he'd sat on the mattress beside her, a sweet, floral aroma had assaulted his nose. He wasn't sure if Addison was wearing perfume, or if her shampoo carried that scent, or hell, maybe it was just the way she always smelled.

With that low moan, she rolled to her back, and then over on her side facing him. Her eyes were shut, her lips slightly parted.

As beautiful as she was, the stress of her job, and probably the strain of dealing with breast cancer, had etched worry lines into her forehead. Now, completely asleep and relaxed, those furrowed brow lines were gone, almost invisible.

Back in November, he'd thought her breathtakingly gorgeous and had been drawn to her external beauty. Now that he'd spent so much time with her, he knew her beauty was more than skin deep. It was ingrained in her soul as well as her face.

He'd gotten the impression from a couple of her comments about her cancer and surgery that she had serious reservations about her future love life, which was ridiculous. She was only thirty-three. She had decades of life and love ahead of her. Any man who was lucky enough to love her and have her love him back would cherish her all the more knowing she could have died and they wouldn't have had a chance at a life together. Any scars she might bear would be battle trauma, like anyone fighting for their life might bear. Didn't he himself bear the scars of war on his body? Fuck anyone who judged people who bore damage from living life.

A cool wind blew around them. Addison scooted closer, as though drawn to his body heat. Her arm flopped across his chest. She nuzzled her head onto his shoulder and released a long, breathy sigh. She slid her arm down until her forearm rested on his waist, her fingers inches from his cock.

Of course, his cock took notice and began to grow and stretch toward her fingertips. Mental commands to his dick to *cool it* went ignored.

He was fucked ten ways to Sunday.

He drew in a deep breath, pulling in the aroma of strawberries from her hair.

How was it possible to be in heaven and hell at the same time?

CHAPTER 14

Addison tried to dig her head into her feather pillow. Her usually soft pillow was firmer than usual. She punched it a couple of times to dislodge the stuffing. The first jab hurt her fist. The second produced a male chuckle. Her eyes flew open and she stared into a pair of laughing eyes.

"Oh! Oh, I'm sorry," she said, scooting away quickly.

"It's fine, Addy. The slug on my shoulder didn't hurt...much." He wiggled and rotated his shoulder. "I'll probably have an impressive bruise, however."

She laughed. "I'm sure." She sobered. "Sorry about climbing all over you. I guess I got cold."

"I'm not complaining." He sat up and leaned against the truck cab. "It's still early. You can sleep a little longer if you want."

She shifted until she was sitting beside him. "Again, sorry about the body groping. I hope I didn't make things uncomfortable for you."

She didn't dare look down at his groin because

while she'd been sleeping, she'd been dreaming. Her dreams had been hot and erotic, involving mouths, and touching, and deep thrusts.

"I'm fine. Are you?"

Irrational thought, but she felt as though he could read her mind and see those dreams. Heat rushed up her neck, making her thankful for the continued dark of the early morning.

"Yes," she said with a whisper.

"I'm going to get up and check on things. Like I said, you can sleep a little longer if you want."

Her phone chimed with an incoming text. She didn't have to look at it. She recognized the custom notification she'd given Denis. His call last night had been crazy. He wanted her back. They should try again. He was so, so sorry for everything. She was the only one for him.

All she heard was he was out of money and wanted into her trust fund again.

As if she were that stupid.

"Don't you need to check your phone for that text? At this early hour, it could be important."

She shook her head. "It's not."

He studied her as though deciding whether to challenge her dismissal of the text or not. Finally, he shrugged and said, "Go back to sleep. I need to get to browning all that ground meat."

"I'll help." She began to move and realized she had other pressing priorities. "Well, I'll help when I get back."

He pointed. "Bathrooms are over there."

"Guys are so lucky. You can whip it out anywhere

and get business done." She sighed. "Sometimes, it would be nice to be a guy."

"Let me say from the entire male population, I'm glad you're not."

"I'll take that as a compliment."

"Good, because that's how it was meant. Your beauty adds to the world."

She put her hand over her heart, which was slamming against her ribs trying to get out to hug him. "Thank you. That might be the nicest thing anyone has ever said to me."

When she returned after taking care of necessities, Eli had rearranged their area, putting the burners on the side instead of the back.

"You've been a busy little beaver," she said,

"I don't like my back to the crowd." He shrugged. "Military mindset."

"Makes sense. What can I do?"

"I would marry you for a cup of coffee."

She laughed, even though his comment launched a million butterflies in her stomach. "I'm sure I can do that."

There were booths at the event that would be selling coffee a little later in the morning, but she was a morning caffeine person. She'd learned he was also. Knowing they'd both be jonesing for that first cup of coffee, she'd packed her coffee pot just in case. Now, she knew she'd made a solid decision.

When the coffee was done, she handed him a cup of black heaven.

"Thank you," he said, then gulped back a large volume.

"That's hot," she cautioned.

"The coffee, or me?" he asked, a mischievous grin on his face.

She laughed but didn't reply. Why? Because she wasn't sure how to answer. The truth stuck in her throat. The honest answer was "Yes."

She pulled the folding chairs out of the Jeep where they'd been stored for the night. After setting them up, she retrieved her knitting tote bag, deciding to knit while she watched a sexy SEAL work. Was there anything sexier than watching a deliciously hunky man work? And honestly, it didn't matter what Eli was doing. Watching him had become the highlight of her day.

The night when she'd first seen Eli standing in the barn apartment, she'd wondered if her chemotherapy had still been affecting her brain. All her reading about her chemo drugs had addressed the possible adverse side effects that could happen. However, hallucinations hadn't been anything she'd been expecting.

Hair loss on head. Check.

Loss of all finger and toe nails. Check.

Mouth ulcers. Check.

Loss of eyebrows and eyelashes. Check.

Loss of pubic hair, along with leg and underarm hair. Check.

Dry nasal passages from the loss of hair and possible nosebleeds. Check.

Weight loss. Nope. If anything, she might have added a few pounds.

Chemo brain, i.e., brain fog, impaired memory, maybe faulty decision-making. Check, check, and check.

But when he'd dropped the bottle of beer, she'd

realized he was really standing in her kitchen. From his shocked expression and reaction, he hadn't been expecting her any more than she'd been expecting him to walk back into her life.

Wendy had been a little vague on when Eli would return. Addison had been under the impression he'd be home in September, giving her plenty of time to get away, instead of the middle of July, when she was still on the ranch.

Now, she watched him in the early morning light, glad to have been wrong. Sure, she'd been furious and hurt by his actions in November. What he'd done hadn't made any sense at all, until recently. Damn Denis. If her ex had mentioned a man in her room, or that he'd called the previous evening, she might have figured it out. Instead, he'd called to ask her to give him the title to the BMW he'd driven while they'd been married. As if. She'd declined and hung up.

Her feelings toward Eli were mixed, leaving her conflicted much of the time. He'd hurt her deeply, even if she did understand the why. Her life had been in an emotional upheaval for the past eighteen months. Denis had injured her pride more than her heart. She'd stayed longer in that marriage than she should have, but she'd worried about the publicity that could surround her divorce, not to mention divorce being the public declaration of a supreme failure.

In the end, the news of her divorce had been over-shadowed by a public corruption scandal involving the Florida state treasurer. While it was a relief her divorce had barely made a ripple in the news, it also made her realize that maybe she thought too much about appearances. But even if that were true, she had no intention of getting rid of her Ferrari!

For the past few weeks, Eli had played a starring role in her life. The drives to Bozeman for supplies. The late-night dinners in a construction zone. The other dinners in her tiny kitchen. The meals in restaurants, lunches and dinners, had been fun with the conversations non-stop.

When she'd met him at the wedding, of course, she'd been drawn by his looks and charmed with his personality, but she might not have acted on that attraction if she hadn't been facing months of breast cancer hell.

They'd been the only single members of the wedding party, so it was natural they would be thrown together at dinner and the reception. After his initial offer of a drink and a table to sit and talk, she'd been the one to take the lead, not him. She'd been the one to make sure they sat together. She'd been the one who'd shown up at his door, her vagina in hand, so to speak.

When he'd ghosted her, she'd blamed herself for being so gullible as to believe a man like him would be attracted to her.

However, the Eli from November, the unforgettable lover, had turned out to be Eli, an unforgettable man. He was loving with his family. His work with the horses showed a gentle, caring side. The day she'd watched him stroke the curry comb along the back of the gelding who'd been boarding at the ranch, the horse had shivered at his touch. She had, too.

"I thought you were going to put up sweaters and vests so people could order from you," he said, glancing over his shoulder, interrupting her thoughts.

"I did, just not in this booth. I've been ordering my yarn from a store in Livingston. I met the owner when I had to make a run up there for a specific yarn and couldn't wait for it to be mailed. She knows more about knitting and quilting than I'll ever learn. Anyway, we hit it off. I called her last week asking her opinion about taking orders like we'd talked about. Come to find out, she has a booth in the arts and crafts area. She offered to display my work and sell anything I had ready, as well as take orders so I could contact the customers after the festival." She looked up at him with a grin. "For a commission."

"Of course." He returned her smile.

Dammit. How could he look so good this early? On second thought, how can he look so freaking sexy no matter if he was cleaned up for a dinner out, or hot and sweaty from work?

The damn man rocked her boat. It was that simple, and oh, so complicated. He'd put her in a friend category, probably not willing to deal with all her baggage, and she couldn't blame him. Cancer. Scars. Fake boobs, even if they were made from her own tissue. Crazy hair. Chemo brain. Questionable job future. Certifiable insane ex. Her baggage was enough to make any rational man run away.

She held up her knitting needles with the purple yarn. "The yarn store owner's son is a senior at Livingston, so I'm making him a pair of gold and purple socks as a thank you for her."

He nodded.

Not long later, the scent of bacon wafted in the air. Her stomach growled.

"I'm starving. You?"

He looked over at her with a raised eyebrow.

"Yeah. Got it. You're always starving." She laughed. "I'm going to wander around and see what I can find for us."

"Good." He sounded distracted, which was probably because he was draining the grease off the Italian sausage.

Like the famous Rudolph, her nose led the way. Carrying her coffee with her, she sipped and nodded as she made her way through the festival booths. Her knitting friend Polly's booth was still boarded up, protecting the goods until she got there to open. She saw Eli's friend, Knox, and she assumed his family. She waved but didn't go over. She could be a bear when she was hungry.

The delicious aromas were drifting from a trailer that advertised home cooking. From the line of people standing at their window, they were either the only ones open, or their reputation preceded them.

She took her place behind the last person and studied the menu. Fortunately for her complaining stomach, the line moved quickly, and she found herself at the window. She ordered, paid, and carried the food back to Eli.

He'd dumped part of the buffalo meat into his pan and was stirring when she got back. He had the giveaway chilis heating so they'd be ready when the crowds arrived.

"What'd I get?" he asked.

"Pancakes and sausage on a stick with a cup of maple syrup for dipping."

"Sounds perfect." He looked at the five pancake

bundles, and then up at her. "What did you get for you to eat?"

She laughed. "We're sharing, and if you give me at least two pancake sticks, I'll go back and get us some fresh blueberry muffins."

He set two sticks off to the side with a grin.

By ten that morning, the sun was up and people were milling around. Smoke from grills filled the air, mixing with the yummy food smells she associated with county fairs, carnivals, and all outdoor events. The sample chilis they were giving away bubbled and added to the aromas. The contest chili simmered on back burners.

Zane and Wendy showed up a little after ten to man the chili giveaway and collect donations. Betty and Henry followed closely behind.

"Good morning, honey," his mother said, kissing Eli on the cheek.

"Hi, mom. Good morning, everyone," Eli said, waving in the air with a large, metal spoon.

"How'd you sleep?" Wendy asked, putting her arm through Addison's.

"Good," Addison said. "Been a while since this gal's gone camping. Remember when my pledge class set up tents in the front yard of the sorority and went on strike? Well, that was my last camping trip."

Wendy laughed. "I was so mad at y'all."

Addison grinned. "I know, but last night was much, much better. I actually had a mattress and didn't have to sleep directly on the ground."

Wendy shook her head. "Those were fun times."

Zane put his arm around his wife. "What are you talking about?"

"Memories. Very good, old, college memories." Wendy leaned her head on her husband's shoulder, and he kissed the top of her head.

Addison's heart sighed at the picture Wendy and Zane made. Two people who loved each other, and even better, liked one another. A spark of envy lit up her insides. This is what she wanted. To love and be loved, of course, but as importantly, she wanted to really like the man she would spend the rest of her life with... someone like Eli.

Wendy turned in Zane's arms and rose on her toes to kiss him. "I've got to run over to the medical tent and check in."

"I'll walk with you," Betty said.

"You okay?" Wendy's brows pulled together in concern.

"Yes, of course. I want to talk about a baby shower for you and for Lori."

Eli's mom's face glowed with joy, and Addison felt a tinge of regret that she wouldn't be here when all those babies came.

As Zane watched his wife and mother walk away, the love he felt for both of those women shone on his face.

Again, Addison felt the prick of jealousy, not only for all the love Zane and Wendy shared, but for him and Eli having their mother active in their lives on a daily basis.

Addison needed her mother. The Miller clan had been fabulous, but she missed her family. When this weekend was done, she would talk with Wendy about leaving. It'd been ten weeks since her surgery, and she felt fine. No fever. No redness.

Incisions healed, so why was she drawing out her departure?

"You know what I heard?" a man said from outside their booth. "I heard that SEALs were weak pussies and the ones who cooked were the worst."

"Well, I heard that a SEAL who wears an apron is more likely to join chair force than belong to a real military branch."

Addison's eyes widened and she glanced toward Eli. His back was turned to the men making the nasty comments. His shoulders and back went rigid. He untied the white apron, calmly folded it, and set it on a table. He tilted his head and cracked his neck. Addison reached out and touched his arm. He shook her off and began a fast walk out of their area.

"Zane," Addison said. "Stop him."

Eli charged the two men, taking one of them to the ground.

Addison expected to hear the crunch of fist to face. Instead, she heard guffaws of laughter as the two men stood, doing that man hug thing.

"You're getting old and slow, Mars," Eli said.

The man just laughed.

"What the fuck are you doing here?" Eli asked. "I know." He snapped his fingers. "You were serious when you called. You really do love me and miss me, right?"

"Fuck no." Mars gestured toward the man beside him. "This is Hank Patterson, owner of Brotherhood Protectors."

Eli shoved out a hand. "You've mentioned him. Nice to meet you, Hank."

"I'm up here fishing with Hank, not too far away. Bear gave me orders to check on you and here I am."

"Of course, he did," Eli said, arching an eyebrow. "You can report back that I haven't fallen off a horse yet."

Hank shook Eli's hand. "Nice to meet you, Wolf. Jack has told me a lot about his team, especially about your cooking skills. My wife would be jealous."

"We had the best team, for sure," Eli said. "Come meet my family, or most of them anyway." He led the men back to the booth. "My dad, Henry, my brother, Zane, and, um..." He looked at Addison. "My good friend Addison. Everyone, this is Jack 'Mars' Marsten from my team and his friend Hank." The men shook hands, and Addison waved from where she stirred the donation chili.

"Jack tells me I should be recruiting you to my organization," Hank said. "We do all kinds of security work. Perfect for a man with your skill base."

Eli shrugged. "I'm not really looking for work right now, but we can talk later."

"Wolf makes the best damned, well, everything," Mars said. "I can't believe you're in a chili cooking competition. The guys are going to get a kick out of this."

"And he's going to win," Addison interjected.

Eli grinned at her. "This is all her fault. I cooked for her once, and wham-bam, she enters us in the chili contest."

"It wasn't exactly like that," Addison said.

Mars arched an eyebrow. "I don't remember you cooking for anyone outside of our team and our women."

Addison found that comment interesting. Did Mars mean that Eli didn't have dates at the team parties? Or did he mean that Eli didn't do private dinners for dates? She hoped it was the later, meaning he only cooked for special people. It was a thin hair of a hope, but she held on to it.

"Hey," a voice called. "Your sign says free samples."

Eli nodded to the man approaching the booth. "Got to get back to work. It was great seeing you, Mars. Hank, I'll look forward to speaking with you later."

All the judging started at one in the afternoon. Each competition had five judges, and no person could judge more than one event, so a different panel of judges was used for each event. Addison wondered how they were able to find so many people to judge.

She walked up and down the contest aisle looking at how others were preparing for the five chili judges. Some of the contestants had elaborately decorated tables covered with linen cloths, fine china, and what appeared to be sterling silver flatware. Others had gone much simpler with real dishes and flatware.

Down at their booth, Eli had planned for a less fancy judging. After seeing the other tables, his was downright spartan. Each judge would be served chili in a soup crock, black on the outside and multi-colored on the inside, with two handles for holding. He had brought flatware, but nothing other than what was in his kitchen.

She hurried back to their booth. "Eli," she said.

"What's wrong?" Concern etched his brow. "Are you okay?"

"Eli, everyone else has such fancy setups for the chili judges. One table had fresh flowers, china, and flatware."

He smiled and pulled her close for a hug.

"That just means they aren't confident about their chili, so they are trying to baffle the judges with bling. We don't need no bling." He squeezed her tight. "And besides, we like the chili. If they don't, then they don't know good chili from fantastic chili."

About thirty minutes after the judging started, the five judges—three men and two women—made it to their booth. They each took a bowl from Eli and took a bite, and then another. Addison couldn't understand how the judges weren't stuffed to their gills if they ate that much at each booth.

Her stomach rolled as acid bubbled violently. She felt like she was going to be sick. A tingle of nausea tickled the back of her throat as the judges ate and swallowed. Then each of them wrote notes into their notebook.

"Nice," one female judge said. "I liked the subtle sweet undertone with the spicy kick at the end."

"Thank you," said Eli.

And they walked on to the next booth.

"Addison, are you ready for your live shot?" a female voice said nearby.

"What?"

Ursula Ramsey stood with her cameraman.

"My station said you're to do a live segment with your station in Orlando."

She nodded. "Right, right. Time got away from me. How long do I have?"

Ursula conferred with someone on a cell phone and said, "Got it." To Addison, she said, "You've got ten minutes."

"Fine."

"You look fabulous," Eli said. "Don't worry about it."

Addison's eyes were wide with surprise. Eli wasn't sure if she'd not known about the live breakaway, or if she'd forgotten. Either way, ten minutes was a lifetime. She had plenty of time if she wanted to primp. In his opinion, she didn't need a thing.

Still, she pulled her bag from the back of his truck and ran a tube of coral lipstick across her lips. "That's the best I can do at this moment."

"Like I said, you look great. Give them hell."

She touched his chest and smiled. "Thank you."

After putting in an earpiece that'd been handed to her, she took the microphone from Ursula's outstretched fingers. She adjusted her shirt and looked forward with Eli and his booth as her backdrop.

"Yes," she said. "Ready."

She paused and then a bright smile bloomed on her face.

"Hello, Sally. What a pleasure to be with WCDA's audience this afternoon."

She paused for a question, or that's what Eli assumed was going on.

"Thank you." She touched her hair. "Something new is always fun. Speaking of new, I'm in Montana at the Annual Buffalo and Beer Festival in Gardiner. Lots of people, games, and fun."

She stepped back and turned toward Eli. "Some of you may have caught our chili segment on The Chat. This is Eli Miller, cook extraordinaire. Eli, tell the viewers what you have going on behind you."

Eli was sure he was wide-eyed. He hadn't expected her to toss it to him, still, he smiled. "Happy to, Addison. These two pots hold gallons of chili made with a mixture of Italian sausage and buffalo meat. As you know, the contest requires the chili contain a minimum of seventy-five percent buffalo, which of course we do."

Addison pulled the microphone back. "And what's your secret recipe?"

"Ah." Eli grinned. "I can't tell you. That's why it's a secret."

She gave a light laugh and turned back to the camera. "Judging started a little over an hour ago. Winners in each category will be announced at three-thirty here, or about five-thirty in Orlando."

She paused and smiled. "And I've missed Orlando." She waved into the camera lens. "Until we meet again." She froze in her spot. A couple of seconds later, her shoulders slumped and she blew out a long breath.

"Thanks, guys," she said to Ursula and the camera-man. "Appreciate the assist."

Ursula took back her microphone and looked at Eli. "Missed you at the dance last night."

"Yeah, sorry about that. I had a ton of things to do to get ready for today, and then got some shuteye. Thanks for coming by."

Yeah, he was giving her the brush-off. Ursula—call me LaLa—was tall, statuesque, and beautiful, and she did nothing for him. Nothing. He could appreciate her beauty—he was a guy, after all—but there was nothing that intrigued him.

Now, Addison? Yeah. She intrigued, amused, and got him.

But he'd just witnessed her taking back her role at

her station. She had the looks, poise, and voice. In other words, she was a natural.

Of course, she would go back to Orlando. Any thoughts of her remaining in his tiny corner of the world were daydreams on his part.

The free chili went quickly. He packaged up some of the contest chili for his family to take home, but then let Zane and his dad giveaway the rest.

The library donation box was stuffed with more bills than coins. Good. He'd spent a lot of time in the library growing up. Money was tight all over. He was glad to do what he could for such a valuable asset to his community.

"Addison."

"Hmm?" She was gathering up loose napkins to put away.

"Have you counted the donations yet?"

She shook her head. "No. I wanted to wait as long as I could before stopping the collection. There were some people who came by and donated without wanting chili." She looked at him. "Mighty strange people in this area if they turn down buffalo chili." She winked.

He laughed. "That'll be my family after all the chili they tasted for us," he joked, which cracked her up.

Okay, so he wasn't that funny, but he loved making Addison laugh. The sound made his heart smile.

CHAPTER 15

"It's about that time," Addison said.

Eli was perfectly aware that the winners would be announced shortly. He was nervous, which was insane. He'd only entered this contest as an excuse to be around Addison longer. He didn't have facts, but he felt he had only a matter of a few days left with her. He'd used the house renovation to keep her there, and now the chili contest. He'd racked his brain for other ways to keep her here. Maybe Wendy would take some pity on him and give him some ideas.

"Eli," Addison said. "Did you hear what I said? We need to head over to the main stage for the winner announcements."

He shrugged. "Sure, but I don't want you to get your hopes up and be disappointed if we don't win."

"But we're going to," she insisted. "Your chili was so good." She walked closer and touched his cheek with her hand. "Didn't you hear what that lady judge said? Sweet undertones with a spicy kick at the end." She smiled and kissed his cheek. "Just like you. A little sweet and a little spicy, just like the perfect man should be. Now, let's go."

She grabbed his hand and began to pull him toward the main stage. Had he heard her correctly? She thought him sweet and spicy and perfect? He let her tug him into the crowd, his mind still trying to process what she could have meant.

His family stood near the front of the crowd. As soon as his mom saw them, she waved them over. He and Addison joined his family.

"Now, like I told Addison, I don't want you to get your hopes up. Like Dad said, Mrs. Worthy wins every year. I don't expect to win, but it would be nice to final."

"Stop it," Addison said, bumping him with her hip. "You are so going to win."

He loved her enthusiasm, but he hated how disappointed she was going to be. Maybe he'd offer to take her out tomorrow night for dinner and a movie to cheer her up. Or maybe they could stay at his house, he'd cook for her, and they could stream a movie. Honestly, he'd sit outside on her mosquito-infested patio without bug spray if it meant spending more time with her. He'd take what he could get.

"Can I have your attention?" A woman on the stage tapped the microphone, which reverberated through the ground speakers. "We are ready to announce this year's winners. I'm Teresa Potter, the Executive Director of Gardiner Chamber of Commerce. Thank you all for being with us this year, only our fifth year in operation. Every year we grow larger and the competition fiercer, and this year was no exception."

Addison took his hand and held on tight. The feel

of her fingers laced with his was nirvana. Like the night they'd met, he felt as if all the pieces in his scattered life were falling into the correct places.

He pulled their joined hands up to his mouth and kissed her fingers. "Thank you," he whispered. "I wouldn't have done this without you. I've had a blast."

Her eyes were wide, and her face flushed, with excitement was his guess. Still, the smile that popped onto her face made his heart sing with happiness.

"Before we get to the winners, I want to take a minute to thank the executive board of the chamber for all their hard work getting this event organized and staffed. I'd like to also thank the contestants for making the winner selection so hard on the judges."

A ripple of laughter rolled through the crowd.

"And finally, we raised over five thousand dollars for the public library, and we aren't finished yet counting donations. So, there's still time to drop a few dollars into any donation station. I'm sure you are all tired of listening to me, so let's get on with the prizes. We are going to start with all the meat divisions before moving on to the microbrews. Starting with the chili division."

Addison wrapped her other hand around their laced fingers and squeezed. Zane patted Eli's back, a gesture of support Eli assumed.

"Third place goes to Team Branson."

A family of six climbed onto the stage to collect their white ribbon from a teenage girl dressed in a long, formal gown.

"Second place goes to Berta and Harold Worthy. Congratulations!"

As Mrs. Worthy made her way to the stage, Addison's hands began to shake.

"You're going to win," she whispered.

He smiled down at her and kissed the top of her head. "We had fun, right? No matter what happens, the most important thing is how much fun we had."

"Wow, Mrs. Worthy is not happy," his dad said with a chuckle. "Not a good loser at all."

Eli glanced up at the stage in time to see Mrs. Worthy snatch the red ribbon out of the executive director's hand and stomp back down the stairs. He bit his bottom lip to keep from laughing.

"First place in the buffalo chili contest goes to..." The director paused, and Eli wanted to yell. In reality, she'd paused only a second or two to amp the suspense, but it felt like an hour.

"Eli Miller and Addison Treadway," the director finished.

Addison screamed and jumped into his arms. He held her tightly and hugged.

"I knew it," she yelled., "You are the best, Eli."

As he lowered her back to the ground, their mouths met. Whose mouth started the kiss might be open for debate, but he made sure he took advantage of the time, pouring all his emotions into the kiss, trying to say with his lips what his voice could not. This kiss wasn't just a meeting of lips. It was the type of kiss he would remember the rest of his life. The kind of kiss that marks a man, makes a man want so much more than a simple pressing of lips together. This kiss was a pledge of his love, but would she get that message?

Loud clapping broke through the mental veil he

had put around them, followed by his family clapping and stomping their feet as noisily as possible.

Addison's eyes were sparkling when their kiss stopped and their gazes met. They were also a tad dilated with lust. He suspected his were also.

"Go get your ribbon," his mother ordered, pushing them toward the stage.

"While the winners are coming up, I'll read a couple of the judges' comments," the emcee said. "This chili had a unique flavor with a sweet undertone that complimented the meat. Then, there was a spicy kick to finish."

Eli and Addison climbed the stairs, still holding hands. On stage, Eli took the blue ribbon, and together, they held it over their heads.

Looking down from the stage, seeing his family clapping and waving, hearing Knox McCrea's deep, booming voice cheering from somewhere in the crowd, holding Addison's hand like he had every right to...all of it felt surreal as though he were dreaming. For a fleeting instant, it crossed his mind that maybe he was still in Tunisia and this was one of his dreams, but then Addison pulled him toward the stairs to leave the stage, bringing him back to reality. She really was here with him. They really had just won the blasted chili contest. What he was feeling was pure elation and joy.

His family met them at the base of the stairs, and the six of them walked over to the side while the next meat category was announced.

"I am so proud of you," his mother said, giving him one of her always-ready kisses on the cheek. "And you, too, Addison." With Addison, Betty not only gave her a kiss on the cheek, but pulled her in for a tight hug.

"Congrats, bro," Zane said, slapping Eli on the back.

"Congratulations. I look forward to sampling all the various meals you're going to make now that you're home," Wendy said, hugging Eli.

"Great job, son," his dad said, and then to Eli's surprise, his dad pulled Addison in for a hug.

"I think a celebration is in order for tonight," Betty said.

"I bet Eli and Addison are both exhausted," Wendy suggested.

"Of course, they are." Eli's mom put an arm around Addison's waist and her other one around Eli. "I figured you two were sick of chili, so I fried a chicken this morning. I thought I'd put some potatoes and English peas with it, along with biscuits. A quick dinner, and you two can get to bed."

Zane snorted. "Um, mom. Do you ever listen to what you say?"

Addison giggled.

Eli shrugged, fighting the grin that wanted to break onto his face. "Sorry, Addison. You heard my mother. We need to go to bed."

His mother pinched Eli's side as she scoffed. "You two boys need to get your minds out of the gutter. You know that's not what I meant."

Eli laughed. He noticed that Addison was excluded in his mother's shaming of dirty minds. And, even though he was thirty-six and Zane was thirty-nine, they were still "boys" to his mom. He didn't mind that at all. This was what being home was all about.

The group stayed long enough to hear Knox's microbrew come in second place. After back slaps and congratulations, the Miller clan left the event park and reconvened at Grizzly Bitterroot Ranch's main house. His mom refused to let Addison beg off what she called "family dinner," but she didn't put up much of a struggle.

The fried chicken meal should have hit the spot after way too much chili. Around Eli, conversation flowed, but he barely registered the topics. He was fully focused on Addison beside him, her leg touching his. His heart raced. His pulse pounded in his ears. His rapid breathing caused him to choke on a piece of chicken, which resulted in Addison pounding on his back.

"Slow down," his mother chastised. "You're gobbling down food like we're in a timed test."

"Sorry." He wanted this meal over. He wanted to get Addison alone, explore her mouth in a little more detail. Glancing at her plate, he asked, "You about done?"

His mother's brow creased into a frown.

Addison's eyes popped open in surprise. "Um, almost. Is there something I forgot to do?"

"Not that I know of," he said. "I was going to walk you home if you were done."

"Dude," Zane said. "She lives close enough that I could throw rocks from here and hit the side of her place."

Wendy gave Eli a warm smile. "That's very nice of you, Eli. I'm sure Addison appreciates having the company."

Zane shifted his gaze toward his wife and then looked at Eli. "So, I can expect you fulltime starting tomorrow?" his brother asked. "I've been saving some projects just for you."

Eli scoffed. "Why do I think these projects are the ones you don't want to do so you're pushing them off on me?"

Zane shrugged. "So suspicious."

Eli chuckled. "Not at all. More like, I know you. But before I jump in with both feet, and while Mom and Dad are still here to help you, I'd like to take a little time off. I came here straight from a mission, jumped immediately into the house renovation, and then the preparation for the festival."

"Well, that sounds reasonable," his dad said. "Your mom and I don't head out for Florida until October. Take all the time you need."

"Thanks, Dad. I don't need that much time. Shoot, I'd go crazy sitting around doing nothing for that long. But I'd like to do some camping and fishing. Maybe a week or so."

"He bought a cool tent that fits in the back of his truck," Addison said and looked at Eli. "Bet you're dying to try that out."

"Exactly."

"Where are you thinking of going?" his dad asked.

"Thought I'd do some fly fishing on the Madison."

"Great spot," Zane agreed. "Can't blame you for wanting to go. What's the good of living in Montana if you don't take some time to enjoy it?"

Eli nodded. "I haven't been fishing in forever. Probably won't catch a thing, but I think I'd enjoy the quiet time."

"Okay, but prepare to work when you get back," Zane said with an evil grin.

The meal wrapped up with chocolate pecan pie. Addison and Wendy insisted on cleaning up the kitchen before leaving, but not without Betty staying to assist. Eli, Zane, and their father headed for the study to pull out some maps Henry had of prime fishing areas on the river. While Eli was glad for his dad's suggestions and insistence he take the maps, he tried to hurry things along. He didn't want Addison to leave without him.

Eli hurried back to the kitchen with maps and recommendations in hand. Addison was hugging his mother and thanking her for dinner when he walked in.

"I'm headed home," he said as casually as he could. "Ready, Addison? We can walk together."

She chuckled. "Oh, yes. Let's walk the fifty feet to my place together for safety."

"We do have grizzlies in the area," he reminded her.

"You know, Eli, we haven't seen a grizzly near the house this year," his dad said from behind him. "But you can't ever be too careful, right, honey?" He put his arm over his wife's shoulders.

"Absolutely. Bears. Mean things," his mother answered, a knowing sparkle in her eye. "You just never know when one will appear."

"Really?" Addison said. "I've been here three months, and we haven't had one bear sighting."

Eli took Addison's hand and looped it over his arm. "Let's go before they start to warn you about the attack of the aliens."

She giggled and let him walk her outside the house.

Her soft fingers rested on his forearm as they walked. Crickets chirped in the darkness of the quarter moon. A light breeze whirled the scent of pine around them. The ranch dogs barked from their pens where they slept at night. A couple of horses whinnied from the corral. Peace. His restless soul felt at peace, as though all the pieces of life fit together and formed a picture for his future. He could see walking with Addison like this, holding her hand in his as they talked about the day.

It wasn't as if he didn't feel whole without her. She wasn't a piece of him he was missing. She was the icing on his cake. She made everything nicer, sweeter, and more enjoyable.

"Listen," he started, "I know I was hesitant to participate in the chili contest, but I'm so glad you pushed me to do it."

"I knew you'd win," she said in a confident voice.

"You never even questioned my ability to win, did you?"

She shook her head. "Nope. Never occurred to me."

"Other than my team, I don't know that anyone has ever put so much faith in my abilities."

"Eli." She pulled him to a stop. "You are a fabulous cook, but you're here on your family's ranch mucking stalls. Are mucking and fence repairs really what you want to do? Does ranch work bring you the same joy as cooking? I've watched you work. You're really great with the horses. Calm. Peaceful. Serene. But in the kitchen? You move as though you are liquid silver. Smooth. Confident. Happy. What are you wanting to do?"

He shrugged. "I don't know."

"Why did you come back to Montana? What were you looking for?"

He shrugged again. "That's one of the reasons I

want to go away for a few days. To think. To fish. To just be."

She gave him a warm smile. "Then that's what you should do."

She took a step to continue their walk, but he stopped her. "I want you to go with me."

Addison's heart leapt at his words, even as confusion flooded her mind. The kiss earlier today had been mind-blowing, almost life affirming. If they hadn't been standing in public, with his family around them, she couldn't say where the kiss would have ended, if it would have ended at all. There were a lot of things she didn't know, but she knew beyond a shadow of a doubt that a kiss like he'd given her wasn't a kiss between friends. It suggested more. It demanded more.

The question for her was could she give more? Was she willing to let a man look at her body?

"Addison," he said in a soft voice. "Did you hear me? Will you come with me?"

"Why?" she whispered back, knowing her voice sounded nervous.

"It's simple," he said. "I need you there."

"But, I'm not the same woman you met, the woman you made love to."

He put his hand flat on her chest between her reconstructed breasts. "In here, you haven't changed, except to become a strong warrior. Come with me. Stay with me tonight. Let me love you."

Her stomach quivered from nerves and fear. No man had touched her since Eli. The idea of showing him how she looked now scared the crap out of her.

Because of Addison's type of breast cancer and her age, the mastectomy performed had been non-nipple sparing. Even though Wendy had been able to rebuild Addison's breasts from her own tissue, the surgery had built only nicely rounded globes of flesh on her chest. She had no nipples, no areolas and she never would again. The plan was for Addison to have 3-D nipples and areolas tattooed on her breasts to give them a more normalized appearance. She could only have the external look of a functioning breast, not the internal function. She'd never have the ability to breastfeed a child.

However, nerve endings and breast sensations were another issue altogether. She was fortunate in that her breasts were constructed from her own tissue, not silicone or saline implants. She was also lucky that she had some touch sensation, but nothing like she'd had in her previous life. While she couldn't know this for sure, she felt as if the connection between breast stimulation and her arousal had been severed. Was she ready to test that theory?

"I...I don't know if I'm ready," she confessed.

"No pressure. You're in charge. Nothing will happen that you don't want to happen. But..." He put his hands on her shoulders and turned her to face him. "But I need you in my arms again. I need to feel you against me, your heat warming my soul. Stay with me tonight." He gave her a smile she suspected made women's panties melt...hers included. "You helped pick out my bed. You should at least give it a try."

Her hands shook with nervous energy. Her breaths were labored and noisy. Her knees quivered.

She nodded. "Okay, but I reserve the right to go home later."

"Of course." He leaned forward and stopped. "I'm going to kiss you now, but I promised you'd be in charge. Is that okay?"

"More than okay."

CHAPTER 16

He led her into his house and gestured toward the kitchen. "You want something to drink?"

She shook her head.

"Do you want to watch a little television?"

She could see he was trying to be considerate, trying to let her decide the next steps. She had to smile to herself. With a man like Eli, it had to be difficult to give up control, but he'd done it in the past for her, and he was doing it again, now.

"I'd like to go to your bedroom, Eli."

With the sexiest smile she'd ever seen, he took her hand and led her up the stairs.

Was she really going to do this? Let Eli see her scars? Her imperfections? Eli's body was perfect. His scars weren't ugly like hers.

Nerves whipped the contents of her stomach. Her heart pounded so fiercely her chest wall ached. Her knees were wobbly, barely able to support her.

When they stepped into his bedroom. her breath caught in her throat. "Eli."

"Shh. You're okay. You're in charge."

Was she? She didn't feel like she was. How could she be in charge when her brain refused to think?

He stood behind her, his chest to her back. His mouth pressed against the area behind her ear. Chills rolled down her spine. Her head lolled to the side, exposing more of her neck for him. He kissed the area again. Ran the tip of his tongue along the rim of her ear.

"You are so fucking beautiful," he whispered. "And so fucking out of my league. How can I be so lucky?"

"Wh...what?" she stuttered.

"Beautiful," he said again. "Fucking gorgeous."

He stroked his fingertips down both sides of her neck to her shoulder then skimmed them lightly down her arms. A row of goose bumps rose in their wake. Placing his hands over hers, he linked their fingers.

"I'll take whatever I can, whatever you give me," he whispered in her ear. "Even when I was so angry with you, I could never forget you. I heard your voice in the ocean waves. I heard your sighs with each puff of the wind. I saw your unforgettable face every time I shut my eyes. I never stopped thinking of you."

She leaned into his firm chest. "I'm scared."

He turned her in his arms. "Of me? Of my hurting you?"

"No," she said, with a shake of her head. "We've been together every day for almost a month. I know you're a kind man, Eli. You're gentle and caring, and..." She smiled. "And a little stubborn, but you'd never deliberately hurt me."

"You're scared to show me your body."

Her gaze dropped to the floor. "My breasts are..." A sob caught in her throat.

He put a finger under her chin and lifted her head until their gazes met. "You don't get it, Addison. I'm not in love with your breasts. Never was. Listen to me. Listen closely. I adore you, Addison. Your heart. Your soul. The goodness deep inside you. You. Not your body."

"Yo...you don't like my body?" Fuck. Tears were building in her eyes.

He chuckled. "I fucking love your body, but it's the person inside who holds me captive."

She stepped back out of his grasp. "You need to see me the way I am now."

He shook his head. "I don't. I really don't."

"Yeah, you do." With trembling fingers, she lifted the hem of her shirt.

"Addison."

"No, Eli. I need to do this."

He nodded.

She slowly lifted her shirt and pulled it over her head, exposing her beige, front-closure bra. Before surgery, she'd worn a double D cup, but she'd never liked the way some people—i.e., men—would talk to her breasts instead of her face. Now, she wasn't a double D. She was a solid C. She was happy with the size, but how would he react to her having no nipples? No areolas?

"You are fucking beautiful."

"You don't understand." She shook her head slowly. "You can't understand."

He stepped up to her. "I can try."

He touched her left breast through her bra. She flinched.

"Did that hurt?" Eli's brow wrinkled with concern.

"No. That's the point. I don't have feeling, or much anyway, in my breasts."

"So? There are lots of other areas of your body we can explore." He ran a fingertip down the front of her neck and stopped in the shallow between her clavicles. "So many other areas."

His finger glided over her bra and down her stomach to the waistband of her shorts.

She sucked in her breath as her abdominal muscles quivered under his touch.

He ran his fingers along the band of her shorts, the tips sliding under and back out. "We just have to be creative and find all your erotic spots."

Her core heated. She knew her panties were wet from her arousal. She expected him to unfasten her shorts, to feel her dampness. Instead, to her frustration, he skimmed his fingers around to her rear and slid the palms of his hands over her bottom.

"Nice," he said, his voice rough and gravelly. "You have the best ass in Montana."

She chuckled, even as a rage of desire rolled through her. "Doubtful."

He swatted her bottom playfully. "Don't argue with me. I said so, and so it's true."

She shook her head, but her lips were pulled into a smile.

"Don't move," he ordered and dropped to his knees, all the while raking his short fingernails down the backs of her thighs to her knees. There, his callused finger did a circle behind her left knee, followed by a tracing of the back of her right knee.

She gasped softly. Never had a simple touch felt so erotic, so stimulating. Her knees wobbled, making her widen her stance for stability. After his fingers made a couple of soft circles there, Eli's fingernails drew five lines down the back of her calves to her ankles.

Addison's breaths were labored. Her heart raced from his gentle caresses. Her bones were slowly dissolving under his touches.

Eli dragged his hands around to her ankles. He outlined the bones with the barest touch of his fingers, followed by the tip of his tongue. Her head dropped back with a gasp. Then, placing his palms on the inside of her calves, he slid his hands up her legs to the hem of her shorts, again letting his tongue follow the path made by his hands. Shoving the material out of the way, his hands continued upward toward her center, which was hot and damp.

He dropped his face against the crotch of her shorts. "You smell like heaven."

He drew in a deep breath, and then to her shock, he opened his mouth and placed it on her over her shorts. His hot breath penetrated the material making an already hot area flame.

She swayed, so turned on she could barely remain standing, but damn it, she wasn't going to tell him to stop.

With his mouth on her crotch, his hot breath heating her core, he walked his fingers up to the button and zipper of her shorts. He made quick work of the fasteners, and her shorts slid freely down, stopped only by his mouth. He pulled away, and her shorts quickly pooled on the floor over her feet, leaving her standing in her white lace bra and a pair of white cotton panties... not exactly the seduction attire of a man's dreams.

Still, seeing the powerful man on his knees in front

of her, his face pressed to her crotch was the sexiest thing she'd ever seen. She moaned as she ran her fingernails along his scalp.

But Eli didn't seem to mind as he sucked her through her cotton panties. "I can taste you," he said, his hot breath blowing between her legs. "Damn, I can't get enough of you. I can't forget how much I craved you."

His gaze rolled up until it met hers. He put his fingers in the elastic of her panties and waited.

She bit her bottom lip and nodded.

Slowly, so slowly she wanted to scream, he pulled her panties down her legs. "Lift your left foot."

She did.

"Now, the right."

And then she was standing in front of Eli wearing only her lace bra. She wanted so badly to unhook the snaps, but she didn't feel ready. What if her fake breasts repulsed him? She wanted him so badly, wanted him to continue his sexy exploration of her erotic zones.

His mouth latched onto her pussy, sucking and licking. The sounds of his tongue lashing along her slit, his guttural moans sent surges of mind-blowing lust through her already aroused flesh.

He pushed two fingers into her as the rigid tip of his tongue played with her sensitive nub. His fingers curled, hitting a sensitive spot that made her eyes roll back in her head. His fingers, mouth, and tongue continued their assault with licks, bites, and long sucks.

She groaned as her muscles tensed. An electrical storm whipped around inside her. She rested her hands on his shoulders as she reflexively rose on her toes.

"You're killing me." Her voice was breathy. "I don't know how much more I can take."

His answer was to run the fingers of one hand down her ass crack until he found her puckered opening. He rimmed the hole while increasing the suction on her pussy.

Her legs quaked. Her hips began to pump and move.

"Eli," she gasped out. "I'm going to come."

"Good. That's the whole idea."

His fingers thrust roughly inside her canal while his mouth pulled on her rigid nub.

An energy tempest built inside. She closed her eyes as she was overtaken by wave after wave of an erotic release. It was too much, and not enough. Tears rolled from her eyes as the powerful storm overtook her.

When she could finally open her eyes again, she looked down at Eli, fully dressed, sitting at her feet.

"Fuck. That was incredible," he said. "Fucking beautiful."

He stood and wiped the wetness from her face with his thumb. "Are you okay?"

"Fucking fabulous."

He gave her a warm smile. "How could I have made it better for you?"

"Only thing I can think of is I'd like to have had you inside me."

The smile on his face widened. He shucked his boots, socks, jeans, and shirt like each item was on fire. His hard cock stood upright from its nest of curls, slightly bobbing as if to get her attention.

Oh, that luscious thing didn't have to bob for atten-tion. She couldn't take her gaze off of it. His cock was as she remembered...long and very thick. Her mouth watered at the thought of wrapping itself around his rod.

When she reached out to stroke his shaft, he jerked his hips back.

"Get on my bed," he ordered.

"So bossy," Addison said as she climbed on his bed and scooted to the center.

"I have to warn you," he said. "I'm like a rocket with the engines already fired. I'm not going to last long."

She grinned. "I wasn't exactly Polly Patience myself."

"It's been a while," he confessed as he pulled a condom from the drawer of the table beside his bed.

"Me, too, like over a year other than our weekend."

He stilled. "You're the last woman I've been with."

"No one in California?"

He shook his head. "No. There never has been a special woman, or wasn't until I met you. Even though I left Texas mad with my heart in pieces, I got home to find I didn't want anyone but you. Since I didn't believe that was possible, I found myself between the proverbial rock and a hard place."

"I'm so sorry," she whispered, leaning up to kiss him. "So very, very sorry."

"Not your fault. Hell, it's neither of our faults. I was an ass by walking out, but I thought I was doing the right thing."

She opened her arms and her legs to welcome him. "I need you."

He unrolled the condom down his stiff shaft, another vision that drove the erotic hunger inside her.

Sliding between her open thighs, he paused

momentarily, and then pushed inside her, inch by inch. She felt herself stretching to accommodate his girth. She spread her legs wider. With a final thrust, he filled her and stopped.

His breathing was ragged against her chest. A light sheen covered his forehead.

She wrapped her feet over his calves. "Move, damnit," she said.

He chuckled. "Yes, ma'am."

He pulled back slowly and slammed back into her, pushing her breath from her lungs in a gasp. When he withdrew to begin another push, she felt a powerful wave of energy building inside her again. Her hips gyrated with his thrusts, the force building inside her almost painful in its intensity.

Eli put his fingers on her nub, rubbing it in concert with his thrusts.

"I'm going to come again," she said, the tension almost excruciating.

"Come then," he said. "You're so fucking gorgeous when you come."

His words sent her over, spiraling into a world of flashing lights behind her eyelids and a raw power surging through her.

A couple of thrusts, and he followed her over to his own release.

He lay on her, his breaths coming in rapid pants. "Holy shit. Give me a minute."

Wrapping her arms around him, she said, "You feel good. This feels good."

"This feels right," he said. After a long kiss, he stood and took care of the condom.

He climbed back into the bed and snaked his arm

around her, pulling her tightly against him. As he pulled her into his arms, the trident tattoo on his thick bicep caught her eye. She'd seen the tattoo in November, but now it bore dates. She lifted a hand to touch it.

"Did this hurt?"

He paused and twisted his head to look at his arm. "Not really. Why?"

"And the dates? Those I don't remember."

He nodded. "My service dates. Why? Are you thinking about getting a tattoo?"

She gave a nervous shrug. "Yeah."

"Really? Where? Is it my name? You can trust me."

"Aren't you curious in the least about this?" She waved a hand across her bra, which had remained in place the whole time.

"Of course, I am. I want to know everything about you, but only when you're ready to show me. No pressure. I promised you that."

"Then I think you should see."

Drawing in a deep breath of strength, she unfastened the bra's front clasps. She held the sides together for a minute before she shut her eyes and slipped the straps of the bra down her arms and off. She'd shut her eyes out of fear. What if he hated her reconstructed breasts? What if he thought they looked as fake as she sometimes felt they were?

Callused fingers touched her cheek. "Hey. Why are your eyes shut? Look at me."

"I'm scared," she whispered as she opened her eyes and looked at him.

"You don't have to be scared of anything around me." He lowered his gaze to her chest.

She knew what he saw. Two globes of white flesh parked on her chest. Nothing about them looked like a woman's breasts, other than their placement. If they'd been on her ass, they would have looked like ass cheeks, but these manmade spheres of flesh sat where breast cancer had invaded.

"Interesting," he said.

"What?" Her eyes opened wide. "Interesting?"

"Yeah, totally cool. Can I touch?"

She nodded as her words failed her.

He lightly stroked one, and then the other. "Soft. Perfectly round. Wendy did a nice job. Can you feel me touching you? I've read that sometimes women can regain feelings in their breasts with an autogenous breast reconstruction. I also read it can take time. Can you feel my fingers stroking your soft flesh?"

"You read? About my surgery?"

He nodded. "Don't you understand? I want to know everything about you. I want to understand what you went through, and how I can help."

"But..." She waved her hand around her blobs of flesh pretending to be boobs. "There aren't any nipples or coloring or anything. They don't even look like boobs."

Damn him. He smiled. "Ah. The tattoo question. I've read about 3-D nipple tattoos." He waggled his eyebrows. "You going to do that?"

"I want to, but I'm nervous."

"Won't hurt," he said. "And if you don't want to do tattoos, don't."

"But..."

"Addison, honey, I don't care if you have nipples tattooed on or not. When you're dressed, no one will know one way or the other. And, if I have my way, I'm the only one whose bed you'll share. I'm the only guy who'll be lucky enough to see you nude." He turned her to face him. "Don't you get it yet? I love you. I love your body, but I love your heart more. I think one of the reasons I was so angry at you was that I fell so fast and hard at Zane's wedding. I don't do things like that, but when we touched..."

"We connected," she finished softly.

He nodded.

She swallowed hard. "That weekend, when we met, I felt like I'd waited my whole life for you. I told myself that my feelings were crazy-lady over the top, but I couldn't help it. But, and don't laugh, I felt like I'd met my soulmate in you."

"Yes," he said emphatically. "That's exactly what I felt. Now, imagine feeling that and thinking I was married."

Her brow furrowed. "I would have died."

"Exactly." He pulled her tightly against him. "I'm not much of a religious man. I've seen too much death and destruction, but I believe in fate, and I believe fate knew we should be together. Not like halves of a whole, you-complete-me sort of way. You're your own woman, but you make me a better man. Stronger. More confident. I don't know how I would've faced the rest of my life if I hadn't found you here."

With a chuckle, she said, "You might not spill so much beer."

He squeezed her. "Spilt beer is such a tragedy," he teased with a mournful tone.

"I thought of you every day, every night. Even though I was so hurt, I prayed that you'd be safe. I honestly hadn't planned to be here when you got home." She slapped his chest playfully. "That's what you get for coming home early."

He laughed and then sobered. "Thank the universe for keeping you here." He kissed her. "I love you, Addison."

She gave him a nod. "I love you, too."

The next morning, Eli woke early and slipped out of the bed without waking Addison. They'd talked long into the night, or rather into the morning. He'd been surprised when she told him she'd didn't have plans to return to Florida, just as she'd been shocked when he'd confessed he'd been looking around the Orlando area for employment opportunities. They hadn't decided where they'd live, but they were sure they wanted to be together.

Eli was whistling as he walked into the barn. Zane snorted.

"By the look on your face, I'm thinking I'll be getting no work out of you today."

"Probably not. I'm packing to go camping for a week."

"And I'm thinking you're not camping alone."

Eli grinned. "Maybe not."

Zane returned his grin. "Wendy tells me that Addison is head over heels for you."

"Why didn't you tell me that before today?"

"Couldn't. Wendy threatened to turn off the fun factory if I did."

"Fun factory?" Eli laughed. "Does she know you think of her as your fun factory?"

"Who do you think made up that name?" his older brother said with a broad smile. "So, you and Addison, huh?"

"Me and Addison."

"You owe me, bro."

"How do you figure that?"

Zane pointed to his chest. "My wedding. Without that, you'd have never met her."

"I owe your wife, you mean. Addison was her friend, and your wife and her sister saved Addison's life. It's Wendy I owe."

"We'll take it in cash," Zane joked.

The two brothers were walking toward the juncture where the new barn had been built when the sound of crunching gravel echoed down the barn aisle.

"Early for deliveries," Eli said.

"Not really. Prince Albert's owner is having a special oat feed shipped in for him."

Eli shook his head. "Prince Albert. He is one spoiled gent."

"You know it. Come on. I'll give you the honor of mucking his stall."

"Gee, thanks," Eli said with a laugh.

Addison woke and stretched her arms over her head. Even though Eli wasn't in the bed, this time she knew he hadn't left. She was in his bed and had spent the night in his arms. She pulled herself from the soft sheets and headed for his shower. Wow. Muscles she hadn't used in a while protested.

A hot shower did wonders for her body. There was nothing that could help her spirit be happier. Eli loved her. He was more fascinated by her boobs than she was. She chuckled as she remembered his close inspection of Wendy's work. He marveled at the texture as well as the barely there scarring. He loved the idea of the tattoos, but hadn't pushed her one way or the other. It was totally her decision. However, he did say that he'd go with her if she decided to proceed, promising he'd get another one too, so they could heal together.

She grinned at the memory. He was such a nut.

But yeah, she was so getting those 3-D nipple tattoos.

In the kitchen, she was sipping on her first cup of coffee when someone looked in the window of the porch. She barely had time to register the Peeping Tom before there was a knock at the front door. Probably Wendy. Eli wouldn't knock on his own door.

She opened the door and stepped back in shock. "What are you doing here?"

Denis pushed his way into the living room. "I've come to take you home. You've been here long enough. Your friend Millie tells me you're well, so it's time to go."

"What?"

She was still in shock at seeing her ex standing in front of her. He didn't look good, either. His usually tanned skin was sallow. His hair had thinned on top. And had he put on weight? His gut stuck out over the waist of his slacks.

He grabbed her arm. "Go pack, and let's get going. I want to get back to Texas today so we can renew our vows tonight. I forgive you for everything."

"What? Are you insane?" She jerked her arm, but he clamped down tighter.

"I'm hurt, darling." His voice held a fake sincerity she recognized. He'd used it for years to make her feel guilty and keep her doing what he wanted. "You've forgotten it's our wedding anniversary, a perfect time to retake our vows and resume our life together."

"Why in the world would you think I'd marry you again? You're delusional."

His face saddened. "I know I said some horrible things, but I was in shock. Complete shock. My beautiful young wife with breast cancer, an old lady disease. You have to realize I wasn't in my right mind."

Old lady disease? What the hell? She tugged at her arm again. "Let me go, Denis."

"So, you can pack," he said, as though it were a statement of fact, not a question of intent.

He really was crazy. When she laughed in his face, his complexion darkened and his mouth pulled tight. "I'm not kidding, Addison. You want kids. I can give you those. Who else would want a woman who wasn't a real woman? I'm willing to take you back and give you all the squalling brats you can manage." He pulled a gun from the pocket of his jacket. "Fuck. Leave your clothes here. You can buy more. Get in the car. I've got a private plane waiting."

Denis had left the front door open. A mistake on his part. Eli and Zane stood in the door. Eli's face wore a mask of rage. She didn't think she'd ever seen Eli look like this.

"Get. Your. Fucking. Hands. Off. My. Fiancée." Each word was said in a menacing, threatening tone.

Denis whirled around, yanking Addison along. "This is none of your business. My wife and I are leaving." Denis waved the gun in the air as a threat.

"No." Again, Eli's tone was deadly.

Denis stepped forward, apparently sure Addison would follow, as she used to do. This time, she froze in place as though her feet were glued to the floor, despite his grip on her arm.

"If you want to walk out of here alive, set the gun down and release Addison. If you don't, there's a strong possibility you'll be carried out by stretcher." Eli shook his head slowly. "Dead or alive. It's your choice."

Denis's nostrils flared, and he turned to Addison. "I need you."

"You need my money," Addison corrected.

"You and your money are one and the same," Denis said. "We had a good life. We can again."

While her ex's attention was focused on Addison, Eli flew across the short space, grabbed Denis and threw him violently to the hardwood floor. Addison fell also, her ex refusing to release her arm. On the floor, Denis's grip lessened enough Addison could pull free.

"Eli, the gun," Addison shouted as Denis's fingers wrapped around the handle.

The sound of a shotgun being racked had Denis freezing.

"Yeah, buddy. My gun's bigger than yours," Eli said as he pointed the barrel of a shotgun at Denis's head.

Zane placed his booted foot on Denis's hand and rested his entire body weight on that one foot.

"You're breaking my hand," Denis whined. "I'm going to sue you."

Zane laughed. "Okay."

"Addison, do something," Denis ordered.

"Okay," she said, and kicked Denis in the stomach. She'd been right. He had a lot more cushion than she remembered. "Let go of the gun, Denis. They will kill you. Eli has killed before, right, honey?"

Eli grinned. "Yep, and ready to do it again if this bastard doesn't let go of that gun."

"Get this oaf off my hand," Denis whined.

"Oaf? I think I'm offended," Zane said, and applied more pressure to Denis's hand.

"You know, I think my brother will stay right where he is," Eli said. "Addison, can you call the sheriff? Tell him we have a garbage pickup."

Two hours later, the interviews were over, and Denis had been hauled away. Eli's living room was filled with his parents, his brother, his sister-in-law, and the woman he planned to spend the rest of his life with. He was sitting in his recliner, Addison on his lap, his arms around her waist. He couldn't bear having her more than a few inches away.

"Well, Eli," his mother said. "You sure brought some excitement home with you."

His dad chuckled. "I'll say. I haven't seen a show-down like that since I ran off your mother's other suiter back in the day."

Betty laughed and swatted her husband. "We promised never to tell that story."

Eli grinned and tightened his arms around Addison.

"I have a question," Zane said, raising his hand like they were in a classroom.

"Shoot." Eli cringed. "Bad choice of words. What?"

"Fiancée?"

Eli frowned in confusion. "What are you talking about?"

"You called Addison your fiancée. You two have some news to share?"

Addison's face flushed.

Eli swallowed. "I...well...I..."

He looked at Addison.

Her smiled gave him the encouragement.

"I haven't exactly asked her yet," Eli said.

"So, ask," Wendy said, leaning forward, her elbows on her knees and her chin in her hand. "We'll wait."

His parents chuckled.

Zane guffawed.

Wendy batted her eyelashes at them.

"Addison," he said.

"Yes," she screamed.

"I didn't ask you anything."

"Oh, right. Sorry. You were saying."

Eli grinned. This woman. She was going to change his life in so many ways.

"Addison, my love, will you marry me?"

She tapped her mouth as though thinking of an answer.

He pinched her side, which made her wiggle in his lap.

She threw her arms around his neck. "Yes, yes, yes. A thousand times yes." She leaned in and kissed him.

"Aww," Zane said.

"I knew it," Betty announced with finality. "I knew you two were perfect together when I saw you at Zane's wedding. I just don't understand why it took so long for you both to realize what was so obvious to everyone else."

"You're right, mom," Eli said. "When it's right, it's right."

"And this is right," Addison said.

"Hey, do I get to drive your Ferrari now that I'm going to be your husband?"

"Hell, no," Addison said.

Eli laughed along with his family as he squeezed Addison tightly.

He was home.

He was safe.

He was in love.

Nothing could top that.

Nothing.

FROM THE AUTHOR

Thank for reading Hot SEAL, Sweet & Spicy. I appreciate my readers. Without you, I wouldn't be here.

Readers are always asking: What can I do to help you?

My answer is always the same: PLEASE give me an honest review. Every review helps.

Cynthia

Acknowledgments

They say it takes a village to raise a child. Well, it took a team of medical professionals, friends, and fellow breast cancer survivors to raise this book!

As some of you are aware, I was diagnosed with Triple Negative Breast Cancer (TNBC) in 2015 and again in 2020. While the heroine in this book has had TNBC, her experience (and treatment) does not mimic mine, so I want to make clear that this book is NOT autobiographical.

I have to publicly thank fellow author, breast cancer survivor, and breast cancer researcher Dana Brantley-Sieders for all the ZOOM conversations and private messages, not to mention the "delicate" sex questions! Thanks, Dana.

Thank you to Lauren Tilley, PA with Dr. James Yuen at the University of Arkansas Medical Sciences for all our chats about the challenges my heroine would face after having an Autologous Breast Reconstruction. Yeah, no horse rides for her!

Thank you for Dr. James Yuen for your excellent surgery skills!

and **SUPER HUGE Thank You** to Cindy Kirk for her afternoon writing sprints with me. I'm not sure I could have done it without you

ABOUT THE AUTHOR

 New York Times and USA Today Bestselling author Cynthia D'Alba started writing on a challenge from her husband in 2006 and discovered having imaginary sex with lots of hunky men was fun. She was born and raised in a small Arkansas town. After being gone for a number of years, she's thrilled to be making her home back in Arkansas living in a vine-covered cottage on the banks of an eight-thousand acre lake. When she's not reading or writing or plotting, she's doorman for her border collie, cook, housekeeper and chief bottle washer for her husband and slave to a noisy, messy parrot. She loves to chat online with friends and fans.

You can find her most days at one of the following online homes:

Website: cynthiadalba.com
Facebook:Facebook/cynthiadalba
Twitter:@cynthiadalba
Pinterest: Pinterest/CynthiaDAlba
Newsletter:NewsletterSign-Up
Street Team:D'Alba Diamonds
Or drop her a line at cynthia@cynthiadalba.com

Or send snail mail to: Cynthia D'Alba PO Box 2116
Hot Springs, AR 71914

Single Title

Hot SEAL, Alaskan Nights

Hot SEAL, Confirmed Bachelor

Hot SEAL, Secret Service (novella)

Hot SEAL, Sweet & Spicy

Hot SEAL, Labor Day

Brotherhood Protectors

(Part of Elle James Brotherhood Series)

Texas Ranger Rescue

Texas Marine Mayhem

Read on for excerpts from
other Hot SEAL books
by
Cynthia D'Alba

HOT SEAL, COLD BEER

DIAMOND LAKES, TEXAS BOOK 2

An ex-Navy SEAL agrees to play fake lover for the Maid of Honor at a destination wedding only to discover that what happens on a Caribbean Island can sometimes follow you home.

Nicholas Falcone, aka Nikko, aka Falcon, is five months out from active SEAL duty, putting his pre-service accounting degree to use while going to law school at night. He'd love to take a vacation between semesters, but every buck is earmarked for his education. When a fellow accountant approaches him about his sister needing an escort for a destination wedding, Nikko jumps at the idea. With the wedding families footing the bill, what does he have to lose?

Surgeon Dr. Jennifer Pierce is still stinging from a broken engagement. Going to a destination wedding at the Sand Castle Resort in the Caribbean would be great if only her ex-fiancé and his new wife weren't also attending. Her options are to find a date or not go, but not going isn't really an option. That means letting her brother set her up with a guy from his accounting office...Heaven forbid. When did accountants start looking like this?

** Cold Beer ** is part of the Diamond Lakes, Texas Series and Sand Castle Resort series. Each book can be read as a stand-alone. They do not have cliffhanger endings.

Hot SEAL, Cold Beer is also in the "SEALs in Paradise" connected series. Each book in the multi-author branded SEALs in Paradise series can be read stand-alone, and individual books do not have to be read in any particular order.

Read on for an excerpt:

If there was one thing Dr. Jennifer Pierce hated, it was not being in control. She'd rather tell people what to do than be told. She despised surprises and was much more comfortable in situations where she had all the information. And, most importantly, she maintained a firm discipline over all emotions, especially her own.

However, right now, she was as nervous as a first-year med student holding a scalpel in surgery, and that irritated her, which only amped up her anxiety.

She agitated the martini shaker violently, the ice clanging against the stainless-steel container like a hail storm. After pouring the dry martini into a glass, she took a long, steadying sip.

Yeah, that didn't help her nerves.

On the other hand, the stiff drink didn't hurt, either.

With a resigned sigh, she walked to the living room and sat to await Nicholas Falcone. Her brother, Robert, had suggested Falcone as her potential date for a fast-approaching destination wedding. She loved her twin brother and trusted him...mostly. Because historically, the men he believed perfect for her had been so far off the mark as to be not even in the same book, much less on the same page. But she was between a rock and a slab of granite.

All she knew about this Falcone guy was he worked at McKenzie, Gladwell and Associates with her brother and had been a Navy SEAL. Weren't they called jarheads? Hell, she didn't know. She took another gulp of the cold vodka. What she knew about the military wouldn't fill a shot glass.

She'd give her brother credit for one thing. If Falcone's online photo was anywhere accurate, Nicholas Falcone looked the part she needed him to play. When Robert had called her to tell her about his solution to her dateless dilemma, she'd pulled up her brother's accounting firm on the internet to look at the staff photos and had been pleasantly surprised. The picture had been of a gorgeous guy with a neatly trimmed beard, a sexy smile, and mischievous eyes.

Man, she hoped he could carry on a decent conversation and not grunt answers to everything.

Her doorbell pealed, and her heart jumped in response. Pressing her hand over her quaking stomach, she drew in a calming breath, not that a calming breath had ever helped. So she took the next best option to deep breathing and finished off her martini.

Carrying her empty glass with her, she opened the door and looked at her potential blind date. Her brain hiccuped or maybe quit functioning altogether. He didn't look at all like she'd expected and prepared for. In person, he was...more. A whole lot more. With his chiseled cheeks and sharp chin, he was a million times more attractive in real life. His green eyes—a billion times more beautiful than that black-and-white photo showed—held an amused twinkle that coordinated handsomely with his amused smile. And his body? Dear lord. Broad shoulders pulled a white, oxford shirt tightly across them. Long sleeves rolled to mid-forearm exposed thick, ropey muscles that bunched and flexed when he extended his hand.

"Dr. Pierce. I'm Nikko Falcone."

She stepped back, embarrassed that she'd been staring at him. "Of course. I'm sorry. I was...never mind. Not important. Come in."

He lowered his hand and stepped into her foyer. The roomy area shrank. She'd expected tall and well-built, but the degree of just how brawny he was registered with a clunk upside her head.

Taking a step back, she gestured with her martini glass. "I'm having a drink. Can I fix you something?"

"A cold beer, if you have one."

"Sure. Have a seat." She flipped her hand toward the living room.

Beer in her refrigerator wasn't the norm. She wasn't much of a beer drinker, but since she hadn't known much about Nicholas Falcone's drink preferences—or anything at all about him really—she'd stocked a six-pack of beer as well as red wine, white wine, and the makings for any mixed drink imaginable. Always prepared, was her motto.

She would have made a hell of a boy scout.

She pulled out a cold bottle, cracked off the top, and got a chilled beer stein from her freezer. While she was there, she also poured herself a fresh vodka martini. Realizing she had too many items and not enough hands, she loaded everything on a tray and went back to the living room.

"I brought you a glass," she said, setting the tray on the glass coffee table in front of him. She lifted her martini and took the chair across from him.

"Bottle's fine," he said and took a long draw off the bottle.

She hid her discomfort with his drinking beer straight from the bottle. The people at the destination wedding they would be attending ran in high-society circles. Beer from bottles had been fine back in college, but now that they were all in their thirties, she was sure her friends, like her, had progressed to more sophisticated drinks and glasses.

Mentally, she made a note to talk with him about appearances.

He leaned back on her white sofa, stretched his arm across the back, and crossed an ankle over his knee.

That's when she saw a tattoo peeking out from where the sleeve of his white oxford had been rolled up. From this distance, she could make out tines. A trident? As a doctor, she knew all about the infections that went with tattoos, and she wanted to disapprove. Instead, she got a little turned on. She didn't like that, or she shouldn't like that.

Damn. He had her all confused.

"So," she said, trying to gather her wits and the reins to the conversation. "What did Robert tell you?"

"In a nutshell, you had a fiancé. A big-time corporate lawyer. Said legal-eagle dirtbag got his secretary pregnant. Married her. Dumped you when he got back from his honeymoon. That about right?"

She winced. "In a nutshell."

He lifted the bottle to his lips—which she couldn't help notice were full and soft. Of course she noticed. She was a doctor. She always observed the human body...especially one like this.

He swallowed. His Adam's apple rose and fell with the action.

She had to get her air conditioning fixed. This room was too warm.

Hot SEAL, Black Coffee
A Dallas Debutante/SEALs in Paradise/McCool
Trilogy (Book 1)

Dealing with a sexy ex-girlfriend, a jewel heist, and a murder-for-hire can make an ex-SEAL bodyguard a tad cranky.

Trevor Mason accepts what should be a simple job...protect the jewels his ex-girlfriend will wear to a breast cancer fundraiser. As founder and owner of Eye Spy International, he should send one of his guys, but he needs to get his ex out of his system and this is the perfect opportunity to remind himself that she is a spoiled, rich debutante who dumped him with a Dear John letter during his SEAL training.

Respected breast cancer doctor Dr. Risa McCool hates being in the limelight for her personal life. Her life's work is breast cancer treatment and research, which she'd rather be known for than for her carefree, partying debutante years. She agrees to be the chair-person for the annual breast cancer fundraiser even though it means doing publicity appearances and interviews, all while wearing the famous pink Breast Cancer Diamond for each public event. The multi-million dollar value of the pink stone requires an armed body-guard at all times.

Past attractions flame, proving to be a distraction to the serious reality of the situation. When Risa and the millions in diamonds go missing, nothing will stop Trevor from bringing her home, with or without the jewels.

At two-thirty Monday afternoon, Dr. Risa McCool's world shifted on its axis. He was back. She wasn't ready. But then, would she ever be ready?

Four hours passed before she was able to disengage from work and go home. As she pulled under the portico of her high-rise building and the condo valet hurried out to park her eight-year-old sedan, her stomach roiled at the realization that Trevor Mason—high school and college boyfriend and almost fiancé—would be waiting for her in her condo, or at least should be. She pressed a shaking hand to her abdomen and inhaled a deep, calming breath. It didn't work. There was still a slight quiver to her hands as she grabbed her purse and briefcase from the passenger seat.

She paused to look in the mirror. A tired brunette looked back at her. Dark circles under her eyes. Limp hair pulled into a ponytail at the back of her head. Pale lips. Paler cheeks. Not one of her better looks.

Would he be the same? Tall with sun-kissed hair and mesmerizing azure-blue eyes?

Tall, sure. That was a given.

Eye color would have to be the same, but his sun-bleached hair? His muscular physique? In high school and college, he'd played on the offense for their high school and college football teams, but she had never really understood what he did. Sometimes he ran and sometimes he hit other guys. What she remembered were strong arms and a wide chest. Would those be the same?

Almost fifteen years had passed since she'd last seen him. He hadn't come back for their tenth nor their fifteenth high school reunions. The explanation for his absences involved SEAL missions to who knew where. Risa had wondered if she'd ever see him again, whether he'd make it through all his deployments and secret ops.

Well, he had and now she had to work with him.

She took a deep breath and slid from the car.

"Good Evening, Dr. McCool," the valet said.

"Evening, John. Do you know if my guest arrived?"

"Yes, ma'am. About four hours ago."

"Do you know if the groceries were delivered?"

"Yes, ma'am. Cleaning service has also been in."

"Thank you. Have a nice evening."

"You, too."

She acknowledged the guard on duty at the desk with a nod and continued to the private residents-only elevator that opened to a back-door entrance to her condo. After putting her key in the slot, she pressed the button for the forty-first floor and then leaned against the wall for the ride.

Her anxiety at seeing Trevor climbed as the

elevator dinged past each floor. It was possible, even probable, that she had made a mistake following her mother's advice to employ his company. She was required to have a bodyguard for every public event since the announcement of the pink Breast Cancer Diamond. Her insurance company insisted on it. The jewelry designer demanded it. And worse, her mother was adamant on a guard. How did one say no to her mother?

Plus, as head of the Dallas Area Breast Cancer Research Center, she'd been tasked with wearing that gaudy necklace with a pink diamond big enough to choke a horse for the annual fundraising gala. The damn thing was worth close to fifteen or twenty million and was heavy as hell. Who'd want it?

The elevator dinged one last time and the doors slid open. She stepped into a small vestibule and let herself into her place expecting to see Trevor.

Only, she didn't.

Instead there was music—jazz to be specific. She followed the sounds of Stan Getz to her balcony, her heart in her throat.

A man sat in a recliner facing the night lights of Dallas, a highball in one hand, a cigar in the other.

"I'm glad to see you stock the good bourbon," he said, lifting the glass, but not turning to face her. "And my brand, too. Should I be impressed?"

Her jaw clenched. Their fights had always been about money—what she had and what he didn't.

"I don't know," she said. "Are you impressed?"

He took a drag off the cigar and chased the smoke down his throat with a gulp of hundred-dollar bourbon. "Naw. You can afford it."

"Are you going to look at me or will my first conversation with you in fifteen years be with the back of your head?"

After stabbing out the cigar, he finished his drink, sat it on the tile floor, and rose. Lord, he was still as towering and overwhelming as she remembered him. At five-feet-ten-inches, Risa was tall, but Trevor's height made her feel positively petite. As he turned, every muscle in her body tensed as she stood unsure whether she was preparing to fight him, flee from him or fuck him.

"Hello, Risa."

Hot SEAL, Alaskan Nights
A SEALs in Paradise Novel

From NYT and USA Today Best Selling Author comes a beach read that isn't the typical sun-drenched location. Homer, Alaska. A Navy SEAL on leave. A nurse practitioner in seclusion. A jealous ex-lover looking for redemption...or is it revenge?

Navy SEAL Levi Van der Hayden, aka Dutch, returns to his family home in Homer, AK for the three Rs...rest, relaxation and recovery. As the only SEAL injured during his team's last mission, the last thing he wants to do is show his bullet wound to friends...it's in his left gluteus maximus and he's tired of being the butt of all the jokes (his own included.)

After a violent confrontation with a controlling, narcissistic ex-lover, nurse practitioner Bailey Brown flees Texas for Alaska. A maternal grandmother still in residence provides her with the ideal sanctuary...still in the U.S. but far enough away to escape her ex's reach.

Attracted to the cute nurse from his welcome home beach party, Levi insists on showing her the real Alaska experience. When her safety is threatened, he must use all his SEAL skills to protect her and eliminate the risk, even if it means putting his own life on the line.

———

Levi Van der Hayden's left butt cheek was on fire. He shifted uncomfortably in the back seat of the sub-compact car masquerading as their Uber ride. As soon as he moved, the stitches in his left thigh reminded him that pushing off with that leg was also mistake.

"We should try to get upgraded when we get to the airport," Compass said.

Compass, also known as Levi's best friend Rio North, was going way out of his way to help Levi get home leave, but at this moment, Levi gritted his teeth at the ridiculous suggestion.

"I don't have the money for that and you know it." Levi, aka Dutch to his SEAL team buds, knew he shouldn't be so grumpy what with all Compass was doing for him but damn it! Why did he have to be shot in the ass? The guys would never let him live it down.

He repositioned his hips so most of the weight was on his uninjured right butt cheek.

"You bring anything for the pain, Dutch?"

"Took something about an hour ago, which right now seems like last week."

The car stopped at the Departure gates of San

Diego International Airport. Dutch climbed from the back seat of the way-too-tiny car with a few choice cuss words and stood on the sidewalk. Compass paid the driver and then hefted out two duffle bags. After slinging both onto his shoulders, he gestured toward the airport with his chin.

Once inside, Compass said, "Seriously Dutch, you need to upgrade. There is no way you are going to be able to stretch out and you know what the doctor said about pulling those stitches."

Levi glared at his friend and answered him with a one-finger response.

Compass grinned back him. "All joking aside, I'll pay for your upgrade. Your ass literally *needs* to be in first class." The asshole then leaned back and glanced down at Levi's ass...well actually the cheek where he'd been shot coming back from their last fucking mission.

"No, damn it, Compass, I already told you I can't afford it and I'm not accepting charity." Levi knew his friend could afford to upgrade Levi to a big, roomy, first-class seat, but he was already taking Compass way out of his way with this trip. When his friend opened his mouth to speak, Levi held up a hand to stop him. "Not even from you. I appreciate it, man, I really do, but no." Levi shook his head emphatically. "I fucking hate being such a pain in your ass, har har har."

To say Levi had been the target of his SEAL team buddies' relentless butt jokes would be an understatement. They'd been brutal in the way only people who love you can. Levi knew that. Understood that. And would have been there throwing out the butt and ass jokes if it'd been anyone else who'd gotten shot in the ass, but it wasn't. It was him and he was tired of it. He lowered himself carefully onto a bench.

Compass looked around and then back to Levi. "Okay, look, I'm going to go talk to the agent over there. I'm not spending a dime, but sometimes they let active duty get upgrades. Let me see what I can do. Okay?"

Levi followed Compass's gaze to an attractive brunette behind the Delta service counter. He chuckled. "Damn man, you could pick up a woman anywhere, couldn't you?"

Compass shrugged, but his grin said he knew exactly what Levi was talking about. "It's a God-given talent. But that's not what this is about. Give me your military ID."

Levi pulled out his card, but hesitated. Compass had more money than God, Dropping an thousand or so dollars to change a plane ticket was probably pocket change to him, but not to Levi.

Compass jerked Levi's military card out his hand with a snort. "Shit that damaged ass muscle has fucked up your reflexes."

"Fuck you, man. It's the pain meds." Levi narrowed his eyes at his best friend. "Not a penny, Compass, not a fucking penny. Got it?"

"Loud and clear." Compass pointed to him. "Stay here and look pathetic."

Compass had only taken a few steps before Levi heard him laugh. God damn asshole.

Jesus, he hated this. Not only was he in pain, but the damn doctors had restricted him from lifting anything over twenty pounds. Twenty pounds! Like he was some fucking girl or something. He was a Navy SEAL. He could lift twenty pounds with his toes...or could before just moving his toes made the exit wound on his thigh ache.

Now that their last mission was behind them—he groaned at his own bad joke—the team had a little time off, which meant he could finally go home for a few days. However, the restrictions from the doctors meant someone had to help him with his duffle bag since it definitely weighed more than twenty pounds. He was pissed off and embarrassed by that limit to his activities. Hell, even jogging was off his activities list until the stitches healed a little more.

He'd been ordered to do medical follow-up at the Alaskan VA Health Clinic. Knowing his commander, Skipper would follow up on that, and if Levi didn't follow orders, his ass would be grass. He groan again and ordered himself to stop with the ass jokes.

Turning his attention back to the action across the lobby Levi watched Compass operate. He was too far away to hear the conversation, but he knew his friend's M.O. well. He'd smile. He'd compliment the woman. Then he'd toss in his best friend's war wound for sympathy. Levi snorted to himself. He'd seen Compass in action too many times to count.

Compass leaned toward the Delta agent and Levi was sure the poor woman had been sucked into Compass's charismatic gravitational pull. She didn't stand a chance against a pro like Compass.

When Compass set both of their duffle bags on the scale and the airline agent tagged them, Levi was at least sure he was going home. What he didn't know was if it would be in the front of the plane or the back of the plane. If it weren't for his ass and leg, he wouldn't care where he sat, but he knew that wasn't true for his friend, who always went first-class when he could.

Compass turned from the check-in desk and started toward Levi with a broad smile he'd seen before when Compass got what he wanted.

Levi eyed him. "Why do you have a shit-eating grin on your face? What did you do?"

"I'm smiling because I'm a fucking magic man." He handed Levi a boarding pass.

Levi studied the boarding pass with first class all in capital letters. "Did you buy this?" His lips tightened into a straight line.

Compass help up his hands. "Nope. Not a penny spent. I swear on my mother's grave."

"Your mother is alive, asshole."

"Yeah, but we have a family plot and we all have real estate allotted. I swear *I* didn't spend a single dime on that ticket man. That pretty little thing over there hooked you up." He motioned over to Brittany who was busy with another customer.

"Sir, are you ready?"

Levi's gaze fell on an attendant pushing a wheel-chair. "What the fuck?"

Hot SEAL, Confirmed Bachelor
A SEALs in Paradise Novel

When a Navy SEAL runs into an obstacle, he climbs over it, under it, around it, or destroys it. So what if it's a woman?

Master Chief Benjamin Blackwell has it all. Adventure, good looks, skills, and women. His life is perfect and he has no intention of changing a thing. Until *her*.

Holly Maxwell is a sexy woman unlike anyone he's met before. A widow for ten years, she's happy with her life even with the trials of raising a pre-teen daughter, and being the only girl in a nosy, boisterous family of Coronado cops.

But what makes her so inexplicable to this Navy SEAL is her total lack of interest in *him*.

"What can I get you ladies?" the server asked as she set cardboard coasters on the table.

"I've got this," Bethany said. "Bring us one, no wait, two pitchers of margaritas-on -the-rocks, and two tequila shots each."

"Are you kidding me?" Holly asked. "Shots?"

Bethany waved her off. "Make that Herradura Silver for those shots."

"You got it," the woman said. "My name's Liz. Be back."

The woman walked toward the bar to place the order.

"First, shots?" Holly asked. "And second, dropping tequila names?"

Bethany laughed. "Trust me. This is sipping tequila. You'll love it. Besides, it's our first night out as family sisters. We are cel-e-brat-ting."

"Remember, I'm driving," Holly said.

"No problem. We'll get you home if you can't drive."

Liz returned. "Okay, ladies. Here we go. Two pitchers of margaritas-on-the-rocks and six shots of Herradura Silver." She set empty margarita glasses on the table. "What else can I get for you?"

"I think we're good," Bethany said. She picked up the pitcher and filled each glass. Then she lifted hers in a toast. "To having the sisters I've always wanted in my life."

"Awww," Holly said and fake sniffed. She clinked her glass to Bethany's.

"You say that now," Diana joked. "Just wait until we drop the boys at your house for the weekend. Then, let's hear what you have to say about family."

The three women toasted with laughter and drank.

That was only the first toast. For the next hour, every freshly poured drink started a new round of toasts. As Bethany had warned, Holly found that the tequila shots slid down her throat like melted butter. Smooth and tasty.

The first round of pitchers and shots lasted almost an hour. Diana offered to buy the next round. After a serious discussion, the ladies decided that changing drinks would be a mistake, so they placed an order for two more pitchers of fresh margaritas. However, Holly suggested—and both women agreed—that there should be nine shots of tequila this time....three for each of them.

They had just toasted to the moon landing in the sixties when Bethany whistled. "Wow. Remember how I said I'd do Tuck-the-bartender for one-hundred K? Well, check out what just walked in the door. I think I'm going to melt off my seat."

Diana followed Bethany's gaze and moaned. "Oh, yeah. He is something. I'm thinking Navy. Maybe SEAL. Patrick would kick my ass for saying this, but Patrick who? That guy is totally yummy."

Facing the bar put Holly's back toward the door. She laughed at her tablemates. "Seriously? No guy looks that good." She turned in her seat and almost dropped her drink in her lap. She whipped back around. "Shit, shit, shit."

"What's wrong?" Bethany asked. She studied the

guy closer. "Hey, Diana. Does that guy look about six-three?"

"I'd say so."

"Silver hair. Body to die for?"

"Yep," Diana said. "Can't see his eye color, but I'm guessing blue. What about you, Holly?"

"Don't call him over here," Holly said.

"Ben!" Bethany yelled. "Ben. Over here." She giggled. "He's coming this way. You were right, Holly. He's totally luscious."

Holly sprang from her chair and rushed to head him off. When she reached him, she threw her arms around his neck and pulled him close in hug.

"Please play along," she whispered in his ear. "It's a long story, and I don't have time to explain, but we're dating. Please."

Hot SEAL, Secret Service
A SEALs in Paradise Novella

As a Navy SEAL, and then as a Secret Service agent, Liam Ghost's best work is done out of the spotlight. When he's assigned to the Vice President's daughter, the magnetic pull between them leads to a hot, passionate affair. But the public attention on him, and on them, shines too bright a light and he backs away into shadows, leaving both of them pining for what they lost.

Liz Chanel is used to the being in the public eye. Through her formative years, her father served as state governor, senator and now vice president. When she falls for a member of her secret service detail, she feels every piece of her life is perfect...until her lover walks away. Even though she doesn't need the money, she jumps back into her modeling career in an effort forget Liam.

During an intense reelection campaign for her father, Liz is snatched off the runaway and held to force her father off the ticket.

Liam assembles a team of ex-SEALs to go get his woman back from the kidnappers, and maybe talk her back into his life.

———

"You know if this goes sideways and I get hurt, my wife is going to kill me. I promised this weekend would include nothing dangerous," said ex-Navy SEAL Nicholas "Falcon" Falcone. "And that I'd make it home by Christmas morning."

"Where did you say you were going?" asked Liam Ghost, aka Dagger One for this mission, aka ex-Secret Service and ex-SEAL.

"A SEAL convention."

The other three ex-SEALs seated on the floor in the back of the transport aircraft laughed along with Dagger One.

"At Christmas? She believed we hold conventions on Christmas Eve? And how did you explain why she couldn't come?" asked Levi Van der Hayden, aka Dutch.

"Didn't have to explain anything to Jen. She trusts me." He shook his head. "Actually, she knows me too well. She kissed me and told me she was going to buy herself a new Benz as a Christmas present from me while I was gone."

Dutch and Banger laughed.

Liam, who'd met Falcon's wife, nodded and asked, "Which one?"

"Who knows? She has expensive tastes so my money is on whichever model is the most expensive."

Liam chuckled. "In that case, my money's on a two-seater convertible."

"Five minutes to target," the pilot said into his mic.

"Man, I hate HALOs. I figured I was done with those when I left teams," said Heath "Banger" Diver.

HALO, otherwise known as high altitude-low opening jump, was one of the least favorite activities for most SEALs.

"Sorry, guys. It was this or a ten-mile hike in the snow with a steep, vertical ascent," Liam said.

"How good's the intel?" Dutch asked.

"Fairly solid. There are other teams being dispatched to other locations, but from the latest debrief, I think we've got the hot spot. Check your gear, gentlemen. Out the door in one minute. And before I forget, thanks for this. I know it's almost Christmas. You're doing me solid. I won't forget." Liam fist bumped each guy. "I promise you'll be home by Christmas Eve."

The plane's tail opened and the ramp slowly lowered. The team pushed up from the floor and shuffled toward the ramp.

"Good luck, guys," the pilot called out.

"Go time," Liam said. "See you on the ground."

Five bodies hurled from the plane.

A recent snowfall left fresh powder over harder, frozen ground providing a welcomed cushion to the landing. After quickly gathering their parachutes and stashing them under the limbs of snow-covered fir trees, each man took a snowboard from his backpack.

"Command. Dagger Team on location," Liam reported to the operations command center.

"Copy, Dagger One," Command responded. "Charlie Team and Beta Team hit dry holes. How copy?"

"Copy, Command. Dry Holes. What are you seeing on sat?"

"Eight heat signatures on the move. One stationary. No vehicle traffic. Copy?"

"Copy."

"VP scheduled to make statement in less than two hours. You have ninety minutes to secure site and locate hostage. Copy?"

"Copy. Ninety minutes."

"Dagger One, engage, but do not terminate. Copy?"

Liam gritted his teeth. Those bastards who held the love of his life deserved to die, preferably in some long, slow fashion.

"Dagger One. How copy?" Command repeated.

"Copy, Command. Engage, but do not kill the fuckers."

"Good luck," Command responded. "Out."

"Listen up," Liam said to his team. "The first two teams hit dry holes. Looks like we've got the prime target. SATCOM reports eight moving heat sigs, one stationary. We will assume that one to be the hostage. When we get within a mile of the cabin, Dutch and Banger break off and circle around to the east. Falcon, you and Mac go west. Once each side is secured, Dutch and Banger will move on to the south. Our orders are to capture tangos for interrogation and secure VIP package. Do not terminate tangos."

"You talking to us, Dagger One, or to yourself?" Dutch asked.

Liam grunted. "Good question, Dutch. I'll try to keep at least one alive to testify."

The five men bumped fists.

"Let's go," Liam said.

SEALS IN PARADISE EDITIONS

SEALs in Paradise: Favorite Drink Edition

Hot SEAL, Black Coffee, Cynthia D'Alba
Hot SEAL, Cold Beer, Cynthia D'Alba
Hot SEAL, S*x on the Beach, Delilah Devlin
Hot SEAL, Salty Dog, Elle James
Hot SEAL, Red Wine, Becca Jameson
Hot SEAL, Dirty Martini, Cat Johnson
Hot SEAL, Bourbon Neat, Parker Kincade
Hot SEAL, Single Malt, Kris Michaels
Hot SEAL, Rusty Nail, Teresa Reasor

SEALs in Paradise: Vacation/Relocation Edition

Hot SEAL, Alaskan Nights, Cynthia D'Alba
Hot SEAL, New Orleans Night, Delilah Devlin
Hot SEAL, Hawaiian Nights, Elle James
Hot SEAL, Australian Nights, Becca Jameson
Hot SEAL, Tijuana Nights, Cat Johnson
Hot SEAL, Vegas Nights, Parker Kincade
Hot SEAL, Savannah Nights, Kris Michaels

Hot SEAL, Roman Nights, Teresa Reasor

SEALs in Paradise: Wedding Edition
Hot SEAL, Bachelor Party, Elle James
Hot SEAL, Decoy Bride, Delilah Devlin
Hot SEAL, Runaway Bride, Cat Johnson
Hot SEAL, Cold Feet, Becca Jameson
Hot SEAL, Best Man, Parker Kincade
Hot SEAL, Confirmed Bachelor, Cynthia D'Alba
Hot SEAL, Taking The Plunge, Teresa Reasor
Hot SEAL, Undercover Groom, Maryann Jordan

SEALs in Paradise: Holiday Edition
Hot SEAL, Heartbreaker, Cat Johnson
Hot SEAL, Charmed, Parker Kincade
Hot SEAL, April's Fool, Becca Jameson
Hot SEAL, In His Memory, Delilah Devlin
Hot SEAL, A Forever Dad, Maryanne Jordon
Hot SEAL, Independence Day, Elle James
Hot SEAL, Sweet & Spicy, Cynthia D'Alba
Hot SEAL, Labor Day, Cynthia D'Alba
Hot SEAL, Midnight Magic, Teresa Reasor
Hot SEAL, Sinful Harvest, Parker Kincade
Hot SEAL, Silent Knight, Kris Michaels